MW00893391

ADIÓS ÁNGEL

A Novel by

Mark Reps

This book is a work of fiction. Names and characters are products of the author's imagination. Any similarities between the good people of southeastern Arizona and tribal members of the San Carlos Indian Reservation are purely coincidental.

ADIÓS ÁNGEL

ISBN-13: 978-1493799282
ISBN-10: 1493799282

Books by Mark Reps

Native Blood

Holes in the Sky

Adiós Ángel

DEDICATION

My gratitude goes out to the following people who helped bring ADIÓS ÁNGEL to completion. Elsa Biel Wilkie edited this book with a fine tooth comb, if ever there was one. Her tireless editing found errors that in a dozen readings I would never have caught. Her dedication to helping me become a better writer is undeniable and ongoing. Thank you, Elsa.

To my wife, Kathy, who puts up with me when things are good and bad in the writing business. Her ideas, suggestions and general look of happiness when I get it right keep me going.

To my sister Jill for her input on the Spanish language in this book. She is my Spanish expert.

Finally I would like to thank Kim, Mary, Jill and Kathy for acting as readers of this book in its various forms.

This book is dedicated to my grandchildren, Max and Yana. They bring light, life and love to everyone they encounter.

CHAPTER ONE

Ángel Gómez's mouth tasted like cotton. His tongue clung unnaturally to the roof of his mouth. The stabbing pain in his stomach radiated straight through to his back. His bowels rumbled, begging to be emptied. Ángel held back for fear he would once again leave the toilet bowl bloody red. Pain zinged through his throbbing head. The rank breath passing through his lips rebounded off the linoleum floor where he had fallen down drunk. His boozy dream state evoked a childhood memory of his sick, dying dog crawling into bed with him and licking his face with its final breath.

"Here, have a shot of mouthwash. It'll wake your sorry ass up." Jimmie Joe's voice boomed from every corner of the small trailer, echoing off the walls into Ángel's pain-filled ears.

Ángel slowly raised his arm toward the tequila bottle dangling in the air just beyond his outstretched fingers.

"A little hair of the dog will cure more than the memory of a bad hangover. Here, take a great big shot of this. Brand new bottle. Freshly opened. It'll calm you. I promise. Here, take it."

Jimmie Joe was insistent, demanding. As Ángel felt the coolness of the bottle in his hand, he wished he had never met, never heard of the big White man, the one called Diablo Blanco by the Mexican brothers and tribal Apaches in the Florence State Prison. Ángel downed a swig of the cold tequila. It was cold in his hand, warm in his mouth, hot as it wormed its way down the back of his throat, burning as it splashed against the walls of his empty stomach."

"A little fire to crank your engine, eh, Ángel?"

He hated the burn of tequila but could not escape its demonic talons. Tequila was the scavenging hawk. Ángel was a helpless rabbit.

Ángel was the name his mother called him. He was her 'Angel'. He also knew that his real name, Cadete, came from his great-great grandfather, Chief Cadete Gómez. The Chief had been a Mescalero warrior who was hostile toward Americans, Mexicans and other Native American tribes. It was said Chief Cadete Gómez paid a bounty of one thousand pesos for the scalps of any enemy that crossed his path. With that heritage Ángel should have been a strong man, not weak like a child. Ironically, the name Cadete meant *volunteer*, a fact that was likely lost on the young, undereducated Cadete Ángel Gómez.

The Mescalero tribal band of native people had survived for centuries with the mescal agave as its main food staple. The White man had turned that food into booze, tequila. Tequila now ruled Ángel's life. Not that he believed it at the time, but the Native American Alcoholics Anonymous program at the state prison had taught him about how alcohol can control every aspect of a person's life. In his most sober moments he wished to regain the power over his own life. Sobriety was, however, always very short-lived for Ángel Gómez.

"Have one more, little muchacha. We have a few weeks before we have to be anywhere. We just have to sit tight and wait. We might as well have a big booze party. What do you say, little one?"

Ángel knew he had no choice. Jimmie Joe controlled him as much as the tequila did. Why not party? What the hell difference did it make?

"Does that bother you, my little muchacha? Maybe you would rather just sit here and think real hard about what it was like for the last two years, cooped up courtesy of the State of Arizona, without the comforts a man needs."

Jimmie Joe swayed the bottle hypnotically back and forth in front of the young man.

Ángel envisioned his time in prison as he downed a large swig of the toxic alcohol. The cheap tequila smelled like cat piss. It bit like a venomous snake. The damned Diablo Blanco probably cut this cheap booze with turpentine. Ángel remembered his grandfather's words. "Don't ever let the devil's drink pass your lips." He had tried to listen. But today the tequila charged his anger, twisted his mind. Ángel could hardly believe the thoughts racing through his mind once the tequila grabbed him. Screw his grandfather and his damned advice. His grandfather didn't understand. He never needed liquor, but Ángel did.

One deep, hard swig and the demons returned, this time as a group. They howled to him that his mother was burning in hell. Then they whispered a secret. Not even the Blessed Virgin would forgive him for breaking his mother's heart by running with the evil man, el hombre malo, as Ángel's fellow Mescalero Apache called Jimmie Joe.

The prison psychiatrist with his fancy suit and shiny shoes had dared to tell Ángel he must quit drinking to be a whole person, to be his true self, and most importantly to know God. Ángel wasn't even sure anymore if there was a God, except maybe the god he felt like when he drank enough alcohol. The doctor had said, "Drinking makes you paranoid, Ángel. It makes you lose control of your thinking. Alcohol makes you do crazy things." Crazy, paranoid, what was the difference? Ángel knew his grandfather had been talking to the shrink behind his back. They conspired against him. The whole world conspired against him, everyone except his lovely Juanita. Juanita and a bottle of tequila were the only two things in the world he could really count on.

His blurry eyes caught sight of the many guns Jimmie Joe had brought back to their hideout after his trip to Safford. A third, then a fourth long drink from the bottle roiled his broken, damaged spirit. Tequila made him forget about his family and the demons that roared inside his head. Newfound courage rose up inside Ángel.

"Jimmie Joe, you never said anything about guns. What do we need all these weapons for? We ain't going to shoot nobody. That's not part of the deal. You said no one would get hurt." It was false courage fueled by alcohol that propelled his words.

"Stow it," growled Jimmie Joe. "For the last time, learn to keep your mouth shut. When this thing is over, you are going to have to learn how to stay quiet and hidden or both of us are going back to jail. One of us might even end up dead."

"I'd rather be dead than back in prison."

"Careful what you wish for mi florita. Wishes have a way of coming true."

Bile raced from Ángel's stomach to his mouth as Jimmie Joe's laughter reminded him of how he managed to crawl under this rock to begin with. His first time behind bars had been the county jail. It was easy time, six months for public drunkenness and burglary. The second judge had not been so easy on Ángel when he was busted for forgery and car theft. The checks were easy to explain. They were written for cheap bottles of tequila and pills for him and his partying friends.

The nice lady social worker had written in her report that Ángel was an alcoholic and very likely cross addicted to narcotic drugs. She said in her report that he needed treatment. When the judge asked him if that was true, Ángel lied. Ángel denied having had a drink in months. He swore he never did any drugs. Drugs were for stupid people. His problems were from a head injury, a concussion he suffered as a child. Ángel claimed it was the concussion that confused his thinking and made him unclear. It was even the reason other children had picked on him. Life had not been fair to him. He pleaded for the judge to give him a break. His mother swore that every word her son spoke was the God's whole truth.

The truth was quite something else. There never had been a head injury, and Ángel was popular with almost all of the other kids his age. The car theft came after a night of revelry and boozing. He did not remember a thing about that night. He had blacked out from the booze and drugs. Ángel did not even remember being arrested after he fell asleep behind the wheel and crashed into a gas station pump.

Three years in the state prison at Florence Junction, with time off for good behavior, was something Ángel thought he could handle. He had heard the state prison had better beds and better food than the county jail. He had even heard the prisoners were better people in there. However, with his slight frame and soft features he was vulnerable. Quickly he became a target for the rapists. They called him la niña, the little girl. Ángel hated it even more than when Jimmie Joe called him mi florita, my little flower. But Jimmie

Joe protected him and maybe even saved his life. It was true that Jimmie Joe beat him, berated him in front of many, but he never asked for sexual favors.

"I ain't never setting foot inside of no damn jail ever again," cried Ángel.

"That's right, hombre. Prison is a place for suckers and losers. We did our time. Now it's time we got some real money...big money."

"Tell me again how much, Jimmie Joe?"

"A million dollars, maybe even two million. More if we're lucky. And I'm feelin' mighty lucky. How about you, my little Ángel? Do you feel lucky?"

Ángel took a deep swig of tequila and grinned with happiness. Luck was running through his veins.

CHAPTER TWO

"Sheriff Hanks!"

Helen Nazelrod's crisp hushed voice sounded unnaturally urgent. The wheels of Sheriff Zeb Hanks' chair sent a piercing squeak through the air as he scooted across the worn hardwood floor. Through his half-open office door he peered over the top of his reading glasses toward his secretary's desk.

"What?" Sheriff Hanks silently mouthed the question. His eyebrows rose inquisitively.

The veins on the back of Helen's hand bulged bright blue as she squeezed the phone. Covering the mouthpiece, she kept the receiver tight against her ear. Her whispered utterance was a desperate response.

"Bomb threat. The high school. Line one. What should I do?"

Gesturing, the sheriff calmly issued unspoken orders that said, "Keep him talking. I'll get on my extension." Sheriff Hanks moved quickly to the phone, and picked it up with extreme caution.

"I place bomb in gym--under bleachers--on other team side."

The accent was Hispanic with an underlying hint of Mescalero Apache, or perhaps mixed Spanish and Apache. Zeb suspected the voice to be at least part that of the Mescalero, the nomads of the Apache family. He had some contact with the few Mescalero in the area. Their voices were distinct enough, but it was hard to be certain. Maybe Helen could confirm this from her church work on the reservation. The slurred speech suggested fear or anxiety. It was apparent he had been in the gym before.

"Could you tell us exactly where you placed the bomb?" asked Helen. "We don't want any of the children to get hurt."

Helen was cool, logical under fire.

"No one ges hurt if you ges everyone out of building."

"What sort of bomb is it?"

The man on the other end of the line paused. His hesitancy sent a bullet of anxiety zinging through the sheriff's heart. Helen kept cool.

"The bomb. Please tell me about the bomb."

"It jes a bomb. Thas all I know. Nothing else I know. Now go get bomb before someone ges hurt. It's go off at nine o'clock on button. Now jes' go get it. That's all I say. Apúrate! Hurry!"

"Please tell me what the bomb looks like. That way we can find it faster," said Helen.

"It jes look like bomb."

"But I've never seen one."

"Is red," said the caller.

"Like dynamite?"

"Sí, sí, like dynamite. Now, please, go get it."

The man's pleading voice sounded near tears.

"Okay. But could you..."

The receiver on the other end rattled clumsily. A blast of static shot down the line and the phone signal died.

"Did you recognize the voice?" asked the sheriff.

Helen's response was terse. "No, I did not."

"Call the principal's office. Have them start evacuating immediately. Move everyone away from the school. Far away from the gym. Call Delbert on the two-way. Have him meet Kate and me at the school. Get the fire department and the EMT's up there ASAP. Call Josh Diamond. Tell him to bring his dogs. He'll be at his gun shop."

"Anything else?"

"Pray the bomb threat is just a bad prank. Pray real hard."

Helen was already dialing the school's number as the sheriff barked out the orders.

"What's going on? Did I hear bomb threat?" asked Deputy Kate Steele.

"You heard right, Deputy. Let's move it. The target is the high school. The device is allegedly under the bleachers on the visitor's side of the gym. It's set to go off at nine."

With sirens blaring and lights flashing the usual three minute trip to the school took less than half that. Sheriff Hanks was surprised to see what appeared to be most of the student body milling about on the football field, away from the gym just as he had ordered.

Principal Newlin, obviously panic stricken, raced toward the sheriff's car shouting. "We've just about got everyone evacuated. What do you need me to do?"

Zeb eyed the newly hired administrator. She didn't look a day over twenty-five. But these days everyone seemed younger. Everyone except him. Her accent, pale complexion and blonde hair spoke of an outsider from the Midwest--Iowa, perhaps Minnesota. He thought of how everyone, everything was changing.

"Should I call the school bus company? Have them take everyone home?"

"Just sit tight," assured Sheriff Hanks. "Keep everyone on the far end of the football field. We will go in and check this thing out. Make sure no one goes near the school buildings. Try to keep everyone calm."

"Sheriff, are you sure everything is going to be okay?"

It was a ridiculously absurd question, but she was young and youth wore ignorance like a tightly fitting glove. He could offer no such assurances.

"Keep your fingers crossed. Whisper a little prayer for us."

"I already am, Sheriff. Please save the school."

He was thinking buildings can be replaced.

"Are the bleachers up or down?"

"They are down all the way. We had an assembly scheduled for nine this morning."

Deputy Steele and Sheriff Hanks exchanged a glance. The same horrible thought collectively passed through their minds. Maybe the idea was to kill and injure a whole lot of children.

"Miss Newlin, a man with two dogs will be arriving any minute. Direct him to the gym through the front door. Tell him to double time it. Advise him that three of us are already in the building."

Principal Newlin's ashen face inferred a woman on the verge of shock. Sheriff Hanks grabbed her by the shoulders.

"Do you understand me?"

"Yes. Yes, I know what to do."

Deputy Delbert Funke stood by the front door. The lumbering man directed the last of the school kids out of the building as Sheriff Hanks and Deputy Steele raced around the corner.

"Why would somebody want to blow up the gym, Sheriff?"

"How did you know the bomb was in the gym?"

"Some teachers said everybody was ordered to get out of the gym first, the rest of the rooms after that. I just figured..."

"We got a threat around eight thirty-five saying a bomb was set to go off at exactly nine. The caller said it was under the bleachers in the visitor's section."

"Jiminy cripes," said Delbert pointing to a large clock in the hallway. "We only got about thirteen minutes."

"The bleachers are down. Hopefully the lights in the auditorium are on."

"If they're not, I know how to turn 'em on," said Delbert. "I used to help the janitor sweep the floor during the summers."

"Use your flashlights to check in the corners. Deputy Steele, you enter at the west end doorway, under the time clock. Stay toward the front of the bleachers. Deputy Funke, you go under the bleachers in the middle by the scorer's table and go along the back wall. I'll enter by the east end and go down the middle of the bleachers. We'll do two quick sweeps, one up and one back. Make certain nothing is taped up underneath the seats. Give the bottom bleacher a real close look-see. Check every corner closely. Got that?"

"Yes, sir," replied the junior officers.

"If we find nothing on two sweeps, check the time. If we have time, we will sweep the home side of the gym in exactly the same fashion. If we find nothing, exit the building at two minutes of nine. Two minutes before nine. Got it?"

Once again in unison the law officers replied in the affirmative.

The bright lights, turned on for the assembly, gave clear visibility throughout the gym. Sheriff Hanks' heart pounded with anxiety as he led his team under the bleachers. Two trips under the opposing team's bleacher section took six minutes. The results were negative.

"Clean as a whistle," said Delbert. "Not even a dust bunny."

"Nothing harmful visualized," reported Kate.

"Let's check the other side and hope we have the same luck. Keep your fingers crossed this is just somebody's idea of a bad joke."

Josh Diamond's silhouette in the doorway cast a sinewy shadow. At his side a pair of highly trained bloodhounds attentively awaited his signal.

"Sheriff Hanks," said Josh. "What sort of device are we looking for?"

"We're looking for a bomb with a timing device. We don't know the size or type. It might be dynamite. It's allegedly set to go off at nine." He used a single finger to outline the already searched area. "We've completed a visual inspection of the visitor's side."

Sheriff Hanks' words echoed eerily off the tall ceiling of the empty gymnasium as somewhere off in a distant part of the building a phone began to ring.

"Take your dogs and search the area where we've just been. You've got three minutes. If you get nothing, you have another two minutes on this side. We are all out of here at eight fifty-eight."

Josh's hand signals set the bloodhounds into action. With great precision the precisely trained animals went into search mode. As the clock above the scoreboard ticked away five fast minutes, nothing resembling a bomb was evident.

"Everyone out. Move it. Now!" shouted Sheriff Zeb Hanks.

Safely away from the building the quartet formed a semi-circle facing the school. The dogs, with their noses in the air, sat by their master's side. Josh pulled a pack of gum from his pocket offering a piece to the others. Delbert took one. The others declined.

"Ten to one it was a crank call. Some pissed off kid getting his jollies," said Josh.

"I bet you're right. I bet it was a prank. When I was in high school, we'd pull the fire alarm just to get a little time off. Kids these days got a weird idea of humor, that's for sure," said Delbert.

"What's the plan, Sheriff?" asked Kate.

"We wait. If there is a timer on the bomb, most likely its next click through will be at quarter after the hour. Right, Josh?"

"If there is a bomb, that would be the most likely scenario. If there was one, Mutt and Jeff would have found it. There is no bomb in the gym."

"They are true professionals," he said, giving each dog a treat. "Nothing escapes their sense of smell."

"I'm inclined to agree with you. Let's give it fifteen minutes. Then we will give the building an additional once over," added the sheriff. "Deputy Steele, would you go inform the principal that we are going to do a building search? With the dogs, it shouldn't take more than an hour. Have her hold tight. No sense sending the kids home for nothing."

"How'd ya' come up with names like Mutt and Jeff for your dogs?" asked Delbert.

Josh Diamond chuckled, patting the dogs on their heads and tickling their ears.

"When they were pups they were exploring around at my store, like young dogs do and they came across a case of Bazooka Joe Bubblegum."

"Mutt and Jeff. You mean those cartoon guys inside the gum wrapper?"

"That's right. The little fellas, at least they were little fellers back then, started in on that gum. The next thing you know they were chewing away. Funniest damn thing I've ever seen a dog do."

Delbert slapped his knee. His body spasmed with uncontrollable laughter.

"Dang, I'da paid a whole week's worth of wages to see that one. They were okay, weren't they? I mean they didn't get sick from it, did they?"

"They were none the worse. I would like to think they were a little smarter for the experience."

"Don't that beat all? Dogs chewing gum. Well, I betcha you couldn't hardly teach a dog to do that if you tried, now could ya?"

Sheriff Hanks stared at the low hanging, sparse clouds over the northwestern horizon of the morning sky. Behind the clouds the peaks of Mount Graham were beginning to reveal the stable unchanging nature of a mountain. The scene calmed him. Something told him they would find nothing--there would be no explosion. Everything about the call pointed in a single direction. Somebody, a disgruntled student, a sick practical joker, had wasted his time, his deputies' time and that of hundreds of children and their teachers. God, as they say, was probably the only one who knew why. Sheriff Hanks glanced at his watch. Nine-sixteen.

"Let's go back in and have another look around. Let's be thorough but make quick work of it. Josh, I imagine you have a plan already?"

"Yes, sir, I do. I'll take the dogs and one of the deputies. We will do the first floor. You and the other deputy do the second floor. Then we will double back and check each other's work. We will finish up with the locker rooms."

"Deputy Funke, come with me," ordered the sheriff. "Deputy Steele, you go with Josh."

A search of twenty-four rooms, six lavatories, two locker rooms, miscellaneous nooks, crannies and janitor's closets took the team exactly fifty-seven minutes. Relieved that nothing was found, Sheriff Hanks gave brief consideration to kidding the young principal about making her students stay late to make up for the classroom time they had missed. The stressed look on her face made his decision for him. Something about the way she carried herself told him she would not find his remark humorous--especially under these circumstances.

"The school is clear, Principal Newlin. You can let the students go back in now."

"You're absolutely certain there isn't a bomb in there somewhere?"

"Yes, ma'am. We have searched the school thoroughly."

"What am I going to tell the parents? The school board? The superintendent?"

"Ma'am?" asked the sheriff.

"How do I explain a bomb threat? Do you know how many reports I'm going to have to file?"

"Yes, ma'am. I believe I do. Deputy Steele will be talking with you. If you need anything, do not hesitate to call us. She can help you with the specific details from our end of things on any reports you may have to file."

Sheriff Hanks knew all too well about report filing rules and regulations. He would have to file multiple reports. Delbert and Kate would have to do theirs. Under new state regulations someone from his office would have to interview the principal, vice-principal, superintendent, and possibly the teachers, janitors and some students. Plus, he would need to get an official statement from Josh Diamond. His head felt light. His stomach rolled with queasiness. It was a bad day to have skipped breakfast. He searched his pockets for an antacid but came up empty handed.

"Delbert, give me your report in a one page summary."

"Can I double space it?" asked Delbert.

"Sure," replied the sheriff. "Just get it done today before you forget anything."

"Right on, big boss man."

"Kate, I want you to interview Principal Newlin. See if she knows of anyone who has made any threats against any of the teachers. Get a list of recently expelled students. If anything looks the least bit fishy, check it out. Josh, I want you to know we appreciate you volunteering your time on this one. Can you give me a paragraph or two for the record? Something simple, give Mutt and Jeff a little mention too."

"No problem. Federal regs I suppose?"

"State, Fed, County, local. Hell, in the old days it was just good enough to do your job. These days it's all paperwork. And when we nab the s.o.b., he'll probably only get a slap on the wrist, if that. This kind of crap, interference with the peaceful conduct of an educational institution, is a class six felony. But even more than that, it's a waste of county time and money. Deputy Funke, Deputy Steele, I want your reports before you go home tonight. Josh, get your statement to me when you can. I'm headed back to the office."

CHAPTER THREE

Zeb felt the acid in his stomach backwash against the bottom of his throat. Gastric reflux? Is that what Doc Yackley had called it? A sharp stabbing pain in his grumbling gut led to a foul smelling belch. The belch contained enough bile to leave a harsh bitter taste in his mouth. Mental note, he thought, always have some food before you drink an entire pot of black coffee.

"Sheriff, is everything okay? You're looking a little green around the gills."

"Yes, Helen. Everything is fine. It was a false alarm."

Helen Nazelrod, long time sheriff's secretary, eyed her boss up and down. He was looking like a horse that had been "rode hard and put out wet", as the local saying went.

"Why would somebody do such a thing, Sheriff? It's just not right. I mean scaring everyone like that. What's wrong with people today?"

"That's a loaded question. Maybe you should write a book and go on one of those daytime talk shows and make a million bucks. I bet people are just begging to know what's wrong with everybody else."

"Oh, Sheriff. You're kidding, aren't you? Me…on the TV…with Oprah?"

Helen primped her hair for an imaginary camera. She was the perfect secretary, calm, tough, sassy and naive all rolled into one. Most of all, she was relieved.

"Before you head off to Hollywood, you got any other bad news for me this morning?"

The attempted humor of the sheriff's remark was short-lived.

"As a matter of fact, since you asked, I do. And, not just a little bit of it either. I've got the freshly compiled, county-wide monthly report right here."

Zeb placed his forehead in his hands, squeezing his outstretched fingers against his temples, pressing against the rising intensity of a sudden headache.

"Three more stolen vehicles were reported, a little car, an old Chevrolet Vega--"

"A Chevy Vega? I don't know one Latino worth his weight in tamales who would be caught dead in one of those babies. I thought they were all on the scrapheap."

"At least one of them is still out there. It looks like you are going to get the opportunity to look for it."

"It's probably better off lost. But, it does tell us one thing."

"What's that, Sheriff?"

"The thief is probably a gringo."

"That kind of talk isn't politically correct, Sheriff."

"Neither is car theft. What's the second vehicle?"

"The second vehicle is a monster truck?"

"What?" He knew what she meant but was surprised that Helen knew.

"A monster truck. One of those that sit way up high." Helen held her hand up as high as it would go. "It has those great big tires. The owner uses it for going into remote hunting areas. He also said one of the taillights glows like a halo. He thought that might help you spot it."

"That's what I call a conscientious citizen," said the sheriff.

"All told that makes for a total of six stolen vehicles, county wide, in the last week."

"Not exactly a crime wave, but it's more car thefts than we've had in a month of Sundays. What about the third car?

"It's a 1987 candy-apple red Corvette. It was stolen right off the lot. It seems as though somebody came in for a test drive and decided to keep it."

"What kind of a jerk would do that?" asked the sheriff.

"The guy at the car lot says it was your brother, Noah."

The sheriff rubbed his knuckles deep into his forehead. Zeb's older brother was the polar opposite of the law enforcing sheriff. He had an embarrassingly long rap sheet, which included multiple car theft charges. He had even done time in the state prison.

As far as Zeb was concerned Noah was nothing but trouble. If blood wasn't thicker than water, he would have cut all ties with him years ago.

"Noah, Noah, Noah."

"A state trooper gave him a speeding ticket on the interstate just outside of Tucson."

"Did the officer arrest him?"

"No. He wasn't aware the car was stolen until after the fact."

"Noah has some drinking buddies up there. I'll contact the locals to be on the lookout for him."

"Unfortunately, that's not the worst of it," said Helen.

Sheriff Hanks leaned back in his chair. There were many things worse than his brother Noah being a car thief, but at the moment Zeb was having trouble figuring out what. Thank God his parents weren't around to know of this.

"Go ahead, make my day."

"One of the vehicles stolen last week--Lorenzo García's classic 1982 powder blue LUV pickup--was found in Tucson. The Pima County Sheriff's Office called about a half an hour ago. They are sending over a report for you."

"Did they say when they were going to release it back to the owner?"

"I don't think that is going to be possible."

"What? Why not? Lorenzo has been calling me every day. He is going to want to know when he can get it back. I just bet it's going to get caught up in some big city paperwork mess."

"It's worse than that. There is no more truck. There is only a pile of melted steel."

"What happened?"

"Somebody torched it."

"Lorenzo is not going to be happy about that."

"The truck went up in flames. To make things worse there were three five-gallon cans of gas in the back."

Among his brother's laundry list of crimes was arson. Could it be that Noah was involved in this one too? Zeb made a mental note to call Noah's parole officer.

"So the car thief was an arsonist as well?"

Helen's expression turned dour. Her voice became deadly serious.

"There was a dead body inside it…burned beyond recognition."

"Was the victim ID'd?"

"No. Oh, and there was one more thing."

"It just never ends around here does it? What other bad news do you have for me?"

"They found Lorenzo García's truck in a part of town called "The Village". The officer who called here seemed to think "The Village" might mean something to you. He told me to be sure and mention it."

"Did he leave his name?"

"Detective Maximilian Muñoz."

Sheriff Hanks had not heard that name in years.

"He said you might remember him by his nickname, Shotgun. Is he a friend of yours? "

"Yes he is. He was my first partner when I worked on the Tucson police force. I haven't talked to him in years. How did he sound?"

"He was arrogant and long-winded. Just like you would expect a big city cop to be."

"Now that is funny."

"What's so funny about that?"

"He's from the booming metropolis of Double Adobe."

"Double Adobe?"

"Heard of it?"

"No," replied Helen. "Should I have?"

"It's a little watering hole on the southern Arizona border, half way between Bisbee and Douglas. Max used to say, if you count the dogs, cats, skunks and coyotes, it had a population of a hundred and six."

"I never heard of it."

"No, I don't suppose. Max Muñoz. Detective Maximilian Muñoz. Talk about a blast form the past."

" A shotgun blast, maybe?"

"You mean his nickname? He's a funny guy, full of baloney. He tells one story right after another."

"I gathered that from talking to him on the phone."

"He liked to say that he and his brothers were the best shots in all of Cochise County. He claimed they would sit on their front porch and practice shooting by holding a rifle barrel between their toes. They took pot shots at a ten penny nail pounded sideways into a board. He claimed he could clip the heads off nine out of ten of them at a hundred yards. He also claimed he could wing a house fly in mid-flight at fifty feet."

"You believed that?"

"He's a funny guy."

"It sounds like he's a little funny in the head."

"Being a little bit loco is a prerequisite for becoming a homicide detective."

Helen gave him a look that said she had no more time to listen to tales of days gone by and that perhaps the sheriff's brief stint working with a man who became a homicide detective had made him a bit loco.

"Do you have any antacids?" asked the sheriff.

"Is your stomach acting up again? Look in the middle drawer of your desk. I put two brand new rolls in there yesterday. I told you. Remember?"

"Oh, that's right. I guess I forgot about them. Thanks."

Helen knew he had not been listening. The sheriff reached into his desk and popped three of the tablets.

"Deputy Steele is interviewing Principal Newlin up at the school."

"Hoping to find a bad egg?"

"Yes, something like that."

"Did you get a recording of the bomb threat?"

Helen held up a cassette tape for the sheriff. She handed it to him without saying a word.

"Make a copy and give it to Deputy Steele. I'm sure she is going to want Principal Newlin to see if she recognizes the voice."

"Here." She handed the sheriff a duplicate. "I listened to it again myself. Sheriff, it sounds like someone much older than a high school student."

"That's all I need, an adult with the brain of a juvenile."

"Criminals are like relatives," said Helen. "You can't pick them."

Being second cousin to Helen, her thinly veiled remark did not help his burning stomach. She had made it clear from the start that she did not approve of his upcoming marriage to a woman of Catholic upbringing, even though Doreen was no longer active in the church. He chose to let the snide comment pass. He had enough trouble as it was. Besides, she was right. You can't pick your relatives.

"When Delbert gets back, have him go out and tell Lorenzo in person about his truck. Old man García loved that truck. For him it was sort of like living his youth all over again. He saved up for years to get it. He told Delbert it took *all* his money to get the truck and because of that he didn't have insurance."

"It seems like bad things always happen to those who can afford it the least."

"Delbert's Uncle Donnie lives a few miles north of García's place. Tell Delbert to stop there and ask around to find out if Donnie or any of the neighbors have seen anything suspicious going on. If anyone has, the word would have gotten around by now."

"Are you sure you want Delbert doing investigation work? You never know what kind of rumor he might accidentally start. Don't you think it would be better if Mr. García heard it from you?"

"Lorenzo García is country folk. Delbert's a country boy. He understands folks up that way. He speaks their language. Delbert can get better information and get it quicker than either Deputy Steele or me. A friendly face is always a better bearer of bad news. Besides, my belly is aching from too much coffee and not enough food. I'm going down to the Town Talk and grab a quick bite. If I'm not back by the time Deputy Steele is done talking with the principal, have her wait for me."

Sheriff Hanks glanced over his shoulder at his secretary as he headed for the door. The look of disappointment covering her face gave him pause.

"What?" he asked.

"Oh, nothing."

It was mid-morning and Helen's blood sugar would be acting up. He should have remembered to ask if she would like him to bring her a muffin. It was a matter of kindness. How could he have forgotten, especially after how well she handled the bomb threat? The pain in his gut was confusing his thinking, but the sheriff knew a little bit of gut discomfort was no excuse for bad manners.

"I was just thinking," he said. "Do you like blueberries?"

"I love them."

"Doreen told me last night she was going to use fresh blueberries when she baked this morning. I was going to surprise you. I kind of figured you must like blueberries, but I wanted to make sure."

"Shame on me," said Helen. "I thought you were going to forget about asking me. I'm glad Doreen is finally teaching you some decent manners. If she says the blueberries are good, well then that is what I will have."

Zeb pulled his cowboy hat snug onto his head preventing the gusting wind from giving it a free ride down the street. If he lived to be a hundred, he might never have a handle on the way women think. God help me, he mused, if women ever become as criminal minded as men are, I won't have a chance.

CHAPTER FOUR

"I was wonderin' when you was gonna show up. Ya' didn't even wake up to kiss your best gal good-bye this mornin'. Just because we're gettin' married at Christmas time doesn't mean you can treat me like some sort of strumpet--which, by the by--I ain't no such thing."

Sheriff Hanks glanced around the cafe. Between the small number of late breakfast and real early lunch diners, the main part of the cafe was mostly empty. In the back part of the café, within earshot of Doreen's sassy remark, the town ministers of Safford were gathered for their monthly association meeting. They stopped a quiet discussion to hone in on Doreen's quip. Zeb could practically see their ears burning as she blurted out strumpet. Now she was almost advertising that the two of them were living in what the churchmen would certainly consider sin.

"I was out like a light. Maybe it was you who should have kissed me goodbye?" said Zeb, keeping his voice low. His personal business was of no concern to the gathered preachers.

"Shucks almighty, you was sleepin' like an angel. Wakin' you up woulda' just been plain wrong." Doreen bent down towards Zeb's ear and whispered. "I suppose then that you might not be able to give me all the details about the bomb threat that forced all them poor kids out onto the football field this mornin'?"

It never failed to amaze Zeb how Doreen got the buzz on whatever happened in town damn near *before* it happened. It always seemed to be telephone, telegraph, tell Doreen and tell the world. Not that it mattered, but once again he asked how she knew what she knew and once again he got a convoluted answer, which seemed to be nothing less than perfectly logical to Doreen.

"Every day Maxine Miller, you know Maxine who worked here on and off for years, she works up at the school now, I don't blame the girl, she gets health benefits and all which I could not afford to give her and God knows she needs them bein' with child and all. Anyway, she works in the principal's office and every mornin' after they get the attendance, that's one of her jobs, which sorta surprises me because she was never very organized, they send her down here for donuts for the teacher's lounge. I swear teachers eat more donuts than anyone. Don't you think?"

The rat-a-tat machine gun answer gave Sheriff Hanks a reason to smile as he glanced down at his protruding belly. Doreen kept firing away. "Well, almost everyone that is, present company excluded, when it comes to donuts. So when she didn't show up on time, she's always here at eight fifty-five on the nose, always on time that gal, never organized but always prompt, even knew exactly when her monthly was coming, that's why I'm surprised she got knocked up. Now that I think about it, she musta' wanted a baby with or without a daddy that might hang around for the duration. That Schmid boy, he's the father, I hear tell he's already outta the picture. Joined up with Uncle Sam is what I heard. Well, when she didn't show, I called up there and no one answered the phone in Principal Newlin's office. That seemed sort of strange, dontcha' think?" Zeb nodded. "Why wouldn't anyone be at the school? Well, I put the phone down and called again, figurin' maybe the attendance was takin' longer than usual or the phones were tied up callin' parents about kids who didn't show up to see if they were really sick. That's one of her jobs too. She does a bunch a weird stuff. No answer agin'. So I got to thinkin'..."

"Uh-oh, thinking might mean trouble," interjected Zeb.

"Oh hush up yer mouth. I got to thinkin' maybe I got the wrong number? I knew I didn't but I looked it up in the phone book anyways. Funny how when somethin don't feel right we stop trustin' ourselves first, ain't it Zeb? I mean why on God's green earth would I think I had somethin' screwed up?"

"I hadn't thought about it quite like you just explained. But, I suppose you're right."

Zeb beamed with a new found personal pride. He might have finally learned to never disagree with a woman when she is making a point. Just maybe he was learning about women in general, Doreen in particular.

"Anyway, then I got to thinkin' that about five minutes earlier I seen ol' Josh Diamond in his pickup truck, with them bloodhounds of his, headin' up the school road. Right away I got to thinkin'--bomb threat."

"Hold on a sec, Doe. That's some mighty fast figuring. How come you thought that? You know he trains those dogs out toward the Mount. He could have just been on his way out there."

"Nope. For sure nope. When he's headed up trainin' on the Mount, he always stops by for a large coffee and some meat scraps for the dogs. Besides he was speedin' and that good ol' boy never moves that fast."

"You got him pegged on that one."

"Both you and Jake told me Josh was a dog and demolitions expert durin' both his military and border patrol time. All hell and tarnation should become me if I couldnta' put something that obvious together. What do I look like anyway? Some sort of ditzoid lamebrain?"

Zeb looked at the lovely, crazy women who would soon be his wife. He knew of no other human being who so succinctly verbalized what went on inside her head. Not even a child could do it so well.

"Then about five minutes later ol' Mrs. Cordoli comes in and tells me every kid at the high school is standin' out on the football field. She says she seen your car is up there too. She seen it pull up with yer' cherry spinnin' and yer siren whoop whoopin' away. Coffee?"

"How about a Pepto Bismol, straight up?"

"Yer stomach still barkin' back atcha? I thought you said it was all better. You been holdin' the truth back on me?"

"Too much coffee on an empty stomach..."

"Hell's bells, sweetie pie. I got just the thing for that. Chamomile tea to calm the tummy ache, a few biscuits to sop up them nasty digestive juices and you just might be feelin' better."

"...and a few too many crimes for a county this size."

Doreen paused. She looked her man in the eye and could see that things were really bothering him. She made an attempt to cheer his obviously dampened spirits.

"Can't do nothin' 'bout that crime wave, unless you deputize me. Say, that reminds me. After we get hitched up am I automatically made into a deputy by the law? It seems I oughta' be. In fact there must be a law regardin' such things."

"There is."

"There is?"

"It's called the Zeb Hanks law. It goes exactly like this. My wife can never have anything to do with anything about the law and should a time come when she thinks she can, I am no longer to be considered her dearly beloved husband."

"Hon, I'm sorry. What's botherin' you? I mean what's really chewin' away at yer innards?"

"Something Helen said to me this morning…"

"Did she shoo you away from her desk agin'?"

"Nothing like that. "

"Snoopin' in on yer private phone conversations?"

"Always. But that's not what I'm talking about."

"Well, hell's bells and buckets a blood spit it out Zebulon Hanks."

"I am trying to."

"Well zip my lip," Doe made the universal symbol of someone zipping their lips shut. Zeb rolled his eyes and smiled.

"After we got the bomb threat Helen asked me, "What's wrong with people anyway?" You know, I got to thinking about it. It sure seems like people are changing. I mean we have had more car thefts, robberies, petty theft and harassment in Safford in the last six months than in the last two years. Now with this bomb threat at the school--well--it just makes you wonder where in the world things are headed. Next thing you know people will be thinking they have to lock their doors at night. Already I see more and more people locking up their cars just to run into the store for a couple of things."

"Zeb darlin', you've burned enough tread off yer tries to know that bad luck comes in streaks. It runs on the same kinda path that good luck does. It just happens to be one of them down times. It'll sure enough change, always does, sure as the sun brightens the day and stars twinkle in the night."

"I suppose you're right."

"At times like this you just gotta grab onto the one ya' love and hold on tight. I think that's why the good Lord put me on the planet."

Doreen slipped around the counter, twisted Zeb's stool around and plopped onto his lap. She planted a huge, wet kiss on his lips while running a pair of wildly caressing hands up and down his back, then squeezed him enough to make the two of them one person. Her movements caught the ministers' attention.

"This one's for you preacher boys."

Doreen embarrassed Zeb by making a loud smacking sound as she kissed him. Her hand then gently pulled up her skirt just high enough to reveal the better part of a creamy white thigh.

"Doe, honey, you're embarrassing me."

The buxom waitress leaned forward and whispered in her man's ear.

"If I'd really wanted to embarrass you, I'd say somethin' about your breath. It smells like the south end of donkey headin' north. I'm calling Doc Yackley. Either you got a rotten tooth or the makings of an ulcer."

"Oh, so now you're a business woman, a detective, a dentist and a doctor."

"A lick a horse sense is all it takes. You might want to take a lesson from that. I probably'd make a pretty dang good doctor if there weren't no blood involved in it."

"How about that tea and biscuits...Doctor Doreen Nightingale?"

"Comin' right atcha, one second after I ring up Doc Yackley. But doncha' think for one minute sweet talking me will get you a pass on seein' the doc. You're gonna go even if I gotta carry ya to his office."

Zeb knew she was right. His stomach hadn't been normal since he had a couple of bouts of the flu a while back. His gut was not that bad, but it wasn't strong like it had been before he got sick. How Doreen knew what was bothering him was another one of those little mysteries about women that puzzled him. He checked his breath by putting his hand in front of his mouth and blowing into his palm. It smelled sickly, a bit like an infection. The chamomile tea seemed to calm his stomach and the biscuits were heavenly. Twice Doreen reminded him he was eating too fast.

"I gotta run, Doe. I have a thousand places to begin the investigation into the school bomb threat. There are almost too many possibilities to know exactly where to begin."

"Why don't you just start at the beginning?"

"Now that you mention it, I guess the beginning is as good of a place as any."

"Don't get sassy with me or your tummy will start howlin' again. That's the way those things work, ya know."

Zeb reached for his wallet. Doreen refused his payment and handed him a blueberry muffin for Helen.

"Somebody's gotta give ya' a break, big guy. Ya' know what they say--charity reaches out its longest arm to a lover."

Zeb grabbed his hat and made for the exit. He tossed Doreen a subtle wink, and after making certain the churchmen were looking the other way, Zeb blew Doreen a quick air kiss.

CHAPTER FIVE

Outside of the Town Talk Diner the air was crystal clear; the sky, with sparse clouds floating over the mountain, was blue and bright. Suddenly Zeb felt physically better than he had in weeks. Maybe he would get a quick break on the bomb threat investigation. He took a deep, relaxing breath. He concluded that probably some angry, foolish kid had made the call to impress his buddies. Odds were pretty good that before long one of the punks would be crowing about how they had pulled a fast one over on the cops. With any luck he would have the caller behind bars in less than a week. It made no sense getting worked up over a lousy day and a bad couple of weeks. He would do his job. He would get to the bottom of all the recent shenanigans. Something this big would bring him leads by tomorrow at the latest. Maybe he would have the bomb threat wrapped up in nothing flat. Even the possibility of his brother, Noah, being the car thief who stole the red corvette seemed less likely. He hoped that the car dealer had mistaken someone else for Noah. But Zeb also knew that with his brother's history, his hopeful thinking was likely unrealistic optimism. Zeb knew Noah had been full of criminal intent since he was a pre-teen. There was no reason to believe that anything had changed.

Zeb was glad his old friend Max Muñoz was the detective involved with Lorenzo García's stolen truck in Tucson. The fact that a dead body had been found in the truck was bad news, real bad news. While the victim was not really his problem, there was an outside chance that there was some sort of connection to the Garcías. He decided to wait to call his old buddy until after he got the report from the Tucson police department, and after Delbert had time to explain to old man García what had happened to his truck.

Maybe the psychological trauma of having a dead body found in his truck would stir up something in Lorenzo's memory. Maybe the old man had seen something and blocked it out or ignored it. Now with his truck gone forever, it might just unlock the part of his mind that held a clue. More than once in this type of a circumstance Zeb had seen people cough up knowledge they didn't know they had. At the state sheriff's convention he had attended a seminar on repressed memory. Yes, this could certainly be that sort of thing. It was no big stretch to see how people put up a protective wall when loss occurred. Zeb's world looked potentially brighter by the minute. His stomach actually felt good as he handed Helen her blueberry muffin.

"Made special just for you."

"You are a sweetheart. So is Doreen for thinking of me."

"Is Deputy Steele back yet?"

"She's in her office listening to the tape."

"Would you tell her I would like to talk with her when she has a minute? And, could you please bring me a cup of cof--never mind. Do we have any chamomile tea?"

Helen, surprised by the request, did a double take. Without asking questions she quickly made the sheriff a cup of tea.

Zeb shook his head in self-disgust as he got down to filling out his report. If he was not thinking clearly enough to know that coffee was burning a hole in his gut, how would he ever get to the bottom of a crime spree in his county, or figure out if his brother was indeed the car thief who stole the Corvette? A couple of deep breaths later he realized it was the thought of a school building, with hundreds of helpless children in it, being threatened that really stuck in his craw. His irritation was rising as Deputy Steele rapped lightly on his door. The sound snapped him back from a progressive abyss of angry thoughts. Her easy demeanor was also helpful.

"Kate, come in, have a seat. Please tell me you've got something. I would like to get this thing wrapped up quickly, for everyone's sake."

Deputy Kate Steele pulled a small notebook from her shirt pocket.

"No recently fired or disgruntled employees at the school."

"That's good. I would hate to think it was an insider who would do such an idiotic thing."

"Principal Newlin did give me a list of recently expelled students, dropouts and major troublemakers. It's not a long list, eight boys and two girls. The boys are all members of a gang called the Little Brothers and Sisters."

"Little Brothers and Sisters? New gang?"

"A mix of Anglos, Hispanic and Native kids. Kids on the edge. Principal Newlin says they are mixed up but mostly lonely types."

Sheriff Hanks shook his head. Lonely boys? In his day even the biggest loser had at least one good buddy. What was the world coming to?

"Tell me about the girls?"

"They have created minor problems compared to the boys. But, they were overheard talking about getting back at the school for being put on detention."

"Why were they on detention?"

"Smoking in the lavatory, fighting with other girls and stealing money from purses. The usual sort of thing that happens with troublemakers their age."

"Budding bathroom muggers maybe?"

"Girls have been settling their differences in lavatories since before my time. I'm going to talk with everyone on the list she gave me. At this time I consider all of them potential suspects. Maybe working together as a group. And don't be naïve, Sheriff, girls can be just as bad as boys."

Deputy Steele read off the names to the sheriff. He knew most of the kids. Three of the boys he had coached in little league baseball. He remembered seeing the girls riding their bikes around town only last summer. How could someone go from bicyclist to bomb threat maker in a few short months? It all seemed so ridiculous.

"Divide the list in half. I'll take five of the boys. What did you learn from the tape?"

"I listened twice. The roughness of his voice sounds like an older man, a smoker. This may sound odd, but to me his voice sounded frightened, even sorrowful, like he was speaking with regret."

"Hmm?"

"The Hispanic accent is rural sounding," continued Deputy Steele. "He also has a bit of a Native American tone to his voice, but not like the San Carlos Apache accent."

"Ever heard a Mescalero Apache accent?"

"No, not that I know of."

"I think that is what we are hearing."

"Okay."

"What else do you have?" asked Sheriff Hanks.

"The caller's sentence structure might indicate a lack of formal education, except for one thing."

"What's the exception?"

"He said the bomb would go off at nine o'clock sharp," said Deputy Steele. "That specific wording doesn't jibe with the rest of his words. Nine o'clock sharp is more the type of phrase a businessman or an educated person would use."

"Maybe he heard it on a television detective show. Lots of dumb criminals get their ideas from the boob tube."

"Maybe. The more I listen to the tape, the less I believe it is high school kids we're looking for."

"An older friend of a high school kid?"

"Maybe."

"We have got to start somewhere. We should focus on these kids and see if we can make a connection."

"Give me five names and let's get started," said the sheriff. "There is going to be a lot of heat from parents and the school board to solve this thing pronto."

"I know. Fifty or sixty parents came and got their kids in the hour I was at the school. Quite a few more called the principal's office and said they were on their way to pick up their kids. This put quite a scare into a lot of families."

"Sheriff! Sheriff!"

The panic in Helen's strained voice sent a chill through Zeb's bones. The shrillness of Helen's statement had a life and death quality to it.

"It's another bomb threat. It sounds like the same man."

Sheriff Hanks picked up his phone. All he heard was static, a loud click and the hum of dial tone.

"Shit! Goddamn it!"

"The grade school. This time the man said he planted a bomb in the grade school--in the boiler room. It's set to go off at one!"

"This is insane. We're dealing with the lives of little children here. Helen, call the school. Have them get everyone out. Now! Kate, call Josh Diamond at the gun shop. Have him take his dogs there on the double. I'll call Delbert on the radio on my way up there and have him meet us."

Zeb's mind did a triple take as it flipped through a catalogue of haunting memories of the grotesque octopus of a boiler in the basement of the grade school building. As a child he had helped his father deliver coal to fire the furnace. As a member of the school board he had led the charge recommending conversion to a gas boiler. Only last week he had called the school to tell them the old coal chute window was open. It was odd he had noticed it at all. What had caught his eye was a stray cat scampering out the backlit window. It would be nothing for someone to push the window all the way open, slip in and plant a bomb next to the gas furnace.

Zeb was only eight when his first glimpse of the basement monster caused him to lose weeks of sleep and struggle with dozens of nightmares. In his youthful, imaginative dreamscape he had envisioned the furnace as a cross between a fire-breathing dragon and a demonic octopus. Nipping at his heels, it had chased young Zeb into a friendless, dead-end alley. Flames rising from the depths of the beast's belly had shot searing spears of heat licking at his face. The machine's pipes had become wildly gyrating arms with suctioned tentacles whose only desire seemed to be to snatch little Zeb and carry him off to the fires of hell and eternal damnation. The memory sent shudders through his spine.

"Deputy Steele, take the emergency patrol car. It has our best first aid equipment. Helen, call the fire department. Tell them to get up there immediately."

A quick call to Deputy Funke assured Zeb his team would be at full strength when looking for the bomb.

For the second time in half a day the sheriff was overcome with a gut wrenching angst. Luckily he caught another break. The kids had finished eating lunch and were outside playing. Teachers were quickly hustling them to a vacant lot.

Josh Diamond's dogs were tugging hard against their restraints as they stuck their noses near the old coal chute. He waived them away from the opening.

"My dogs are onto something, Zeb. Let's get in there and have a look."

Sheriff Hanks was the first of his team on the scene, or so he thought. He stuck his head through the old coal chute opening. Josh, his dogs settled ten feet back, joined Zeb at the opening. A ray from a flashlight jerked across the cement floor in tandem with the stride of an intruder. The sheriff took his weapon from his holster and drew it up by the opening. He looked again as the flashlight beam appeared with a body coming around the corner. He lifted his gun and found Delbert in the crosshairs. "Shit." Delbert was in the boiler room. Had he forgotten to tell Delbert to wait outside the boiler room door? He distinctly remembered otherwise. Zeb began to shout, "Del..." at precisely the moment Delbert looked toward the coal chute window. Delbert could not have heard the sheriff's voice over the explosion.

"No," cried Sheriff Hanks. His plea was in vain. In what seemed like an eternity a brick flew through the air, destined for Delbert's skull. Another brick flew through the air striking Josh in the ribs and wrist. Josh's position protected Zeb who caught only a smattering of loose mortar across the face. Kate, approaching the scene, ducked just as a brick flew within inches of her head. Broken bits of brick and mortar struck her face. Her only injury was a tiny cut over her right eye.

The explosion and its immediate effects happened in slow motion and seemed more like a dream than reality.

CHAPTER SIX

The sand-colored Toyota Camry had been easy to steal. The man had simply driven his pickup truck to the base of Mount Graham. He had hidden his truck in the dip of a small wash behind a large boulder. From there he had walked a mile or so along a low mountain trail to the parking lot used by day hikers. Just in case someone called in the car as stolen during the short time he was going to be using it, he had quickly switched the license plates for a stolen set. If all went well, the hikers would not be back until after his job was completed.

Using the same screwdriver he had used to change the plates, he popped it into the ignition and was gone. The whole operation had taken only three minutes. It was a seven minute drive back to town. The clock on the dashboard read 12:15 as he pulled onto the street in front of Diamond Gun & Ammo. His timing, so far, was impeccable.

He stopped a half block before the gun shop and parked on the opposite side of the street. This gave him a clear view of the gun store and any movement inside. No one could come or go without his immediate awareness. The tinted windows on the Camry were another reason he had chosen it. He opened a map and set it on his lap as cover in case someone should walk by. They would assume he was a tourist, probably checking directions. Slouching low, he pulled the brim of his baseball hat to the top of his sunglasses.

He stuffed some Copenhagen chewing tobacco between his cheek and gums. His reconnaissance had paid off in spades. He knew the movements and habits of Josh

Diamond, Proprietor, Diamond Guns and Ammo as well as anyone could have, right down to the fact that he would be working alone today. The inside layout of the store and where specific guns were kept was etched into his brain.

In the next fifteen minutes, one lone truck passed by. An old woman was driving, likely on her way to the grocery store three blocks down the street.

At 12:25 p.m. he sharpened his focus on the front door of the gun shop. If things went as planned, the owner of the store and his two dogs would soon be racing out the door and into a pickup truck parked at the side of the building. The gun shop had only one additional employee. A caricature of a man in a small boat catching a whale in the front window of the gun shop wished 'Gabby' good luck in an annual fishing contest over the next three days in nearby Rocky Point, Mexico. The thief knew this was the worker who was out of town.

As the clock switched to 12:34, Josh Diamond and his dogs zoomed out the front door. Josh stopped only for a brief moment to make certain the door had locked behind him. He kenneled the dogs in the back of his truck, popped a flasher on his roof, and tore off in the direction of the grade school.

Twenty minutes, the man figured, twenty minutes to get what he needed; get in, get out and then get the hell out of town. As the owner's pickup truck made the first available left turn, the man in the Camry put the car in gear and drove into the alley behind the building that housed the gun shop.

He parked behind the abandoned, boarded up building next door. As he stepped out of the car, small gym bag in hand, he eyed the alley up and down--nothing. The only sound was a slight wind flapping a forgotten, tattered old advertising banner that had seen better days.

At the back door the man went right to work. First things first. The electrical box that fed the building and controlled the alarm system and surveillance cameras was padlocked shut. He was prepared for this. He grabbed his cutters, sliced it off, and put the padlock in his pocket. Reaching inside the box, he flipped off all power to the gun shop. He shut the electrical box cover and slipped a duplicate padlock in place. No sense arousing suspicion if someone wandered by. The gym bag was on the ground. In went the metal cutters and out came a thin piece of metal. He knew there was enough space to slide the metal tool through the small crack between the door and the jamb. In it went. He felt for the resistance of the wood that sat in the U-hooks. With a quick, hard, upward jerk of the instrument he dislodged the two by four piece of wood. He heard it crash to the floor. If there was a secondary alarm system, it either hadn't been triggered or was a silent one.

He returned the tool to his gym bag and grabbed another tool of his trade. This one was more sophisticated and perhaps even one of a kind. The man had made it himself. It was also a thin piece of metal with a small hinge six inches from the end. When a trip mechanism at the opposite end was pushed, the hinge flipped to ninety degrees and the self-locking mechanism made it rigid. It slid through the narrow space. He pressed the end and heard it click into place. He maneuvered the tool, something he had practiced hundreds of times, to precisely where he wanted it. With a simple twist of the wrist the dead bolt flipped open. He pushed on the door and was inside. No alarms sounded. He smiled victoriously.

He dropped his tool into the small gym bag, picked it up and carried the tools of his trade inside. The door behind was quickly, noiselessly shut. Making his way from the back of the store to the sales room, he kept his eye on the street. Much to his satisfaction there was no movement out there. He walked deliberately to the front door and flipped over the open sign. With the lights off and closed sign showing anyone passing by would assume the owner was still at lunch and likely not lean against the glass to peak in.

He made a bee-line to the case that held handguns. It was locked. He knew smashing it might cause an alarm to go off. Reaching into the large outer pouch of his pack he grabbed a glass cutting tool. Placing the suction cup on the countertop, he arced a perfect circle, clicked the release and removed a six inch diameter piece of glass. His shopping took a matter of seconds as his gaze fell upon his personal preference, a .38 Colt Diamondback. He grabbed four of them, fondling the first for a few seconds. He then wrapped each, before carefully placing them into the small gym bag. The .22 was a no brainer, a Walther P22. It was for his partner. It needed to be small for his little hands. He turned to the case that held the ammunition, grabbed what he needed and stuffed that into the gym bag. A display rack held some gun cleaning kits. The Otis Elite was an easy choice. He eyed a wide variety of holsters. One grabbed his attention. It was a special military style that held two guns. It was perfect for a man who might get into a shootout. It disappeared into his gym bag too. He glanced at the clock. Eighteen minutes had passed since he entered. Two minutes to spare.

With one last look around he headed for the back door. Something on the owner's chair in the back office caught his eye. It was a Kevlar flak jacket that appeared brand new. Grabbing it, he chuckled, "Frosting on the cake." With that he was out the door. On his way to the Camry he hurled a glob of tobacco laden spit at a board that covered the window of the abandoned building. It hit dead center, precisely where he had aimed.

The chemicals in his brain lit up. Just one more thing he did perfectly. Life was great and it was about to get a whole lot better. Self-congratulations were in order.

CHAPTER SEVEN

Almost two days later Delbert had yet to regain consciousness. Doc Yackley said his vitals were stable. Other than that he told the sheriff all they could do was wait.

"Delbert? Delbert can you hear me?" Little could Sheriff Hanks know that his voice landed on deaf ears and a badly damaged brain. Nothing was registering. The hodgepodge of signals coming from the command center of Delbert's brain was functioning only enough to keep him alive.

"Delbert? Delbert, can you open your eyes?"

It seemed like such a simple request. All Delbert had to do was flip up his eyelids. But somewhere between Zeb's directive to perform such a basic task and the reality of putting it into action laid an unseen barrier.

"Jesus, Doc, his eyeballs are fluttering beneath his lids. That's a good sign, isn't it?"

Zeb's voice seemed to stir a reaction from Delbert.

"Look, Doc. Look at that damn silly grin he's got on his mug. I'd be willing to bet you lunch that he knows I'm standing right here by his side. Hell, yes. He knows it."

Doc Yackley looked glum. "Say something else to him."

"Delbert? Delbert, it's Zeb. Just relax and open your eyes. Come on, Del, old buddy. You can do it.

Delbert's eyelids may as well have been cemented shut. He could not produce a single voluntary action. Frustration flooded every inch of the sheriff's being. He felt tremendous guilt, as though Delbert's injury was totally his fault. Somehow this seemed even worse because the injured man was not only his deputy but also a longtime friend.

Mrs. Corita Funke, Delbert's mother, stood helplessly by, watching her son.

"Corita, why don't you stand on the other side of the bed and hold his hand? Grip it tight," said Doc.

"What are you going to do, Dr. Yackley? Is it going to hurt my boy?"

"Don't worry, Corita. I am going to use a bit of horse sense. It's nothing I learned in medical school."

Doc Yackley placed his thumb and first finger over his patient's shoulder muscle and bore down with the power of a vise grip. Nothing. Not even a reflex reaction. The expression on Doc's face, if anyone had been looking directly at him, turned from glum to downright dour.

His mother tried again. "Delbert, honey, you are lying in a hospital bed. Just keep your eyes shut and listen to me. You have suffered a concussion. You were hit in the head by a flying brick. You have been unconscious for two days. Del, my son, did you hear what I just said?"

Nothing. Not even a single muscle twitched on the injured deputy.

The attentive doctor watched closely for the smallest of reactions from his injured patient. A signal from Delbert's injured brain moved his eyes making the eyelids appear to flutter by some purposeful act. His mother and the sheriff felt a ray of hope. Doc Yackley knew better than to be optimistic. Corita Funke placed her cool hand over her son's forehead. She caressed it with all the love a mother has to give her only son. She was certain her calming assurances would quell his pain, help heal his damaged brain and bring him closer to consciousness.

"I'm staying right by your side, Del," said Corita. "You are going to be better real soon. I can feel it in my bones."

Delbert did not move a muscle. Delbert could not move a muscle.

CHAPTER EIGHT

"I'd say you have a lucky star shining over your head. Maybe even a guardian angel or two. For sure the Ga'an are keeping their eyes on you."

Eskadi Black Robes, tribal chairman of the San Carlos Apache Reservation, shut the door to Deputy Kate Steele's office and wrapped his arms tenderly around her. The blunt truth of his comment about the Apache Gods keeping an eye on her sent a peaceful awareness through her. A flying brick had missed her head by inches. Broken pieces of brick had struck her face causing a small cut over her right eye. Her uniform had been splattered with dust and shattered bits of concrete and clay. Both she and Sheriff Hanks had only minor injuries.

"You are right, Eskadi. Someone or some greater power was looking after me."

Josh Diamond was not quite so lucky. Now, almost two days after the explosion, Josh was fresh out of the hospital with three fractured ribs, a broken wrist and enough cuts and bruises to make him look like he had been sucker punched in a street fight. Doc Yackley had made him stay the extra day as he was concerned about possible internal bleeding and organ swelling. Deputy Funke, according to Doc Yackley, took a direct hit from a ten-inch brick to the base of the skull and has a skull fracture, a severe concussion and maybe worse.

"You must have the luck o' the Irish, eh, lassie?"

Eskadi's attempted Irish brogue left more than a little to the imagination.

"I don't know what it was, the Ga'an or leprechauns or…" Kate patted her left shirt pocket. Inside was her inherited good luck charm, a baseball card of Lefty Mathewson, the great New York Giants pitcher from the early 1900's.

"Whatever it was that saved you, I, for one, am awfully glad about it. What do you hear about Deputy Funke? Is he doing any better?"

"The sheriff just called from the hospital. Delbert's the same. Dr. Yackley didn't give the sheriff any good news. Sheriff Hanks said Doc sounded uncertain as to any progress Delbert might make any time soon."

"How about the other guy? The one with the bloodhounds? What's his name, Jim somebody?"

"Josh Diamond." Kate was sure Eskadi knew Josh's name.

"Josh Diamond," cackled Eskadi. "Now there's a White man's name for you."

"Josh is okay. He just got released from the hospital according to Helen. I guess they wanted him to stay one more day, but he wouldn't have it."

"Tough guy, eh?"

"Independent might be a better word for it."

"He's new around here, isn't he?"

"He's an old border patrol friend of the sheriff's. They worked hard to bring in some very bad people who were trafficking both humans and drugs across the border. You sound like you don't like him?"

"He's just another White man living in Indian Territory as far as I'm concerned."

Kate knew it was time to change the subject.

"Can we get down to business?"

"What? It's not good enough for me to come into town just to see you?" asked Eskadi. "We have to do some business together?"

"What's with you? You come in sounding like an Irishmen and the next thing I know you're sounding like a Jewish banker."

"Good one, huh? I'm just getting in some practice for the Morenci Rodeo Days talent contest. I'm going to mimic as many different tribes of White people as possible," laughed Eskadi.

"You never let up do you?"

"A guy has to have his shtick."

"Okay, funny man, let's have a listen to the tape. I want to know if you recognize the voice. I know it's a long shot, but everyone around here seems to think the person is at least part Mescalero."

Eskadi Black Robes stood silently staring out the window, hands clasped behind his firm muscular back, as Kate played the tape.

"Play it again, please."

Kate admired Eskadi's physique. His shiny, black hair traveled over his broad shoulders, stopping near his waist and firm buttocks. The sleeves of his black tee shirt stretched tightly over his upper arms exhibited perfectly formed triceps.

"It's definitely not the voice of a San Carlos Apache. The man does speak like a Mexican, excuse me, Hispanic, who spent more than a little time conversing with Apaches. He has stolen a little inflection from our dialect. I do have to say, he does have a Mescalero accent."

"I don't suppose you're going to tell me you recognize the voice?"

"I can't help you with that. That is going to take real police work. That is the reason you make the big money and the rest of us just scratch out a living."

"You're a laugh a minute," chided Kate.

"I'll bet you anything he speaks Hispanic with a Mescalero accent, just like he does English," said Eskadi.

"I'll keep that in mind," said Kate. "You also mentioned you might know something about the stolen cars?"

"I've heard some talk that might interest you. It's one of those little stories one person mentions to another and another until finally it passes through enough people it make its way to the tribal office. Sometimes I feel like I live in gossip central."

"That's the way the whole world works. Please tell me what you have."

"By the time the story reached me it went like this. Eugene Topy was fishing for small mouth bass over at the big lake. He fell asleep and dreamed of wild animals. In his dream he heard a coyote howling. Naturally he woke up and looked around. After he realized it was a dream he noticed his rod and reel were missing. To hear him tell it, some big fish nabbed it and took it right to the bottom of the lake.

Hannah Udom, his cousin, told me about it. She claims it serves him right because he was probably drunk anyway. I talked with Eugene. He says he only had two beers and was as sober as a White man at work."

The absurd human details of Eskadi's stories were endearing to Kate.

"It started to rain pretty hard and Eugene decided to go home in case a big storm was coming in. He moseyed over to his truck and took a back road home. He wasn't in any particular hurry because his wife's twin sister and her five kids were staying with them. He knew he would catch holy heck from the both of them when they found out he lost his fishing gear. Eugene had been bragging earlier about all the fish he was going to bring home. Now, not only was he empty-handed, he had to find a way to scrape together a few dollars to buy some new fishing equipment. His wife controls the money, and Eugene says she's pretty tight with a buck."

Kate knew Eugene Topy. He and his wife ran a little burrito stand at community gatherings on the reservation. He was a big man, four hundred pounds and six and half feet tall. His wife, Melina, couldn't have been five feet tall and was as thin as a reed in a dry lake.

"When Eugene pulled up to the house, they figured out pretty quickly that he had been skunked at the lake. They put on an act like they were practically starving to death and ready to eat any old bottom fish he might have been able to drag up. Melina, her sister and all those kids were sitting there at the table with a knife in one hand and a fork in the other. They were pounding on the table, making a great big scene. When he told them he didn't have any fish, they chased him out of the house. He said they were screaming that they were going to cut off his leg, cook it up with some sour greens and eat it for dinner. Poor old Eugene hopped back into his truck, rolled up the windows and locked the doors. He was sure they had gone crazy. He started honking the horn and shouting at them. Finally, he got up enough courage, opened the window just a crack and asked them if they had eaten locoweed. When those sisters heard that, they started laughing so hard they fell down on the ground and started rolling around. That's when Melina noticed it."

"Noticed what?" asked Kate.

"When she was rolling around on the ground, she looked up and noticed the license plate on the truck was missing. Eugene bought the truck over in Tucson. He never bothered to get new plates when the old ones expired. Maybe he didn't want to pay for them. Maybe his wife wouldn't give him the money. Who knows? He never got arrested because he only drove the back roads from his house to the lake."

"But now without any plate at all, Melina figured he might get pulled over?" asked Kate.

"Exactly," said Eskadi. "I guess she scolded him so bad it didn't take him long to make the decision to come into the tribal office and tell me about it."

"What did he think you were going to do?"

"He figured if he told the tribal police he had been driving the truck for over three years without legitimate reservation plates, they might run him in. He asked me what to do. He wanted me to straighten out his mess for him."

"What did you tell him?" asked Kate.

"I told him if he brought me the truck's registration, I would help him get some valid plates. He didn't have the registration card. I don't think he even knew what it was. So we got the vehicle identification number off the truck and I called the motor vehicle department in Tucson. That was yesterday morning."

"What exactly is this leading to?"

"You were telling me about all the stolen cars. It seemed ironic to me. Whites steal cars, Hispanics steal hubcaps and Indians just steal the license plates. Now that's what I call progressive poverty."

"Is that part of your shtick for the talent show too?"

"It wasn't. But now that you mention it..."

Kate rolled her eyes.

"About the DMV?"

"The DMV called me back this morning. They wanted to know who owned the truck. I explained all I wanted was to transfer the title. I told them since it was a reservation vehicle it was none of their damn business who owned it. Which, it isn't. I was polite as punch. They demanded to know who owned the truck."

Kate shook her head.

"I'll just bet, knowing how much you like government officials, nothing they said sat too well with you...especially after how you tried to be so cooperative."

"When I wouldn't kowtow to their jack boot style of questioning, they got all huffy. I hung up on them. All ghost skins want to do is make life miserable for the rest of us."

"Did you ever hear the old saying, 'You attract more flies with honey than with vinegar'?"

"Why should I be nice to them? When was the last time the government did anything to help America's First People?"

Kate knew Eskdai had a bit of a point. "Was that the end of it?" asked Kate.

"Hell no. About two minutes later a detective with Arizona Highway Patrol called. He asked me a bunch of questions about the truck. According to him it wasn't possible the plates had just been stolen. He claimed they were in the hands of the Tucson police and had been for over a week. The detective said the state was going to send an investigator down to talk to me. I'm sure they think it's my truck."

"Did they explain why the police had the plates? Did they say what they wanted?"

"Not exactly. They said they found them on a stolen car that had been abandoned at a wayside rest. They just said they were coming down to the reservation today to have a little chat with me."

"Today? When today?"

"I imagine they're out there waiting for me now."

"Are you purposely trying to put a bee in their bonnet?"

"Hell, yes."

"You should show at least a modicum of respect."

"Why? Let them wait. We Apaches have been waiting for over a hundred years for any kind of satisfaction from those scoundrels who stole our land. Why should I go out of my way to make their life easier?"

"It wasn't the state highway department or the state police who stole Apache land. You know that."

"It's close enough. Both of them work for the big White machine in Washington."

Kate found Eskadi's incorrigible, anti-establishment behavior both charming and alarming. As tribal chairman he knew working cooperatively with the powers that be could prove beneficial. If he angered the wrong political people, the amount of hassle brought on the people of the San Carlos Reservation could be significant. Yet, when it came to dealing with the bureaucracies, he was as stubborn as a mule and as troublesome as a wild child.

"What are you going to tell them?" she asked.

"It depends on what they ask me."

"You're going to be forthcoming with them, aren't you?"

Did you ever meet an Indian that wasn't honest?"

Eskadi raised his hand, mimicking and mocking the stereotypical pose of a cigar store Indian.

"I swear, you are a little bit loco," laughed Kate. "Promise me you'll let me know what happens?"

"Of course. Why do you think I'm here right now?"

"I thought maybe you just wanted to see me," replied Kate.

"Then maybe after I talk with them, I'll have a reason to come back and see you again. Or maybe you'll have a reason to stop by and see me. It's been a while since you've been up to the Rez."

Helen's knock on the door interrupted what had become a far too infrequent personal moment between the pair.

"Deputy Steele, Josh Diamond is here. He's asking to talk with you."

"Tell him it will be just a minute."

"Official business, I presume?" asked Eskadi.

"Don't get jealous. He is a very good man, but not necessarily my type."

"Mmm-hmm."

"Besides, someone's already got their designs on me...or so I've been led to believe."

Eskadi's deep ebony eyes smiled as broadly as his lips.

"I will call you."

Eskadi cast a stern expression in the direction of the ruggedly handsome Josh Diamond as they passed.

CHAPTER NINE

"Josh, have a seat."

"Thank you, Deputy Steele."

"Call me Kate, please."

"Yes, ma'am."

Josh Diamond's soft southern accent puzzled her. Sheriff Hanks had mentioned that Josh had moved to Safford from Bisbee, a small town near the Mexican border in central Arizona. The sheriff had also said they had served together as young men working for the border patrol. Before that, Josh had enlisted in the Marines and had served in Desert Storm, the first Iraqi war.

In the few short months he had lived in town, rumors about his past were plentiful. He had allegedly been a member of the Special Forces in Iraq and Kuwait, a military operative behind enemy lines in Bosnia, and a Texas bounty hunter. Most of them were just that, rumors. The serenity and calmness in his face deeply contrasted with the image of a man possibly involved in such a vast array of human hunting endeavors.

The truth, in fact, was that he had worked with bomb sniffing German Shepherds in combat and non-combat situations in Kuwait. He trained, handled and ultimately was deployed in the field with these dogs. He referred to himself as a military dog handler when asked by those close to him.

"The county has arranged to take care of your hospital bills." Kate slid an official form across the desk toward him. "Just sign on the dotted line. Press hard, it's in triplicate."

"Thank you," said Josh sliding the form back at Kate. "It's not necessary. I have health insurance and I never get the chance to use it. I might as well get something for all those premiums I pay," laughed Josh.

"Are you certain? All I have to do is send this form over to the hospital and everything will be taken care of."

"I'm sure it will. But let's keep the taxpayers from footing this bill."

"Then let me extend my official thank you from the sheriff's department and the citizens of Graham County for helping us."

"For getting in the way of flying debris?"

The injured man raised the arm cast and beamed broadly.

"And the broken bones," added Kate, returning the smile.

"Your thanks is officially noted and accepted," said Josh.

"Fair enough."

Sheriff Hanks walked past Deputy Steele's office and stuck his head in the doorway, interrupting what was quickly becoming a flirtatious encounter.

"How you feeling, Josh?" asked Zeb.

"Doing all right," replied Josh. "Even better now."

Zeb looked at his old friend, looked at his deputy and looked back at Josh.

"What are you doing here?"

"Reporting a crime."

"You've only been out of the hospital for a couple of hours," said Zeb. "What's happened?"

"While I was looking for bombs and getting patched up in the hospital, somebody broke into my store. Five handguns, a fair amount of ammunition, some merchandise and a personal item, a flak jacket, were stolen. I made a complete list of the missing items. The guns are all registered to the store. I need you to come check it out. I already left a message with the Bureau of Alcohol, Tobacco and Firearms. They told me to talk to you. Here is the list of what is missing."

"The ATF was here yesterday looking at the bomb site at the grade school. They are still around. I imagine they will add the break-in at your store to their list of work to do."

Josh nodded and handed a meticulously typed note to the sheriff. He briefly studied the list, handed it to his deputy and glanced back at his friend. With his hand in the cast, he must have pecked the list out one key at a time. The stolen handguns included four .38's and a .22. The ammunition included 24 boxes of one hundred count NyClad HP for the .38's and one 250-count box of .22 cartridges. The holsters were a special type of military issue that each held two guns, shoulder variety. The flak jacket was standard police issue. The gun cleaning kit was top of the line, Otis Elite.

"You have an alarm system. How did they bypass that?"

"I do. And it was armed. But ultimately it didn't make any difference."

"What do you mean?" asked Zeb.

"Somebody used a bolt cutter on the padlock on the electrical box. They cut the wires to the alarm system and to my cameras."

Zeb immediately assumed the job was done by a professional. Very likely it was somebody from out of town as he would know any locals with that kind of skill and mindset.

"What do you make of the specific stolen weapons? Are any of them antiques or collectibles?" asked Zeb.

"No," replied Josh. "From the looks of it someone knew exactly what they were after. They passed over many more expensive guns to get to the ones they took. My guess is, five handguns and that much ammo, it isn't about collecting."

"You're probably right about that," replied Zeb.

"What about the holsters?" asked Deputy Steele.

"They are a specialty item fast draw competitors use in an event called the double draw."

"What about the flak jacket?"

"That was mine. I picked it up at a gun show. A guy owed me some money. When he couldn't pay me back, I took it as collateral. It wasn't for sale. I know better."

"A flak jacket and that many hand guns add up to trouble. Any suspects come to mind?" asked Zeb.

"When you sell guns for a living like I do, it's pretty easy to get suspicious about anyone and everyone who walks through your door. Sometimes even little old ladies who buy cap guns look like criminals. If I ever get that paranoid, I'll get out of the business. "

Zeb and Deputy Steele nodded. They had both seen plenty of criminals who didn't look the part.

"I've only lived in Safford for a short time. I don't personally know all the people who walk in the door."

"But you're suspicious of our seasoned citizens?" asked Zeb with a smile.

"I wasn't being glib when I made the remark about little old ladies. When my dad had a store down on the border, two grandmotherly types robbed him. One stuck a gun in his craw and pistol-whipped him while the other cleaned out his till. My old man was in the business for twenty-five years. They were the only people who ever got the upper hand on him. He got kidded about that until the day he died."

The image of a pair of blue haired grannies knocking over a gun shop brought a silly grin to Kate's face. What she had heard was true. Josh Diamond could spin a yarn.

"Is that really true?" Kate asked.

"With God as my witness," said Josh raising his uninjured arm. "Worst part was they hog tied him. He had to lay there all trussed up for a couple of hours before anyone came in. When he finally was rescued, it was by the biggest gossipmonger this side of the border. It wasn't long before the neighborhood was talking about how Big Ed Diamond was made a fool by a pair of grandmothers. He took a lot of razzing. His store traffic doubled on the curiosity factor alone."

Zeb was familiar with his old border patrol buddy's style, and Josh's easy-going manner was beginning to grow on Kate.

"We had better go down to your business so I can have a look around. Is now a good time for you?" said Zeb.

"Yes, Sir," replied Josh. "Never better."

"Don't 'Sir' me," said Zeb sternly.

"Okay, boss," said Josh sarcastically.

Kate knew that Josh had served under Zeb's command as a United States Border Patrol agent, so she figured that was an inside joke.

"I'll meet you at your gun shop in fifteen minutes."

From the corner of her eye, Kate watched Josh Diamond amble out of the office. Even in his injured state he carried himself with a uniquely dignified panache.

"Helen, Josh Diamond's gun shop was robbed when he was in the hospital. Could you put the paperwork together and put it on my desk? I'm headed over there to have a look around. Here's the list of stolen items."

"Certainly. Do you want me to type in the particulars I already know?"

Zeb knew Helen's ears had acted as sonar detectors during his conversation with Josh.

"That really would be helpful."

Sheriff Hanks slipped into his office to finish off a bit of paperwork. From his office he listened as Helen spoke to his deputy.

"Oh, I almost forgot," said Helen. "Eskadi left this for you."

Helen handed Kate a sealed envelope.

"If you ask me, I think Eskadi Black Robes is jealous of Josh Diamond."

Kate's response to Helen's statement was to examine the envelope. If Helen had tampered with it, there were no obvious signs. Even though she had been civil to Eskadi Black Robes, Helen's independent nature would not allow her to forget the run-ins she had with him over the years.

Kate opened the envelope. Eskadi had drawn a single star at the top of the page. Beneath it he had printed the Apache word Son-ee-ah-Ray--Morning Star--the Apache name he had given her at a gathering less than a year earlier. Maybe Eskadi did have a bit of a jealous streak in him. She wished her mother was alive so she would have someone to talk with about the strange ways of men and how they express their affection.

Kate tucked the letter into her desk drawer.

CHAPTER TEN

During the four-block walk to Diamond Gun & Ammo Zeb concluded mind that the words spoken in the bomb threat did not jibe with the tone of the caller's voice. A man calling in a bomb threat…two bomb threats…would have no regret in his voice. Yet, the voice of the caller was seemingly full of remorse. His job was to figure out why.

Josh Diamond's gun store was on Second Street, just past Jilberto's Mexican Eatery and a pair of abandoned buildings. The old livery stable, dilapidated when Josh took it over, had been freshened with a new coat of paint and security doors.

"Yo, Zeb," said Josh. "That was quick."

"I hardly recognize the place," said Zeb. "It looks great."

"Thanks. I'm converting the upstairs into a deluxe apartment. The future of Safford looks bright, wouldn't you say?" asked Josh. "I mean for a businessman like me."

"If we can keep the downtown alive, the mines open, the price of cotton up and keep the young people from moving away, I'd say Safford will thrive."

"I hope it does. I like what I see so far."

"Sounds like you're talking about Deputy Kate Steele. I saw the way you two were eyeing each other."

"She is quite a gal," said Josh. "Don't know her that well yet, but I'd like to. That is just between us boys, if you don't mind."

"I'll keep it on the down low, but you've got competition," said Zeb.

"I'd be surprised if I didn't," replied Josh.

An art deco clock, a series of first edition Zane Grey novels and a signed, framed Picasso were among the many new additions since Zeb had last been in the store.

"Is that a Picasso?" asked Zeb, eyeing the painting. "What kind of money is there in the gun business, anyway?"

Josh laughed. "Not that kind of money. My dad got it in a swap a long time ago. I don't think the owner knew what he had. Coffee?"

"I've got time for one cup. I would prefer tea if you have it."

Josh eyed his old pal and said, "Sounds like someone is domesticating you at last."

"Kiss my ass, amigo. My guts are acting up. Tea calms them."

"Good, but I still mean what I said. One tea coming up."

"I see you're making this a fancy gun store," said Zeb.

"I prefer *eclectic,*" replied Josh. The men chuckled.

"Eclectic ain't exactly what got us through some tight circumstances along the border now did it, or kept you alive during your time in Kuwait," said Zeb.

"I'm a complex man," replied Josh. His comment caused both of the men to laugh uproariously.

"Maybe we should get down to the details of the robbery," said Zeb.

Josh stood, taking his coffee mug in hand, and strolled behind the counter. He thumped the top of a glass enclosure with the first finger on his good hand. He pointed to a small hole in the glass, not much bigger in diameter than a softball.

"The handguns were taken from this case. They managed to break the glass fairly cleanly. Hardly left a mess at all. The *neato bandito.* How about that for an m.o.?"

"I'll note it in my report," replied Zeb.

Zeb pointed to a hunter's display created from an impressive collection of antlers.

"That's a unique gun rack. Did you make it yourself?"

"Hell, no. I bought it at a bankruptcy sale over in west Texas," replied Josh. "Some phony oilman claims to have shot every one of them himself. I suspect he was full of b.s."

"I bet there's a story behind that."

"He was the fattest human being I have ever seen. When I met him, I wondered if it would take a stick of dynamite to blast him out of his chair."

Zeb shook his head. Same old Josh. Always full of bull.

"Most of these horns are from mountain animals that would require a fair amount of walking to get to. The schmuck even had a bunch of phony photographs with himself dressed in a safari outfit standing by freshly killed animals. He couldn't remember where he had been hunting and couldn't match the animals with the horns in his collection. It doesn't matter. I bought them for display purposes. I like the way they look."

Josh had a keen eye and a clever tongue. Zeb eyed the trophy horns and the tersely worded sign hanging just below them.

ALL EXPLOSIVES REQUIRE PROPER PERMITS.

NO EXCEPTIONS!

DON'T EVEN ASK!!

"What about the ammunition? Where was it taken from?"

Josh motioned the sheriff behind the counter and through a pair of swinging doors into the back half of the store.

"Those old doors came with the place. I think they're originals. I fell in love with them the minute I saw them. They give the building an honest to goodness old west flavor. They make me feel like a kid again."

"Like you ever grew up," said Zeb.

"This is my business office. That's being a grown-up, isn't it?"

Zeb shook his head. The room, lit by the bright glare of incandescent bulbs, was divided in half. Toward the front was an old-fashioned green bank safe with *SANTE FE STAGECOACH COMPANY* written in faded black lettering. Next to the safe was a roll top desk with several piles of neatly stacked paperwork and a small number of framed pictures. Against the back wall, on either side of a massive door, in padlocked metal lockers were cases with hundreds of boxes of ammunition. He already had what he needed. The weathered oaken door had two locking mechanisms--a dead bolt and a two by four piece of wood in a U-shaped bracket. It appeared fairly impenetrable. The rest of the room was bare except for an area rug and a calendar. The calendar was headlined FRENCH LIVERY and STABLES with the date 1914.

"Did the calendar come with the building too?"

Zeb walked over to the calendar and took a look at the pictures sitting atop Josh's desk. One of them was of Josh wearing a cowboy shirt, hat and holster. He looked to be about four years old. Next to it was a wedding picture. The man looked happy, beaming broadly and not looking at all uncomfortable in his ill-fitting suit. Darkened skin and a tan line across the forehead made it obvious the man worked in the sun and wore a hat. The stunningly beautiful bride looked radiant in her wedding dress.

"Yes, it did. The French family put up this building in 1906. They used it as a livery stable until the Second World War. I checked it out at the library. I found some early pictures of the building at the Safford Historical Society. I'm thinking of having them enlarged and framed. I think they would look great hanging in the store."

"Hell, you know more about my hometown than I do," said Zeb.

"People are paying homage to the past more and more these days. My dad used to tell me you can't know where you're going unless you know where you've been," said Josh.

"A philosopher too?" said Zeb.

"Well rounded. This is where the ammo was taken from."

"It doesn't look like anything else was disturbed."

"I didn't touch a thing. If I hadn't just completed an inventory, I might have not missed it at all."

"How did they manage to enter the building? I didn't notice any damage to the front door," remarked Zeb.

"Stay right where you are and look toward the back of the building," replied Josh.

Josh flipped the lights off. The overly bright room became instantly darkened. For half a second, while his eyes adjusted, Zeb could see almost nothing. Then he noticed a crack of light streaming in through the doorframe. Josh flicked the lights back on.

"Watch your eyes."

Zeb walked to the back door. His eyes winced from the sudden change in light.

"Here's what I think happened," said Josh. "There's enough of a crack in the door frame to stick a thin piece of metal through and lift up the two by four."

"What about the dead bolt?"

"Unfortunately, I didn't pay attention to it. But it's an old lock, a flip down style. Look at it closely."

Zeb reached up and put the bolt through its normal positional changes. It slid easily having been recently cleaned and oiled. He left it in the open position.

"The dead bolt could be opened with a second piece of metal, an angled one--insert through the crack--flip up--pull back--and voila, you're in like Flynn."

"Two people, you figure? One for the lock and one for the two by four? Maybe a thief and a lookout?" suggested Zeb.

"That's the way I had it figured when I first thought about it," said Josh. "But I changed my mind."

Using his right hand and left elbow, Josh deftly removed the large beam from the back door and leaned it against the back wall. He pulled the door open into the natural light of the sun.

"I found only one set of footprints that weren't mine in the alley around the door. They go from the back door to near the dumpster, where he must have parked his vehicle. One distinct set of prints coming. The same exact footprints going."

Josh gave Zeb minute details of the distance between the prints, the toeing out of the right foot, an approximated foot length and size, even the number of steps the person had taken.

"Have you ever been burgled before? I mean at your other store."

"No. A few times teenagers have tried to shoplift. Never a burglary."

"Robbed?"

"Never. It takes a desperate fool to rob a gun shop."

"I'll come back and make some impressions of the footprints. Was anything else disturbed on the outside?"

"Nothing that I noticed."

A cowbell hanging over the front door clanged loudly signaling Josh that a customer had arrived.

"I'm going to have a look around back. Bar the back door behind me. I'll come through the front when I'm done."

The dead bolt clicked and the wooden crossbeam clunked into the U-hooks. Zeb's hand rested against the adobe wall of the old building. The French family had built a respectable building, one that would stay cool in the pre-air conditioning era.

Following the footprints in the hardened dirt from the back door to the dumpster he imaged the route of the thief. It was a short one that could have been covered in mere seconds. Entry into the building with the right tools would have taken a professional less than a minute. Across the street were railroad tracks and a pair of empty, dilapidated industrial buildings. Directly across the alley was the back of a windowless storage shed. Zeb had been standing there for over three minutes and not one vehicle had come by. If the crook cased the alley, he might have guessed he could pull off the break-in even during broad daylight.

The building next door had a boarded up window. The plywood cover was stained with pigeon droppings. In the center of the excrement was a dried, brown stain. A thin trail from the center of the stain ran down the wood. Overhead, the tin roof slanted toward the alley. In a metal eave at the corner of the roof was an abandoned pigeon nest. Zeb marked the imprints with orange flags, walked down the alley and around the corner onto the street. He kept his eyes open for other clues but saw none. He re-entered Josh's gun shop through the front door.

"Find anything useful?"

"Maybe. Mind if I take a closer look at the gun case?"

"Be my guest. The sooner you have a look at it the sooner I can replace the broken glass."

Zeb touched the ridge of the entry point on the glass case. It had been etched, leaving only a smooth cut. Inside the case were ultrafine shards of glass. The thief had been quiet, clever and obviously experienced.

"Would I be likely to find anyone else's finger prints on this cabinet?"

"On the top glass you're going to find anyone's who leaned on the cabinet. You know how people are. They put their finger on the glass and point at something they want to have a look at. I clean the glass every day. I'm certain I cleaned it the day before I ended up in the hospital. I was only open a short time on the morning of the robbery. I don't recall anyone browsing this case, but I could be wrong. If there are any prints there, they could be from my unwanted guest. My prints should be the only ones on the back side of the case. I keep it locked and have the only key."

"Can you keep people away from it until I can get Deputy Steele over here later to dust it for prints?"

"No problem. In fact have her come over as soon as she can."

"You seem eager to see her."

The men exchanged a knowing smile as the cowbell above the entry door clanged again. Zeb turned to see a local man whom he recognized. He tipped his hat to the man and they exchanged hellos. He had come for a box of twelve gauge shells and some .22 cartridges. He mumbled something about varmint hunting which caused Josh to laugh and make a quip about it being varmint season.

When Josh walked through the swinging doors to get the ammunition, Zeb got a clear view of the back office. A professional could have easily staked out the inside of the building. An eerie feeling came over him as he thought about Josh Diamond, expert tracker and man hunter, having his office space and business stalked by someone with a devious and clever eye for plotting a crime.

CHAPTER ELEVEN

Ángel took a long pull on the tequila bottle. He began to feel better. It had been another sad and empty night without his beloved Juanita. His longing for her brought her to life in his daydream. During his prison lockup he counted the days, the hours and finally the minutes until he was paroled. His beautiful Juanita had written him a letter every day. Sometimes she would scent it with sweet perfume. Sometimes he could smell the heavenly fragrance of their lovemaking. He ached to run his fingers through her long black hair. To caress her silky soft skin would be divine. Ángel sighed until his lungs ached with emptiness. His love for Juanita was larger than just about everything else in the world.

But the demonic tequila despised his thoughts of love. Suddenly the devil recoiled in his mind. Tears pooled heavily beneath his eyelids. He had no strength to fight against the Demon Tequila that stole his sense even when he thought of his sainted mother. She had died while he was in prison. His grandfather had written the warden asking for a simple, humble favor. Could Ángel be released from prison for one day so he could go to his own mother's funeral? His grandfather even promised the warden on his dead daughter's soul that he would return Ángel to prison the minute the funeral was over. Other men had received this sort of favor. These men had committed much worse crimes than Ángel. The warden had laughed at his grandfather. The warden even spit on him. He said Ángel could not be trusted in the hands of a frail, old man. The boy would "run like a dingo dog". Those were his exact words. He had called

Ángel's grandfather frail and untrustworthy. He had called Ángel a dog. Ángel knew the warden hated him. The warden hated all the brown skins. He despised the Apache, who he called "goddamned redskins with no souls". He called any prisoner with Mexican blood "the bastard sons of Spain". The damned warden knew Ángel was first Mescalero, second Hispanic and last a Mexican-American. Such disrespect roused feelings of vengeance in his heart.

Ángel took one more long drink from the bottle hoping to put a lid on his growing hatred. The effect was quite the opposite. Ángel's blood was boiling. All he wanted was his dream of a beach life in Mexico. With Juanita by his side he would drink cerveza on the beach and fish in the ocean. He would buy his little mujercita a house on the beach. They would live happily ever after, just like in the storybooks his mother had read to him when he was a child. Ángel's mind raced between his hatred of the warden and the love of his Juanita.

"Jimmie Joe?"

"Sí, Ángel. You need more tequila so soon?"

"No. The tequila is tasting good."

"What is it then?"

"I am worried about Juanita driving around in a stolen pickup. It is such a beautiful truck. She is such a beautiful woman. Somebody will notice her. People will wonder why a lovely woman in a fancy truck is without an hombre by her side. It is bound to make someone suspicious."

"I told you a thousand times, Ángel. You never listen. When the pigs are looking for a stolen vehicle, they only check the license plates. I put a clean set of plates on that little truck before I handed her the keys. She will be just fine in that little baby blue Chevy pickup when she meets you in Tucson. Quit worrying. Have a little more fire water."

"I'd be feeling so much better if I had been able to see her face and touch her."

"Ángel, you know that would not be the safe thing to do. If you had taken the truck to her, you two would never come back. You and Juanita would be drinking and partying and having fun."

"Sí, sí. This sounds so very good. Me and my baby dancing all night long."

"But Ángel, you would have nothing, no money, no future. Now you wait only three short weeks."

"But three weeks is a long time, Jimmie Joe."

"How long were you in the prison, Ángel?"

"Two years, four months, six days, nine hours and forty-two minutes."

"Then what's a few more weeks out of your short life if you can be rich?"

"But, my Juanita..."

"You think Juanita won't love you a whole lot more if you have a million dollars in your pocket?"

"I know she would love me if I had no money at all. She would love me if I was as poor as the little white mouse in the Iglesia Catedral back home. She doesn't care about money. Juanita only cares about loving me."

"Bah! Ángel you know nothing of women. You may look like a girl but you don't think like a muchacha."

"Cut it out, Jimmie Joe. Quit making fun of me. You shouldn't do that."

"Who saved your cute round ass from the homosexuals, Ángel? Huh? Who protected your cute little mouth from being a lollypop sucker?"

Ángel took a deep pull on the tequila bottle to put out the fire in his heart. That day in the shower--would Jimmie Joe never let him forget about it?

"Mi abuelo--my grandfather. You are sure he is okay? I know he is worried about me. Ever since mi madre buena went to heaven he prays from the Bible every day. If I could only have seen him one time, I would feel so much better."

"How many times do I have to go over this? You could not see Juanita because she would steal your heart. You could not see your grandfather because he would talk to his friends. If one word slipped to the wrong person, then people would know you are in the area. That is exactly the sort of thing that could ruin our plan. We don't want anyone to know we are anywhere near here. One little slip and we're back in the big house. Look Ángel, use your head. We don't want any trouble. I have got this thing all mapped out. We won't vary from my plan. It is too late now to have it any other way. Don't go screwy on me, Ángel."

"I know, I know. I just miss my family so much it hurts me. They are the only ones left--Grandfather Felipe, Juanita..."

"You can't really count on them. They're no different than anyone else. They would turn on you like rats if the money was right."

"That is not true. Family is blood," said Ángel.

"I know from experience that family members are nothing but bloodsuckers."

"I can count on my family no matter what."

"You had better hope so," said Jimmie Joe. "You had better hope so."

Jimmie Joe fired a glob of spit next to Ángel's hand. He pulled a tin of chewing tobacco from his right rear pocket. Ángel watched as the older man stuffed a fresh plug of chew between his cheek and gum. Pulling out the drippy gob of used tobacco the sinister older man held it out to Ángel.

"Chew? Its better the second time around, already broken in, if you catch my drift."

Ángel turned away from the rancid smell of the stringy brown leaves pulled from between the rotting teeth of the diablo blanco. Why did the big White man insist on playing such stupid little tricks? Maybe his amigos were right. Maybe el diablo es loco.

"Doesn't go good with tequila, huh? Here let me show you how."

Jimmie Joe Walker grabbed the bottle from the tightly gripped fingers of his young partner in crime. Slowly he brought it to his mouth. An evil grin, full of black teeth, ran cheek to cheek. With one swallow he chugged down half of what remained in the bottle.

"See? Nothing to it when you're a real man."

The big White man with the huge tattoo of a laughing devil on his arm smiled broadly. A rancid display of tobacco juice hung between his widely gapped rotting teeth. The pain in Ángel's stomach escalated in waves. His gut creaked like a rusty gate. Nausea surged through his body from head to toe. Stumbling out of the run-down trailer house he fell to all fours. Ángel began up-chucking a mixture of bile, tequila and blood. A wave of self-hatred rushed through him as he realized good liquor had barely been given a chance to do its job.

Ángel didn't hear the footsteps behind him as he used the back of his hand to wipe the red and green brackish fluid from his face. As the putrid smell of the vomited liquid reached his nose, turning his stomach yet again, the big White devil placed a boot squarely in the middle of Ángel's neck crushing his face directly into his own vomit. The boot striking his spine sent a lightning bolt of pain through his body. Ángel puked a second time. He struggled for breath. His anxious painful breathing forced some of the vomited liquid back into his stomach.

"Learn to hold your liquor, you stupid little bastard. So help me God, if you screw this up, you are going to be one dead fucker."

CHAPTER TWELVE

Deputy Steele closed the door to her office. She slipped her copy of the bomb threats into the cassette player. Listening to the hum of the rewinding tape she stared intently at a painting on her office wall titled "Where Beauty Begins". Eskadi had drawn it for her shortly after he had given her the traditional Apache name of Son-ee-ah-Ray--Morning Star. The painting was a lifelike rendition of Jimmy Song Bird, Medicine Man at the San Carlos Reservation. Something caught her eye. Something that she had not seen in all the times she had stared at the painting. Eskadi had carefully constructed an obscure celestial design with the tiniest of stars painted into Song Bird's dark and mysterious pupils.

The cassette player clicked. Kate rested a lithe finger lightly on the play button. She pressed it on slowly, softly. Her mind replayed the taped conversation a fraction of a second ahead of the actual recording. Every hesitation, every inflection, even the scratchy hang up noise from the caller's phone was etched into her consciousness and seeping more deeply into her subconscious. The slight slur in his voice--was it alcohol or simply nervousness? Was she hearing regret in the man's voice or not? The accent was Mexican Hispanic but the thick-tongued inflection carried hints of what she now knew to be Mescalero Apache. Whatever it was, it was definitely not a local accent. The caller's cadence was neither precisely Spanish nor exactly Athabascan Apache. It was an unfamiliar rhythmic blend.

She looked at the regional map beneath the glass covering her desk. With a magic marker she drew a circle. The telephone company had confirmed the call was local.

Thirty miles in any direction was the area she needed to know. That area involved a half-an-hour drive, a mere thirty miles. But it may as well have been the moon…or the stars in Song Bird's eyes. Lost in thought, Sheriff Hanks' voice took her by surprise.

"Kate? Mind if I listen to the tape with you?"

"Certainly, Sheriff. Have a seat. Maybe you can hear something I missed."

"I'm sure you've heard everything there is to hear. It's just that every time you listen to it I can hear it in my office. It sounds all jumbled through the wall. It was starting to annoy me. You know, hearing it without being able to make out what it said. I thought maybe if we listened to it together, we could hear something neither of us heard separately."

"Actually, Sheriff, I am a little stuck. It might just be helpful if you would sit down with me and have a listen."

Zeb placed his elbows on Kate's desk. He leaned forward resting his chin on a closed fist. He gave his full concentration as his deputy replayed the tape.

"The voice isn't familiar sounding. It doesn't sound exactly like Mexican-American nor does it sound like Athabascan. Worst of all, it sounds wrong. Something isn't right about it. The tone, the way it's worded, something."

"We need to figure out what it is that we don't know. Any small hint might be helpful."

"Wait a minute," said Sheriff Hanks. "I remember something Delbert told me a while back."

"Yes?"

"I think that phone call might have come from north and east of town."

"What? How do you know that?" asked Kate.

"That scratchy sound when the man hung up. You know that squeaky sound when he set the phone down. Did you hear that?" asked Zeb.

Kate mimicked the sound of a phone being put back in its cradle.

"Say, that's it and a pretty good imitation," said Zeb. "I didn't know you could do that."

"Just one of my many talents. Actually, Eskadi and I have contests doing mimicry. It's a long story," she said with a smile. "When I hear that sound, it seems to me as if he was nervous, like his hands might have been shaking and hung the phone up too fast."

"That could be," said Sheriff Hanks. "Remember when we had those big winds about four months ago? The weather reporter on Channel 6 called them dry Santa Ana crosswinds."

Kate nodded.

"The high winds knocked down a bunch of telephone wires out that way. That funny noise in the telephone wires started right after that. I remember Delbert saying that an uncle on his mother's side lives out that way. He told me that every time she called him that high pitched sound irritated the dickens out of her hearing aid. Delbert said she was going to sue the phone company for the price of a new hearing aid if they didn't get it fixed."

Zeb and Kate suddenly realized how much they missed Delbert's unique ways around the office. He wasn't the sharpest knife in the drawer, but he had a keener sense of observation than most. To top it off he had a memory that was rock solid.

"Delbert told me none of the other local lines were having that particular problem. I remember he told me his mother asked him to call the lineman supervisor and tell him to fix it. Delbert talked to him. He said the supervisor told him there had not been complaints anywhere else about line interference, but he did say he was surprised more poles hadn't been blown over in those big winds."

"So the phone company was fairly certain those are the only lines with that type of static on them?" inquired Deputy Steele.

Kate ran a finger over the map. The huge territory she had been looking at was quickly reduced to a workable area. A call to the local phone company might narrow her search area even further.

"Sheriff, do you remember exactly where the telephone poles were blown down?"

"Sure I do. I did a drive along with Delbert to check and see if any poles had fallen onto the road. Thank goodness, none had."

"Do you remember what road the poles were downed on?"

"On County Road 6, just off Highway 191. I'd say about nine miles north of the turnoff on the west side of the road. Just a little past an old abandoned cattle corral."

Kate scoured the map.

"County 6, here it is. It joins up with Indian Route 11 on the lower end of the reservation, near the Gila Box."

"Yes, that is exactly the spot."

"Do the telephone poles that were downed serve that area of the reservation too?"

"I don't think so. I am fairly certain they stop before the reservation land. I can check with the telephone company line supervisor. I know him. He's a good guy."

"When you talk with him, would you find out where the line ends? If we can find out who the customers are on the lines, we might catch a break."

"Good thinking, Kate. You better watch it or you might be next in line for my job."

Kate was surprised to hear Zeb talk that way. It was out of character to speak so freely to her about something as important as a sheriff's election.

"Sheriff, do you drive out there often?"

"No, that is, I mean was, Delbert's turf. Hardly anyone lives out that way. It is sort of a no man's land as far as people are concerned."

Kate eyed the map. County 6 joined up with Indian Route 11. From there it angled off to the northwest and ran along the edge of the southernmost tip of the San Carlos Reservation. After a distance it shot back up to the northwest and joined up with Indian Route 8, the major road through the heart of Indian land. Tracing her finger backwards along the same route something caught her eye.

"Sheriff, have you ever driven on the lower end of the reservation?"

"I've hunted out there. I think I know it quite well."

"Are there any roads where County 6 joins up with Indian Route 11?"

"There's an old washed out road. It meanders through the reservation. I heard it used to go most of the way up to Indian Route 8. You would need a four-wheel drive vehicle with high clearance--or a horse--to make it through there."

"Where does it go?"

"It runs up to an abandoned copper mine. It hasn't been maintained since they shut the copper mine down years ago," said Sheriff Hanks.

Without speaking Kate continued to eye the details on the map.

"Anything else?" asked Sheriff Hanks. "If not, I think I will call the phone company."

"No, nothing right at the moment. Once you've talked with them, please let me know what you found out."

"Certainly," replied the sheriff. "Is the evidence you have leading you down the road to a specific theory?"

"Maybe. I hope so."

"Work on it. Let me know. I am headed out to tell old man García about his truck," said the sheriff.

"Good luck."

Kate studied the detail map of Graham County. At the intersection by the high school she wrote a large X. She put a second X at the grade school. Half way up County Road 6, in the area of the downed telephone poles, she put a third X. It was a long shot at best. Suddenly Kate had the distinct feeling that maybe Delbert had come out of his coma. Maybe he could add something to all this. She could not have been more wrong.

CHAPTER THIRTEEN

Zeb headed out to see old man García who was not going to be very happy when he heard the news about his truck. Being the bearer of bad news was a part of the job Zeb had come to dislike intensely, but it came with the territory and it was his responsibility.

As he approached the García homestead Zeb saw Lorenzo, his wife and a couple of their grandchildren sitting on a front porch swing. They all smiled and waved as they saw Sheriff Hanks approach.

"Shit," he muttered under his breath. Sheriff Hanks parked in Lorenzo's yard. He hesitated a moment and then got out of the car slowly.

"Hello, Sheriff Hanks," said Lorenzo García with a broad smile. "Have you brought me good news about my truck?"

Zeb walked up to the porch and greeted Mrs. García, who offered him tea and Mexican shortbread cookies. He had known Mrs. García since he was a child, when his own grandmother used to have Mrs. García tell her fortune or read her future in the Tarot cards. Zeb had a particular affection for the Garcías. They seemed like the perfect couple. They were solid citizens, good Catholic church-going folks and down to earth, hard-working people. None of the Garcías' extended family had ever had a run in with the law as far as Zeb knew. The grandchildren stood next to him admiring his gun and uniform. The older of the two, a little boy about seven years old, spoke to Zeb.

"Señor, are you really a Sheriff?"

"Yes, I am," he said tousling the young boy's hair.

"Can I look at your gun?" asked the boy.

Sheriff Hanks looked at Lorenzo and his wife for approval. Their nods said it was okay. Taking the gun from his holster, Sheriff Hanks unloaded the weapon and held it out for the boys to touch. The boys looked at their grandparents for approval.

"Sí," said Lorenzo. "You may touch it but be careful."

Wide-eyed the boys each ran a gentle finger across the barrel of the gun then quickly ran off together giggling, using their fingers as pistols, pretending to shoot at each other.

"Boys," said Lorenzo shrugging his shoulders, "will always be boys."

Overhead clouds rolled in from across the desert expanse. The day darkened along with the sheriff's mood. Small talk would be pointless. There was no getting around the fact that the outcome here was going to be bad. Lorenzo was going to be disappointed, perhaps even angry. The presence of Mrs. García made things only a little easier. Sheriff Hanks got right to the point.

"Lorenzo, I am afraid I have some very bad news for you."

"You did not find my truck?" asked Lorenzo.

"No, I'm afraid your truck has been found."

"Where?"

"In Tucson."

"So far away," said Lorenzo pointing toward Tucson. "Can I go pick it up?"

"I'm sorry," said Sheriff Hanks. "Your truck has been destroyed."

"No," gasped Lorenzo.

"I'm afraid it is a total ruin. It was burned up in a fire."

"No," gasped Lorenzo a second time. "Was anyone hurt?"

Sheriff Hanks hesitated a minute before telling the Garcías that a dead body had been found inside their Chevy LUV truck. When he finally told them, they both made a fast sign of the cross. As the sheriff further explained the body had not been identified and that the truck had stolen license plates on it, the Garcías seemed to go into a state of shock.

"This is an omen," said Mrs. García. "A very bad omen."

"I'm sorry," said Sheriff Hanks. He knew they had no insurance on the vehicle and that it would be a while before they had enough money to buy anything but a high mileage used junker. He departed the García homestead with Mrs. García's words "a very bad omen" ringing in his ears. Five miles from town he got a message on the two-way radio that proved her words prophetic.

CHAPTER FOURTEEN

"Delbert has passed on."

At first Helen's words made no sense to Zeb. It was almost as though his ears refused to hear the words from her mouth. He asked her to repeat what she had said. "Delbert died twenty minutes ago. Dr. Yackley just called looking for you. He gave me the sad news."

Zeb was stunned. The shock of it all prevented tears from forming. His heart sank. He had known Delbert since they were kids. Delbert was one of the nicest people he had ever known. It was not fair. It was not right. Corita Funke had only Delbert. Now, in her old age, she would have no comfort. Worst of all was the guilt Zeb felt. It was his fault Delbert was dead. Delbert was only following his orders. For a few seconds that seemed an eternity, Zeb let every cell of his body feel the horrible sensation that had just jolted his mind.

It felt almost identical to the time when a fellow border patrol agent, one of his team members, Darren Wendt, was shot and killed not twenty feet from where Zeb and Josh stood. It was a bad time in the history of the Arizona Border Patrol. They had lost five men in a single month. Bad memories came rushing in like a canyon flash flood in spring. All of the dead Arizona Border Patrol members were murdered by thugs from a drug running and people smuggling gang, the Crazy Cachandos.

Now it was Delbert who was dead. Zeb felt rage roiling inside him. He forced a cap on his emotions. It was quite possible he might come apart at the seams if he let Delbert's death get to him. He had been down this ugly road before. He knew nothing would bring Delbert back. Delbert was gone, hopefully and most likely, to heaven. Zeb's faith, what he had of it, was being tested once again.

The viewing of the body and the funeral came three days later. Zeb thought Delbert, in his full uniform, never looked so handsome. Zeb had a curious reflection at the viewing. The funeral director had somehow managed to put a smile on the face of the dead deputy.

The townspeople of Safford and nearby Thatcher mourned in unison over the loss of a native son. Doreen sang a hymn that left no one in the church with a dry eye. The Bishop of the Church of Jesus Christ of Latter Day Saints spoke from his heart. Friends testified to the good works of Delbert Funke. It seemed as though no one wanted the service to end as it would mean the last of Delbert. Sheriff Hanks spoke from the pulpit and allowed some of the guilt he harbored to be shared with the community. His words may have helped others, but they only intensified his own feelings of guilt. No one blamed him for Delbert's death, not even Delbert's mother who wept uncontrollably as the casket was rolled into the church, and again as the last shovelful of dirt was tossed on the coffin.

Whoever set the explosion was now also a murderer. Sheriff Hanks and Deputy Steele were going to make certain that the crime was paid for, in full. Their investigation needed to be put into high gear. In the minds of Sheriff Hanks, Deputy Steele and just about everybody in the area, each moment that passed with the murderer of Deputy Delbert Funke walking free was a bad moment. Justice needed to be served and it needed to be served quickly.

CHAPTER FIFTEEN

In the days between the death and burial of Deputy Delbert Funke, the entire town of Safford seemed to be on hold. Now, with the funeral proceedings behind them, the time to move forward was at hand.

Deputy Steele felt the greatest sense of urgency she had ever felt in her life. The need to solve the murder of her cohort was taking precedence over any other professional issues, and certainly her personal ones.

"I have some information you need, Kate," said Zeb. "It might be the break we've been seeking. Let's have a look at your map."

Removing a pencil from her desk drawer she handed it to Zeb who pressed the rubber eraser head against the map and drew a box. County Roads 6, 11 and 14 marked the eastern, southern and western borders. The northernmost boundary angled off to the northeast and formed an imaginary line through the jutted out southeastern tip of the San Carlos Reservation. The map clearly showed there were no marked roadways in this area.

"Joe Escarte, from the phone company, told me that inside this area they are still getting some static from the downed lines. He thinks the noise is transformer resistance complicated by some sort of a dual coupling problem or an electrical technical issue that I didn't really understand. He says those poles out there all need to be replaced. The ones that got blown down were termite infested. He said not only were they old, but had not been treated correctly with creosote. The way he has it figured is this--somebody shortchanged the county when they sold them the poles. He asked me to look into that issue. I referred him to the local purchasing agent for the county."

Kate studied the sheriff's drawn outline. The area inside the box was twenty by forty miles. The eight hundred square miles seemed huge until Zeb reiterated a point the phone company man had made.

"There are less than one hundred phones serviced by that line. Some of them are shared lines, party lines, but almost everyone who uses that line lives on County Road 6."

"It looks like we're going to do some legwork and knock on some--"

Deputy Steele's comment was interrupted by a shout from Helen.

"Sheriff. Line one. It's the man who made the bomb threat. He wants to talk to whoever is in charge. He won't give me his name."

Zeb Hanks stepped quickly toward his office. As he passed Helen's line of sight he silently signaled her to record the call. He picked up the phone as Helen pointed to the already turning tape recorder.

"This is Sheriff Hanks."

"Are you policia in charge?"

"Yes, I'm in charge."

Zeb's mind raced. He had the murderer of his deputy only a phone line away. Was this man a psychopath checking to see how the sheriff's office was reacting to the loss of one of its deputies?

"I hear on radio your deputy die. I am terrible sorry."

The man's voice was heavy with remorse. Could it be genuine? Sheriff Hanks did not believe it for even half a second.

"I want turn myself in. I go to jail for calling in bomb threats. Can you do that? I didn't kill no one. I promise I don't kill no one."

The man on the other end of the line began to sob. Sheriff Hanks was not only stunned by the man's confession, but by his tears. He sounded soft, sincere and contrite.

"That can be arranged. What is your name?"

The man on the other end of the line suddenly froze. Anxiety arose in the sheriff's chest. He did not want to lose the killer now.

"We can come and pick you up right now. Just tell us where you are."

The crackling on the line increased dramatically. The man's voice became barely audible amid the hissing. His next words became incomprehensible as the static turned to white noise before dying.

"Damn it!" said Sheriff Hanks slamming the phone. "The line went dead."

"Maybe he'll call back," said Deputy Steele.

"We can only--."

A shrill ring interrupted her comment.

"Please." Deputy Steele's voice was but a whisper. "Please."

The sheriff and his deputy hurried to Helen's desk. They hovered over her, listening in silence as she picked up the phone.

"It's him again. He apologized for the line going dead," said Helen. "He wants to talk to you again, Sheriff Hanks."

The man was already talking as Zeb took the phone from Helen's hand.

"If you come and get me, that be good. My truck, she is broken. I am sorry to not drive myself to jail. Please come put me in jail so I can rest."

This is way too easy, thought Zeb. It could be a set-up, a trap. If the caller were a true psychopath, he might even have another explosion in mind, something to send another lawman to his grave.

"Tell me where you live," said Sheriff Hanks. "We will come and get you."

"Please just one to come and get me. I no want to get killed."

"Tell me where you live. I'll come alone. You have my word."

"You know County Road 6."

Sheriff Hanks had been right.

"My place four miles north of turnoff on east side of road. My name is on mailbox. Can you come now?"

"Yes I can come right away. What name should I look for on the mailbox?"

"Felipe Madrigal."

The man sounded forlorn at the utterance of his own name. The line crackled. Sheriff Hanks listened as the man once again began to cry and apologize about the death of the deputy.

"Mr. Madrigal?"

"Sí."

"When I come to the house, I want you to come outside with your hands over your head. Do you understand me?"

His quiet response was drenched in sobs.

"Sí, yes, yes. I am very, very sorry. No one supposed to get hurt. That already happen. No more hurting."

"I will be right there to get you. It will take me about thirty minutes. I will honk the horn two times. You come out with your hands over your head."

"Sí."

"No weapons! Put your hands over your head. Do you understand me?"

"Sí. Comprendo. I understand."

CHAPTER SIXTEEN

Zeb's heart thumped heavily, partly from anxiety, partly from hatred and a desire for revenge. The near certainty of a trap raced through his mind.

"Sheriff, do you recognize the name Felipe Madrigal?"

"Sure, I know right where he lives. Delbert used to memorize the names on the mailboxes. One time when I went with him I saw Felipe in the yard. He's an old man. He walks bent over at the waist. He waved to us. I don't know why I remember that, but I do. He seemed like a nice old guy."

"Did he just confess to the bomb threats?" asked Deputy Steele who had overheard only one end of the conversation.

"Yes."

"How about the murder of Delbert?"

"No, he apologized for Delbert getting hurt. He said he didn't hurt anyone."

"Let's go get him," said Deputy Steele.

"He's nervous. He wants me to come alone. You heard me tell him to come out of the house with his hands over his head. As I remember, his house sits down low, in a little glen. How do you feel about covering me? You have to be ready to shoot to kill, if it's necessary."

Deputy Steele had intense training in her background, but never had it been necessary to pull the trigger. At this moment she had no doubts of her ability to do so.

"As Delbert used to say…never keep a criminal waiting. Let's roll," said Deputy Steele.

The patrol cars crossed over the Hanksco River, headed north on County 6, as Zeb's concern about an ambush slipped into a state of perplexity. Nothing about the case made sense. Why would a friendly old man blow up the grade school? Then it dawned on him. The bomb was less about producing physical damage than it was about inflicting fear. If Delbert had not been in the wrong place at exactly the wrong time, he would not have been injured. What message was Felipe Madrigal trying to send? Why the remorse in his voice? When he had called to turn himself in, he had broken down and cried like a child, not a sociopath. Beneath it all lay a fear that it all might just be a set up. The crackling of the two-way radio broke the sheriff's concentration.

"Sheriff?"

It was Deputy Steele.

"I was thinking…why don't you let me go on ahead? I can park my car, climb up over the hill and get close to Mr. Madrigal's house. That way I can be ready in case he is planning something."

It was a risk, but a good one.

"Good idea. Just don't let him see you."

Kate felt the adrenaline rise as she shot past the sheriff's car leaving a cyclone trail of dust. Zeb slowed down, rolled up his window and let her get some distance between them. Kate pulled over a hundred yards short of a silver metal mailbox at the end of a long driveway. She opened the trunk and pulled out the .30-.30. She checked the safety and quickly loaded shells into her weapon. As she worked her way to the back side of the house she noticed a smiley face painted in yellow that accompanied the handwritten name of Felipe Madrigal on the mailbox. The idea of drawing a gun on an old man who drew smiley faces on his mailbox seemed like utter madness.

Zeb pulled into the old man's driveway. Kate, perched on a small knoll ninety feet away, tipped her cap and pointed to the small house. The yard in front of the old adobe building was littered with twisted pieces of metal, chunks of gnarly firewood, a garbage pile and a run-down doghouse. A truck with the hood propped open by a tire iron was parked under a mesquite tree on the north side of the house. A pair of windows in the front of the house had broken panes. One was partially boarded over from the outside. The other was stuffed with rags and dirty insulation. Tumbleweed remnants lay trapped under a rusted television antenna at the back of the low, slanting roof.

Exiting the car, Sheriff Hanks heard the unmistakable squeak and low groan from the rusting blades of an ancient windmill. An easy wind from the south wafted the sweet aroma of late season sage bloom. Everything appeared normal--abnormally normal.

The run down ranch house showed no signs of life. Deputy Steele trained the sights of the .30-.30 on the door. A timid voice from behind a window squeaked out.

"I don't got no gun. You tell señorita on hillside to no shoot me."

Felipe Madrigal sounded meek, almost childish. He was definitely scared.

"She won't shoot," replied Sheriff Hanks. "Come out of the house with your hands over your head. Nobody wants to hurt you."

The door of the house, with its broken screen mesh fluttering in the wind, began to open. Slowly one hand, then the other, poked through the open space. The old man's hands trembled as he held them above his head. His rounded back and shoulders forced his head into such a position where his eyes could only see the ground. He shuffled along with great difficulty as he made his way toward the sheriff.

Could this man possibly be Delbert's killer? Sheriff Hanks didn't think so, but then again the things he had seen along the border of Mexico, when dealing with human and drug trafficking, did not make sense either. He shook his head clear of the thoughts of the border patrol agent's death and focused on what was in front of him. The lingering doubt he lived with, that the deaths of Darren Wendt and now Delbert Funke had been caused by his lack of attention, haunted him at a level few could understand.

"Please, Señor Policia. Don't kill me. I did no harm no one."

The sheriff's eye trained on the man caught something off to the side moving through the underbrush. He instinctively crouched behind the door for additional protection when he realized it was Deputy Steele slowly making her way into his peripheral vision.

"Deputy Steele, check the house."

She made her way to the door and quickly ascertained that Felipe Madrigal was alone, at least at this moment.

"No one is going to shoot you," said Sheriff Hanks.

"Gracias, Señor Policia. Gracias."

Felipe Madrigal fell to his knees, weeping.

"Suplico clemencia. Clemencia. Please have mercy on me, Señor Policia."

Sheriff Hanks grabbed the little man under the arm and helped him to his feet. The man's left eye was discolored and swollen. His face was sad and defeated. A salt and pepper beard surrounded a mouthful of yellowing teeth.

"Are you Felipe Madrigal?"

"Sí. I am Felipe Madrigal."

"Did you phone the sheriff's office in Safford and say you wanted to confess to the bomb threats at the high school and grade school in Safford?"

"Sí."

"Do you know your rights?"

The old man responded with a puzzled look and turned toward Sheriff Hanks.

"Under the laws governing the State of Arizona and the United States of America you have the right to remain silent."

The tired and haggard looking old man stared at the ground. His body trembled as Sheriff Hanks rattled off the Miranda mantra.

"Do you understand these rights as they have been read to you?"

The old man said nothing. He stood rigid, gazing open mouthed toward the ground.

"Should I read them to him in Spanish?" asked Deputy Steele. "I'm not so sure he understands everything you said."

"I think you had better do that," replied Sheriff Hanks.

Deputy Steele removed a Spanish copy of the Miranda rights from her pocket. She read fluently, sometimes not even looking at the words. When she asked the old man if he understood, the weathered old man responded by nodding his head up and down.

"Let's put some cuffs on him and put him in the back seat of my car. I want to ask him a few questions on the way into town. Deputy Steele, you close up the house and follow me back to town."

Sheriff Hanks headed south on County 6. He waited for Felipe Madrigal to say something. If the old man was the first to speak, he might feel less pressure. He might simply let things out, maybe even explain what he had been thinking by threatening the lives of hundreds of children. The sheriff drove slowly. His prisoner remained mum. Near town Zeb flipped down the visor to shade himself from the setting sun. In the rear view mirror he noticed Felipe holding his head forward. The prisoner wore a humble, sad expression on his face. The sheriff flipped the passenger's side visor down to block the sun from his eyes.

"Gracias."

"De nada"

"Habla Ud. español?" asked the old man.

"Un poco, no, not really," replied the sheriff.

The old man returned to a stony silence.

"Felipe?"

"Sí?"

"Why did you call in those bomb threats?" Zeb glanced over his shoulder. The old man was quivering. "Felipe?"

"Sí?"

"Did you think that no one would get hurt when you made a bomb and put it in the grade school?"

"Señor Policia. I didn't make no bomb. I didn't put no bomb in the school!"

His meek voice suddenly became adamant. His dull eyes sharpened as he spoke.

"Who made the bomb, if you didn't?"

Felipe cast his eyes toward the floor of the car, tipped his head forward and once again became mute.

"Is there anything you'd like to say to me now? We're almost at the jail. The more you can tell me now the easier it will be for you. My deputy is dead. This won't go easy for you."

The old man's voice was forlorn, fearful as he muttered three words.

"Mercy, mercy, mercy."

CHAPTER SEVENTEEN

Felipe Madrigal barely uttered a word as he filled out some paperwork he obviously didn't understand. His confusion and disorientation heightened as Deputy Steele inked his fingertips for identification. The look in his eyes spoke of a man who carried a heavy burden bearing down on his soul. Yet some unseen force rendered him mute.

A hand braided leather billfold revealed twelve dollars cash, a social security card, an expired Local 616 Morenci Copper Miner's ID card and an Arizona driver's license. According to the driver's license Felipe Madrigal was sixty-five years old, five feet two inches tall, weighed a hundred twenty pounds. He had brown eyes and black hair.

Tucked away in the wallet was a Spanish version of a prayer to the Blessed Virgin and three small photos. One photo was Felipe dressed in a fine white suit with an Indian or Mexican woman in a traditional wedding dress. The second photo was a smiling, young girl in a white dress holding flowers and a Bible. From the age of the photo, Deputy Steele assumed it was his daughter. The final one was a young boy in a cap and gown. The deputy held the picture of Felipe and his wife on their wedding day. She held it close so her prisoner could see it clearly. Felipe shook his head.

"Ella está con Dios."

"Que?" said Deputy Steele.

"She is with God," said Felipe.

When she flashed the second photo, his eyes welled with tears.

"Ella está en un lugar mejor ahora."

"I'm sorry but I don't understand spoken Spanish very well," said Kate.

The old man looked away, speaking silently, "She is in a better place now."

"Felipe?"

"Sí?"

Deputy Steele showed him the picture of the young man.

"Who is this young man?"

Felipe Madrigal shook his head, almost defiantly.

"Is he your grandson?"

"My grandson has gone to devil," replied Felipe.

"Is he dead?"

"I don't know."

Felipe spoke the words with a harsh determination. Deputy Steele once again asked about Felipe's grandson but his unwillingness to discuss the young man stopped the conversation cold.

"Would you like something to eat?"

"No. No quiero comer…quiero fumar."

Deputy Steele shrugged her shoulders.

"Could I have cigarette?"

"I'm sorry," replied Deputy Steele. "There is no smoking in the jail."

The tired looking old man lay down on the bed and rolled towards the wall. Breathing heavily through his mouth it sounded to Deputy Steele as though he was fighting back tears of distress and pain.

Kate was stymied. If Felipe made the bomb threat, why would he confess and then clam up? Maybe the old man did not have respect for her because she was a woman?

She walked to her office and removed the bomb threat tape from the locked desk drawer. She slid it into the tape player. There was no doubt the voice on the tape was that of Felipe Madrigal. A part of her genuinely wished that the recording was not this seemingly humble old man. A glance at the clock told her it was after nine. She knocked on Sheriff Hanks' door.

"Come in. What have you got for me?"

"Not much, I'm sorry to say."

Zeb kept his head down over some paperwork and grunted. Her response was more or less what he had anticipated.

"Sheriff, I think you might be able to get more out of Felipe Madrigal than I can. I think he would rather talk to a man. If he's awake, I am willing to bet you can get him to chat. I think he might feel better if he got things off his chest."

"I agree with you. It seems like things are weighing pretty heavy on him. I get the feeling he wants to tell us something. Did you learn anything that might help me to get him to talk?"

"He seems to open up when you get him to talk about his family, his wife and daughter that is, but not his grandson. I think if he believes we are here to help him, he might talk. But I don't know for sure. I suspect he is very troubled."

"We see a lot of troubled folks in here, but we don't see many like him do we, Kate? We don't see many that had a hand in killing one of our own."

It took everything the sheriff had inside him to hold back his anger.

"No, we sure don't. Thank God for that. Sheriff," said Kate.

"Yes?"

"It's just not the same without Delbert around."

Stony silence was the sheriff's response. He did not need to be reminded that it would never be the same again. When you lose a man, a good man, you never forget. Zeb felt his anger rising as he headed for Felipe Madrigal's cell. Felipe was lying on his side, half asleep and half weeping. Zeb put his hands on the cell door and listened. Could this whimpering old man possibly have made the bomb and planted it in the boiler room of the grade school? Could this man really be Delbert's killer? The whimper turned into a soft snore. Zeb decided he would let the old man sleep on his guilt. Tomorrow would be here soon enough. The sheriff headed home. He gave orders to the night staff to check in on the prisoner to make sure he did not try to kill himself.

CHAPTER EIGHTEEN

Doreen greeted Zeb with a hug and a kiss. His response, or rather the lack of his anticipated response, told her his mind was somewhere else.

"You okay, sugar dumplin'?"

He wasn't. There was no sense lying to Doreen. He knew she could read him like a map.

"Not really."

"Delbert?" she asked.

"We arrested the man who called in the bomb threats. He may be the guy that murdered Delbert. He could be part of a group of crazy people with bad ideas. I don't know for sure."

The thought of Delbert created a painful tear that slipped down Doreen's cheek as she asked Zeb who he had arrested.

"An old man. His name is Felipe Madrigal. To look at him you wouldn't think he had a bad bone in his body. Most sociopaths can fool you though."

"Felipe Madrigal? I don't recognize the name. I thought I knew everybody around town."

"He probably has never been in the Town Talk. He lives off of County 6, just south of the San Carlos Reservation."

Zeb slipped out of his boots, hung his cowboy hat, unbuckled his holster and walked to the refrigerator for a cold beer. Doreen had not seen him drink in a month of Sundays.

"Do you believe him? I mean about not having made the bomb?" asked Doreen.

Zeb took a few sips of the cold brew. It was a good question. He did not have a good answer.

"I don't think he is lying to me. But, on the other hand, I doubt like hell that he is telling me the whole truth either," said Zeb staring blankly at the television screen.

Somewhere in the back of his mind he knew Felipe wanted to tell more than he was saying. Was Felipe so full of remorse that he couldn't speak? Was he in shock knowing that he had killed Delbert? What was the reason behind his half-truthful story? Maybe Felipe Madrigal had something to fear. Maybe he was a true sociopath. The sheriff knew for certain that being behind locked jailhouse doors was not what scared Felipe. The more he thought about it, the more Zeb realized it probably was not even the thought of prison that scared him. What was behind Felipe Madrigal's fear? If he could answer that question, he might understand a whole lot more.

Doreen, usually quick with the quip, said nothing as she watched her man pondering his troubles. Her own experiences told her there was more, much more to this than he was saying.

"What are you thinkin' about, Zeb?"

"Everything, Doe. It just doesn't make sense, any of it."

"I was thinkin' about Corita Funke and how she must be feeling, losin' her only son."

Zeb's heart felt as though it were about to explode. His mind raced between seeing Delbert dead in his casket and Border Patrol Agent Wendt, also an only child, dead from a bullet wound, in the remote desert near the Mexican border. Both men had been under his command, his direct orders when they died. Who was he to have power over anyone's life or death? Then Michael Parrish sprang into his mind. He had put a bullet in him and never given it a second thought, until now.

"I think I am going…"

"Crazy," said Doreen filling in the blank.

For a few moments neither Zeb nor Doreen said a word.

"I think I'm just feeling sorry for myself," said Zeb.

"A pity party for one?" asked Doreen

"Yup," said Zeb taking another pull on the beer.

"Been there. Done that," said Doreen. "It don't work. It only makes you run from reality."

"Are we talking about the same thing here?" asked Zeb. "Or do you have something you want to tell me?"

Doreen took the beer from Zeb's hand and set it on the end table.

"Zebulon Hanks, if you are going to be my husband, there is something I have to tell you and I have to tell you now."

Zeb sat up straight. He stared his wife-to-be in the eyes. What was she about to tell him? She had mentioned up on Mount Graham that she was waiting for the right time to tell him something important. He had sensed that it was an important secret she held deep in her heart. Was this what she had been talking to Father McNamara about before he was murdered? Was this about her crisis of faith? Was this the thing she needed to get off her chest so they could finally get married? It had to be. For a fraction of a second he considered her timing bad, but just as quickly let go of that thought. Right now there wasn't a good time for much of anything, so there wasn't a bad time for anything either.

"I am not who you think I am," said Doreen.

Zeb looked into her eyes. He loved her dearly. But why was she bringing this up right now?

"Wha..."

Doreen gently placed her finger over his lips and began to tell a story he could never have imagined. Indeed, Doreen was nothing like she seemed to be.

"Doreen isn't my real name. My real name is Holly Munson Jewell. I grew up in Atlanta, Georgia."

Zeb was taken for a loop.

"You grew up in Atlanta? Georgia? I guess that explains your accent."

"Yes, hon, it sure enough does."

Zeb and Doreen stared at each as if they were seeing each other for the first time.

"What? Why?" asked Zeb.

Before Doreen could get another word out of her mouth she began to weep. What began as a few drops turned into a river of tears, then abruptly inappropriate laughter. Zeb's confusion morphed into concern.

"Don't worry, Zeb. It's all right. I'm all right. It just feels so dang good to finally get it all out there in the open. I have been waitin' for years to tell someone the whole truth. I've wanted to tell you since the day we met. Father McNamara knew most of it, but not everything."

"What is the truth? Why haven't you told me before now?"

"I didn't know how to tell ya' about me. I guess I was hidin'. It seems like keepin' it all hid somehow protected me. I knew I had to tell you sooner or later. Just listen, please, without judgin' me. Then you can decide if you want to marry me or not."

"Fair enough," said Zeb, now intrigued as well as more than a bit confused.

"My family, what there are of them, are good southern folks. But I have disappeared out of their lives…for now."

Zeb's head was spinning. "Why?"

"It's very complicated. Someday, maybe even soon, I will see them again. Maybe not. I dunno for sure what's right anymore."

"Should I call you Doreen or Holly?"

"Let's stick with Doreen for now," she replied.

"And your family?"

"My father is alive and living in Georgia. He's a retired high school agriculture teacher. I miss him. I wanna see him agin. I will when the timin' is right. My mother was a sickly woman who died shortly after my birth."

Zeb managed to say he was sorry to hear that before being floored by Doreen's next statement.

"I was married..."

"Married?" Zeb felt the anger of being lied to rising through his flushed face. "To whom?"

"That's what I couldn't tell ya'. Please be patient. I'll explain it all."

"Okay," said Zeb. "I can't even begin to imagine what the rest of the story is."

Zeb gulped down a beer in one swallow and opened another.

"Less than two months after I graduated from high school I got married to Loren James Jewell."

"Married? You did say married?"

"Yes, you heard me right the first time. This isn't any easier on me than it is on you, so please be patient."

Zeb felt heat, anger, jealousy and rage as he downed another half of a beer. "Who in the hell is Loren James Jewell?"

"My high school sweetheart. I was young; I was in love."

Zeb's heart sank. He knew he was not the first man in Doreen's life, but he did think he was going to be her first and only husband. Having that illusion shattered was painful. It was all like a swirling eddy in Zeb's brain. Was she Holly or was she Doreen? The questions in his mind far outnumbered the answers. He knew she was not a virgin when he first made love to her but had no idea that she had been married. The mere thought of Doreen having been married was unsettling. Even as he sat there pondering, he realized how ridiculous that thought was, yet the pain remained. Still, he had to know about her past as it might concern their future together.

"What about your marriage? Are you divorced?"

"I was tryin' to tell you about that. Loren and I dated in high school. We got married right after graduation, when I found out I was pregnant."

"You have a child?"

Doreen looked deeply into Zeb's eyes and began to cry. He could tell this cry was different from any tears he had ever seen anywhere. These tears originated from a place deep in her heart. He held her close and then smothered her in his arms as the tears did not, seemingly could no,t stop. When she was mostly cried out, he was more confused than ever.

"I don't know if I can make it through this," said Doreen.

"Please try," said Zeb. "I love you. No matter what you say, nothing will change that."

His words felt slightly hollow as he spoke them. Doreen looked so deeply into Zeb's eyes he could feel the track of her stare right down to his heart. He shivered. That anyone could see so deeply into his very being shook him.

"I feel like I can believe you," she said. "Yes, I really do believe you." Her words also carried a twinge of doubt. "Seven months after our marriage our son, James Wellington Jewell, was born."

Zeb's heart sank to the floor. His mind raced in a thousand directions. He was at a loss for words. He didn't want to hear another word. How could she have possibly kept this from him? He was about to find out.

"When young James was two and a half years old, he and I went to meet Loren for lunch at the Green Dragon Tavern. Loren had just stepped out of a cab and was waiting for us. Little James saw his father and began to run toward him." Doreen's complexion turned ashen. Tears welled in her eyes but none came. "Just as Loren bent down to pick him up a car veered out of control and hit them. Both of them died almost instantly. I held them both as they breathed their last breaths."

With those words, Doreen collapsed into Zeb's arms and fell onto his lap where she wept tears of pain. Zeb caressed her hair. Untold thoughts raced through his mind. Who was this woman he now held? Was she so broken that she could not be put back together? Did the horrible event she just described prevent her from ever being whole again? Or was she healing from a horrible trauma right in front of his very eyes. What did this mean for their relationship? Was it over? Was this the real beginning? His mind went everywhere. His mind went nowhere. Zeb had seen the look in Doreen's eyes as she went back to the time and place of the deaths of her husband and son. It took him back to the Mexican border and the death of Darren Wendt and to the school basement and the explosion that had killed Delbert. If he had periodic flashbacks to Agent Wendt's and Delbert's deaths, he could not even imagine what went through her mind. What went on inside Doreen's head had to be truly horrifying. Felipe Madrigal flashed through his mind. He tried to push it away, but Felipe was another person who was not what he seemed to be. The whole world seemed jumbled and crazy. Eventually Doreen sat up, dried her tears, silently made some tea, opened another beer for Zeb and announced she wanted to tell him the whole story.

"The doctor said I was sufferin' from an acute stress disorder. You and I would call it a nervous breakdown. I couldn't face myself. I couldn't even look in the mirror. I couldn't face anyone. And, I really couldn't face the world."

"What did you do? Were you hospitalized?"

"The doctor tried to dope me up with them crazy people pills to hide my feelin's and emotions. I couldn't do that. The medications made me feel suicidal. I went to a shrink. That only made me feel worse. I even went to a Cherokee medicine man. I think that mighta helped some, but not a lot. I had to face my monsters in my own way. So, I did what I knew how to do. Loren was a motorcycle enthusiast. He taught me how to ride."

"So that's where you learned," said Zeb feeling irrationally jealous that Loren had been the first to share the thrill of a motorcycle ride with her.

"I had a Harley Davidson, a 978 FLH Electra-Glide. I sold everythin' I owned. I had some money from a settlement of the deaths of Loren and James. I called up a lawyer and he put the money into a trust. Far as I know most of it is still in that trust. I never check on it."

Zeb could only shake his head in disbelief. This was all too much, too fast.

"I took off on my Harley and rode across the country and up to Alaska. I rented a house on Kodiak Island for a year. I got drunk or stoned out of my mind every day for the better part of that year. I watched television and movies twenty hours a day. When I was really messed up, I wandered off into the woods hoping the bears would eat me, but they never did. Oh they saw me and watched me," said Doreen with a laugh. "But they must have figured I was crazy and that a crazy woman's meat wouldn't be no good for eatin'."

Zeb looked at her with alarm.

"Don't look at me like that."

"Like what?" asked Zeb.

"Like I am crazy. I was crazy. 'Was' being the operative word. I ain't crazy now. In fact, this is as sane as I've ever been.

"Okay, you're not crazy."

"Thank you for noticin'. Then one day I got a job waitressin' at a local greasy spoon. I had done it back in high school. It was about all I knew how to do. I made some quick cash, hopped back on my Harley Davidson and headed south. I was goin' to ride to the tip of South America and jump in the ocean."

Zeb's head jerked back in astonishment.

"Cool it cowboy, only kiddin' about jumpin' into the deep blue sea. I coulda' done that any time in Alaska."

Zeb was only half convinced she was joking.

"But as fate would have it, my motorcycle broke down right here in Safford. While my Harley was at the shop gettin' fixed, I walked up and down Main Street. I found myself starin' at my own reflection in the window of the Town Talk. I truly saw myself for the first time since my husband and son had been killed. I had to change. In the window of the Town Talk were two signs, *Help Wanted* and *For Sale*. I walked right in and bought the place. Best move I have ever made."

"And the Town Talk? Why did you choose a restaurant to buy?"

"My husband's family was in the restaurant business. They spent every minute of the day yammerin' on about their cafe. I just sort of listened and learned. Like I told ya, I worked in diners in high school and up in Alaska. I figured how hard could it be to run a place like the Town Talk? I always took a shine to the idea of a small town diner so I bought the Town Talk. And the rest, as they say, is history. Or, in my case, the present."

Doreen felt like an elephant had been lifted off her chest.

"I can't say that I have ever felt as free as I feel right at this very moment," she said.

Zeb scratched his head.

"I love you," he said trying to convince himself it was true. "I need a little time to digest all of this, and to think it over."

"You can take the rest of yer life to think it over. Nothin' about it is gonna change. Facts are facts and history is history. What you see is what you get."

Doreen opened her arms widely. Zeb accepted her embrace, but something didn't feel quite right.

"For now, let's keep this between us," said Doreen. "Sometime we'll let the world in on our little secret. But let's not complicate things for a while, at least until after we been married a while."

After their heart to heart talk Zeb tossed and turn throughout the night. Doreen's life story was giving him second thoughts about their impending wedding.

"Doreen, I know this is bad timing, but I think I need some time to work through everything you told me last night."

"I sort of was suspectin' you might need some extra time," replied Doreen.

Zeb sighed. He really hadn't thought Doreen would take it so easily.

"We'll talk about it soon. Give me a few days."

"I love you," said Doreen.

He kissed Doreen and headed to the sheriff's department. It was time to find out for certain if Felipe Madrigal had killed Delbert.

CHAPTER NINETEEN

"Do you think Felipe Madrigal was capable of blowing up the grade school?" asked the sheriff.

"Do you think someone else is involved in this? Mr. Madrigal is a meek, mild-mannered old man. His voice is full of sorrow when he talks about what he has done," replied Deputy Steele.

"Every con man sounds like that."

"He really doesn't seem like the sort of man who might make a bomb and plant it in a grade school, if that's what you mean."

"What have you found out about the bomb?"

"I talked with your friend, Josh Diamond," said Deputy Steele. "I take it he hasn't talked with you yet?"

"I've talked with him about the break-in at his store. I am up to date on the injuries he sustained. He's tough. He'll be fine. What did he tell you about the bomb?" asked Zeb.

"He called it a well-placed, amateurish, low-power, pipe bomb. It was armed with a fuse, a blasting cap and a three-inch pipe packed with low grade explosives. Josh thought it likely had a timer. Whoever planted the bomb knew when it was going to go off and had plenty of time to be somewhere else when it did."

"So we must assume whoever set the bomb knew it didn't have a lot of power behind it," said Zeb.

"It looks that way to Josh. He said it was the type of bomb that anyone who knows how to read a library book could make."

"That doesn't narrow our list of additional suspects down much, does it?"

"No it doesn't." replied Kate. "I've been over to the grade school boiler room and looked at it closely. The mortar between the bricks is old and loose. Only eight full bricks were knocked out of the wall by the explosion. One of those was the one that hit Delbert."

"Well then we have a situation, don't we?"

"Sheriff?"

Deputy Steele's response was a stall for time. She knew precisely what the sheriff was thinking. A phone call from a scared old man sending the sheriff's department to a crudely made bomb placed in an area where it should never have hurt anyone did not add up. It had to be a ruse, a simple diversion to get the sheriff's department looking the other way.

"The day the bomb went off…the day of the threats. What else is on the crime sheet for that day?"

Kate simultaneously had the same thought.

"Not much…three speeding tickets, one act of vandalism, a broken window that coincides closely with the phone calls and a stolen car. The car was an old junker. The type kids steal and joy ride until it runs out of gas."

"How about the day before and the day after the bombing?" asked Zeb.

"Only routine traffic violations, a few writs were served, some divorce papers, nothing overtly suspicious. Josh Diamond's gun shop was broken into while he was in the hospital. That could have been the same day or a day or two later. We don't know for sure."

"Let's have a look at that list of stolen items," said Sheriff Hanks.

"Five handguns, four .38's and a .22 and plenty of ammunition for all of those guns. A flak jacket, a double holster, military style, and a gun cleaning kit," said Deputy Steele. "But no money was taken. According to your report the cash in the register wasn't even touched, nor was anything taken from in or on his desk."

"No doubt about it, the thief knew exactly what he wanted. Entrance was made through the alley door. The door was opened using a thin, but obviously strong piece of metal to lift up a two by four that was used to barricade the door."

"I also saw in your report that Josh Diamond noted only one set of tracks in the alley behind his store," said Deputy Steele. "I agree with your findings that it was a thief, not thieves. You don't suppose Felipe Madrigal is a robber, too, do you?"

"It would surprise the heck out of me," replied Sheriff Hanks. "However, he doesn't seem like the type who would call in a bomb threat either, but he did. He admits to that. Have you completed the background check on Mr. Madrigal? Work history, marriage, kids, criminal history, tax liens, anything."

"I am working on all that. My report will be on your desk the minute it's complete."

"If he didn't act alone, we need to find a link. I'll take a ride out to his house and search it from top to bottom," replied Zeb.

"Are you thinking you might find the stolen guns?"

"I doubt it, but I will look for them anyway. I don't exactly know what I am going to be looking for. I just hope I know it when I see it."

"You heading out there now?" asked Kate.

"Yes, right now."

"What do you want me working on today?"

"We need to triple check to see if anyone in the area saw Lorenzo's pickup after it was stolen."

"What are you thinking?"

"A powder blue LUV pickup like that, somebody had to see it," said Sheriff Hanks.

"Do you think Lorenzo's truck is tied to the bombing?" asked Deputy Steele.

"I've known the García family forever. They are what you call a superstitious bunch. Mrs. García reads tea leaves and palms. She even makes predictions about the future. God knows what thoughts she is going to put into Lorenzo's head over this whole deal. I will bet you anything he will be spooked into believing the dead woman's spirit is going to affect him. If we can explain what happened, it will make a great difference to his peace of mind. Did you get any updates on the body they found in his pickup?"

"I got one follow up from Detective Muñoz," said Deputy Steele. "He sent a note saying the body was a Hispanic female, between twenty to twenty five years of age, approximately five feet tall, weighing one hundred pounds. Most importantly the fire isn't what killed her."

"What did?"

"She had a broken neck and a crushed windpipe."

"Murder?" inquired Sheriff Hanks.

"It looks like it. The message from Detective Muñoz indicated the investigation is open and ongoing. The Tucson police department is trying to locate any missing persons who fit the woman's description. They haven't had much luck."

"To them this is a routine case of an undocumented illegal alien in a stolen truck." said Zeb.

"That doesn't make the young woman any less dead."

"I didn't mean anything by it," he replied, realizing how cold his statement sounded. "It's just that the odds of finding out the who and the why are less likely when you are possibly dealing with an illegal alien as the victim."

Kate knew the sheriff was right.

"We have to remember in this case we are here to serve the victim, a dead young woman," he added.

Kate's head told her not to follow her imagination. Yet her mind could not shake a horrifying vision of the young woman's death scene--a brutal pair of hands gripped tightly around her neck, squeezing her life away, breaking her neck, crushing her windpipe. It was not a pretty picture.

"Maybe your friend, Detective Muñoz, can beat the odds on this one," she said.

"I wouldn't bet against him. As soon as you finish that report, why don't you head out to the Garcías and check around. See if anyone remembers ever seeing the powder blue LUV pickup truck with someone other than old man García behind the wheel, or if anyone saw the vehicle driving faster than he would have driven it. Somebody had to have seen something the day it was stolen. Someone out that way must know something. Jar some memories. Give me a call on the two-way if you learn anything."

CHAPTER TWENTY

"Snap to attention, amigo, siesta time is over. We're burnin' daylight."

The half-asleep Ángel felt a rough hand on his shoulder shaking him back and forth.

"Come on ass-wipe, we got work to do."

Opening his eyes, Ángel Gómez yawned widely and slowly stretched his arms over his head. The harsh command from Jimmie Joe Walker had roused him from a pleasant, sweet dream of his beloved Juanita. In his dreamlike condition Ángel could practically smell the lovely rose water she splashed behind her ears and sometimes even between her breasts for him. It was her firm breasts that had been the focus of his dream. His flesh tingled as he thought of her holding the hemline of her skirt away from her body in one hand and snapping fingers on the other as she danced a sensuous salsa she called El Gato Caliente.

Ángel drifted back into semi-consciousness as he imagined his lovely woman dancing closer, closer, enticing him to be a man, a hot-blooded man, making him ready to pounce on her like the animal he was.

"Wipe that silly, shit eatin' grin off your God-damn mug. I said wake up, boy."

This time Ángel awoke fully. Standing above him the man who had become his compadre and master was slowly loading bullets into a handgun one at a time.

"One--two--three--four--five--six. Bang, número uno, bang, número dos shot, bang, número tres, bang, fourth shot, bang, fifth bullet out of the gun. Just one shot left." He pointed the gun directly at Ángel's forehead. "Kapow--you're dead. Gone to hell forever, my little muchacha. Gone directly to hell."

Diablo Blanco was playing with his guns again. The evil game of pointing the gun at Ángel and pretending to fire the bullets frightened him. The look on Jimmie Joe's face was the look of an hombre loco who might just pull the trigger. Ángel felt a rush of dread run through his veins. In prison he had seen Jimmie Joe do so many crazy things. He knew the White devil did not feel things in the same way other people did. He was crazy like a rabid lobo and mean like a cornered rattlesnake. Maybe one day the devil inside the big White man would make him pull the trigger and Ángel would be blown to bits. If the devil shot him, he hoped it would be a quick one through the head, not a slow one in the stomach.

"You don't like to play my little game, chiquita? Then you'd better be a real good driver because I don't want to shoot you--and you know why I don't want to shoot you, don't you?"

Ángel smiled at the apparent reprieve but did not know how to answer. Shake your head one way and Jimmie Joe would go crazy, shake it the other and who knows what might happen. Jimmie Joe erupted into a fit of insanely disturbing laughter. Ángel broke into a cold sweat.

"I don't want to waste no stinkin' bullet."

Jimmie Joe's smile faded to hard steel. Bending down toward Ángel he caressed the young man's cheekbone with the barrel before resting the cold metal against his ear. He rubbed so lightly it tickled. But Ángel did not laugh.

"Let's go for a little ride. We need some practice in driving the big truck fast around corners. You drive."

"I've got to take a leak first," said Ángel. Then I'll be ready to go."

Ángel stepped outside the ramshackle trailer and behind the mesquite tree. He unzipped his pants and gave a small morado cactus a good dowsing of yellow water. As he tucked his private parts into his underwear, he looked over his shoulder. He wanted to be certain Jimmie Joe was not watching him. Reaching into his boot, he took out his switchblade knife, checked its action before tucking it tightly into a secret compartment he had sewn into the waistline of his pants, and untucked his shirt for additional cover of the hiding place. Reaching back, he double-checked the positioning of his blade. A second knife in his boot was also ready. Jimmie Joe, sitting inside the cab of the big four-wheel drive truck, appeared oblivious to Ángel's actions.

"Come on, angel face. Let's see what kind of action this machine we stole has," whooped Jimmie Joe. "I'll betcha a dollar to a dingo it can go one hundred and twenty miles an hour on a straight away and ninety, ninety-five around corners. Here, partner."

Jimmie Joe tossed Ángel the keys. As the men took their seats, Jimmie Joe reached into the glove compartment. Removing an unopened pint of Cuervo Gold tequila, he handed it to the driver. Ángel hungrily twisted off the cap. One deep swallow drained a quarter of the bottle.

"Ah, sí, sí. That is some mighty good juice. Now I drive like lightning."

"Come on, little buddy," laughed Jimmie Joe. "Let's go for a nice, long ride and break these wheels in."

"Where we heading?" asked Ángel.

"Take some back roads over to Highway 191 and scoot down towards York. We'll catch Route 75 and cut back up toward Guthrie and Granville. I want to see what you can do when you put the pedal to the metal."

Ángel began to better acquaint himself with the big truck. Five speeds, eight cylinders, it rode high but cornered well. It did not make the ninety miles an hour Jimmie wanted, but seventy even seventy-five miles an hour without shaking was no problem. Ángel punched it up to a hundred and ten on a straightaway but it shimmied badly when he hit an unexpected pothole in the road. When they hit the paved roads, one twenty was no problem and it cornered like a racecar. Ángel did not know the plan, but he knew he was the man behind the wheel of the getaway vehicle.

"About ten miles north of Granville, just past the Mitchell Peak Road, there's a dirt road that cuts over through the Rez and catches up with Indian Route 801. Eventually it runs into Indian Route 8. Let's head that way," said Jimmie Joe. "We need to get to know those roads."

"Hell," said Ángel taking another pull on the bottle. "I already know those roads out there like the back of my hand."

"That's what I am counting on," replied Jimmie Joe. "That's exactly what I am counting on."

After three hours of crisscrossing every side road three or four times, Ángel had every bump and rut memorized.

"Head back over to Duncan," said Jimmie Joe. I know a cut off up that way that will take us to the Blue River. Rich folks from Safford, Tucson, Phoenix and even El Paso got fancy houses up that way. Most of them are vacant ten months out of the year. I thought we might like to "rent" one of them for a few days. Maybe even drink up some of the rich man's liquor. What do you say to that?"

"Rich man's liquor? You mean like Bombay Gin and Johnny Walker Black Label Whiskey? Maybe Patrón Anejo Tequila?" asked Ángel.

"Sure. Maybe even that fancy-ass tequila with the worm in the bottle."

"Cuervo Anejo. The drink of kings," said Ángel dreamily.

"We can even sleep in the rich man's bed. I heard every one of those places has feather pillows. Maybe even sleep with the rich man's daughter, eh, eh Ángel? What would you think of that? I bet you would like that, wouldn't you? Some real pretty long legged blonde with cha chas grande, eh Ángel?"

Ángel's halfhearted chuckle was meant to placate the evil one. It was only Juanita that Ángel wanted. His letters to her from prison had promised his everlasting devotion. Nothing would make him break that promise. She was his gato. He was her tigre. He would see her in a week. He could wait for her. Not even Jimmie Joe could bully him into sleeping with a woman other than Juanita. But he knew he had to play along with the White devil or things would go very badly for him.

The sinking sun shimmered across the lazily flowing waters of the San Simon River. Ángel relaxed as he eyed an old man and a boy standing on the bank, casting for trout. Ángel honked twice. They smiled and waved. He remembered the days after his father's death when his grandfather took him fishing. "Fishing," his grandfather said. "You can go fishing instead of going to church and it's okay with the Man Upstairs because he would just as soon be fishing too." Fishing with his grandfather had made the pain of his father's death more bearable. Soon he would again see his grandfather's kind face. He would buy his grandfather a new fishing pole. Ángel's spirits soared as he saw light at the end of his dark tunnel.

"Jimmie, do you like fishing? I love everything about fishing. I love to fish trout, bass, and crappies. When we're done with this job, I'm..."

He almost let it slip but caught himself. Once the job was done, Ángel was headed to Mexico with Juanita. He would never see the big White devil again. Ángel was going to change his life forever. Jimmie Joe Walker was going to be but a faint memory.

"Maybe you and me will go fishing? Maybe the big house we're going to stay at will have some fishing poles?"

Jimmie Joe cast an evil eye over the San Simon River.

"I hate fishing," he snarled. "I can't imagine one reason in a million why anyone would eat the slimy little bastards. I'd rather eat worms."

Just ahead the city limit sign of Morenci marked the outskirts of the small mining town.

"Pull into downtown. Let's see what's happening. Maybe get a drink. How about that, Ángel? You must be getting a little thirsty by now?"

The White devil too well understood Ángel's lust for alcohol.

"I can always use a drink," replied Ángel.

Ángel drove slowly through downtown Morenci. He wanted to draw zero attention to himself, Jimmie Joe and the stolen pickup. Even though they had snatched it in Tucson and changed plates in Benson, Ángel didn't want to screw things up when he was so close to being rich.

"You drive any slower and the cops are going to pick you up for blocking traffic," growled Jimmie Joe. "Pull in next to that bar, it looks friendly enough. Let's go in and have an ice cold brew."

Ángel pulled into a parking spot in the alley behind the bar. A faded mural of a pair of muscular men in hard hats covered the side of the building. Beneath, a motto read, COPPER--KING OF METALS-- Morenci Miners Union, Local 616. The front of a rundown wood sided building displayed the name of the bar in neon letters, some of which were in working order and many that pulsed and flashed intermittently. The sign hanging at the front of the bar read "Earl's Firebelly Lounge   Cold Beer   Set Ups".

"It looks like a redneck joint," said Ángel. "It's probably dangerous for us to go in there."

"It is exactly my kind of joint," replied Jimmie Joe. "Rednecks got the same right as everyone else to drink in a bar. Are you prejudiced against white trash like me?"

Ángel did not bother to answer that one. He hated Jimmie Joe's guts but needed him if he was ever going to be rich.

It was a dimly lit establishment with a dark wooden bar; a pair of grizzled old men smoking cigarettes slumped round-shouldered over the bar. It smelled of beer-stained carpet. A jukebox played old fashioned country music. The disheveled regulars remained slumped and unmoving as the newcomers passed by. In the corner a muted television played a sitcom with a perfect looking young couple kissing deeply and passionately. Ángel stood behind the men and stared at the actors. The television lovers made him ache for his beloved Juanita. The ache was one of both love and desire. He felt pangs from his heart to his groin.

But a few drinks of smooth whiskey would shift his focus and fill his head with thoughts of easy money and the luxurious life of a rich man. The job that would make them rich was less than a week away. Ángel was getting anxious for his partner to tell him what exactly they were going to do and how they were going to get all that money.

"Tell me, Jimmie Joe. I need to know the plan. Don't you trust me?"

Ángel feared his partner might think he was chicken because the job was too dangerous. Everyone who knew Ángel knew he was not some sort of stinking pollo.

"You, my young pardner, will find out real soon," replied Jimmie Joe.

Sitting at a corner table with his back to the wall, Ángel ordered another whiskey, this time with a tequila chaser. He watched from a few feet away as Jimmie Joe rubbed his ugly paw against the oversized round bottom of a fat gringo woman. The woman's long, narrow face reminded him of an old caballo his grandfather had kept for many years. She even seemed to whinny when she talked. Ángel watched her push

Jimmie Joe's hand away many, many times. Each time it found its way back until the woman ignored it altogether as she smoked cigarette after cigarette, blowing smoke rings to impress Jimmie Joe, Ángel assumed. Ángel would never let Juanita smoke cigarettes. It would not be healthy when she started having babies and they became a real family. Ángel grinned widely as he imagined himself and Juanita running on the beach at San Miguel while their beautiful children made castles in the sand. He would be a proud padre. He would teach his son how to fish, how to play baseball, how to drive, how to fix things with his hands. Juanita would teach the girls how to be good people and make sure they had a good education. He dreamed of a thousand things they could do. He visualized the future he would build around his family. His heart felt good, at ease and hopeful.

"Hey! Hey, Ángel."

The harsh order from Jimmie Joe's mouth yanked him from his peaceful place.

"Are you sleeping on the job again or just daydreaming about being a gringo?"

The Diablo Blanco screeched out a fit of hideous laughter as Ángel opened his eyes. Standing by his side was the White devil with his hairy, tattooed arm draped around the fat woman, cupping her enormous breast. He pointed a deformed finger at Ángel.

"This here little fella," said Jimmie Joe nodding toward Ángel. "He falls asleep when he's awake and daydreams about his darling Juanita. You can tell just by the look on his face that is exactly what he was thinking about. Did you ever see such a stupid looking grin?"

Ángel smiled politely at the obese, smelly woman who was too drunk to pay attention to Jimmie Joe's ramblings. He noticed she was barely able to stand without the big man's support. Ángel worried that the fat woman might fall on top of him and crush him.

"Here."

Jimmie Joe spun the woman around and pushed her down onto Ángel's lap. Ángel grunted as he braced and steadied himself under the enormous weight of the fat horse-faced woman.

"Maybe you'd like a little piece of dark meat as an appetizer?"

The stout gringo woman reeked like a dirty bathroom floor. Drool rolled through her lips as she nibbled on Ángel's ear. He swooned at the wretched odor of her stale perfume and offensive body odor.

"I don't think I want to..." began Ángel.

"Wha..?" belched the woman. "You don't like what you see? You don't like these."

She lifted her mammoth breasts and shoved them into Ángel's face. Ashamed, he looked down. He saw only the dirt under the chipped polish of her broken fingernails.

"No, señorita, it is just that..."

His mind raced to find a way to explain to her about his beloved Juanita. He was in love. As a woman, even a drunken, ugly woman, surely she would understand. Ángel looked up to see the angry fire in Jimmie Joe's eyes as he lustily ogled the woman's drooping breasts. Ángel could only find false words for the plump woman. He told her she was beautiful and offered her a drink and some cigarettes.

"Are you shaying you don't want me? You don't want this?"

She lifted up her filthy skirt, showing off unshaven legs and pair of filthy panties. Her slurred words were carried on the air of her hideous breath. Before Ángel could answer a hand came out of nowhere, walloping him across the face.

"Well, I never! I never been turned down by no greasy, little Mexican taco. What are you, some kind of fudge bunny? What kind of man turns down a woman like me? Maybe you like boys instead of girls? I bet that's it. Faggot. Sex freak!"

Before Ángel had a chance to answer, she slipped off his lap. Crashing onto the floor, her large rear end went ass over teakettle sending her shoes flying into the air. One of them smacked against Jimmie Joe's forehead.

The ruckus caused the two old men sitting at the bar to turn just far enough to see the woman sprawled over the floor. Unimpressed, they turned back toward the television. In silent unison they reached for their beer glasses, tipped back their heads, and swallowed their beer.

The bartender walked out from behind the counter. He helped the drunken woman to her feet. She cursed at Ángel, flipped him off with her middle finger and stumbled into the ladies room.

"We can't have that kind of ruckus in here, young man. You had better leave now," said the bartender.

"But I didn't do nothing," protested Ángel.

"And you had better go with him," he said to Jimmie Joe.

The bartender pulled back his vest, revealing a holstered pistol. Ángel knew the knife hidden in his right boot would not be much of a defense against the big gun. For half a second he considered cutting the man, slicing him across the wrist or in the face near the eye. Then suddenly, Juanita came to mind. He envisioned her smiling face, the silver cross he had given to her before he had gone to prison, gleaming on her beautiful skin as it hung around her tender brown neck. He reached down and touched the identical necklace she had given him. If he wanted to see Juanita, he needed to stay calm. He glanced toward Jimmie Joe whose hand slowly began creeping under his jacket toward the back of his belt where he carried his gun. Ángel jumped to his feet.

"It's my fault and I am terribly sorry. We are leaving now. Come on, Jimmie Joe. Let's go somewhere else and spend our money."

Jimmie spit on the bartender's shoe.

"Next time," he said glaring into the bartender's eyes. "I might not be in such a good mood."

The outburst of laughter from Jimmie Joe brought a relieved smile to the bartender. The old men at the bar shook their heads ever so slightly as the strangers made their exit.

"We don't need no trouble, Jimmie Joe. Let's get out of town. It is bad luck for us here."

Jimmie Joe seethed. Turning into the alley, he grabbed Ángel by the throat and stuck the gun against his temple.

"Don't you ever tell me what to do. I make the decisions for both of us. I should have shot that son of a bitchin' bartender right between his fucking eyes. But I didn't know if you were with me or not. You screwed up in there. Don't ever let it happen again--that is, if you want to live long enough to see Juanita."

Instantly, the effects of the alcohol on Ángel's brain passed.

Morenci and Earl's Firebelly Lounge were bad luck. Morenci was the town where Ángel's father had died almost twenty years earlier. He had been run off the road and killed by a drunken gringo. Even his blessed grandfather, who worked so many years for the Morenci mine, had bad luck here. The town was a cursed place for his family. Ángel closed his eyes. His prayers to the Blessed Virgin were juxtaposed by the cold steel of a gun barrel against his temple. Jimmie Joe slowly ran the barrel of the .38 around Ángel's ear, tickling the cartilage, caressing the lobe.

In prison Ángel had heard one well-placed shot directly behind the ear would kill a man or, worse, leave him a vegetable. Juanita would not want to spend her life taking care of a cripple. Ángel would not wish that on her. He always knew the day might come when Jimmie Joe might kill him. Ángel prayed harder. The cold steel of the gun penetrated, it seemed, all the way to his brain. Sweat rolled down Ángel's cheeks and onto his lips. An insane explosive peel of laughter shot from his partner's mouth.

"You look so worried, my little muchacha. You think I am going to waste a bullet on you when we are so close to being rich? Ha ha ha. You little fucking idiot. You don't even know how close we are to the money right where we stand."

Ángel looked down the alley and across the street. What was Jimmie Joe talking about? Next to the bar was a clothing store, the gas company, a drug store, a small building with hand painted sign in the window that he couldn't read and a bank. The bank? Was the Diablo Blanco crazy? Ángel wasn't a bank robber.

"The bank? You think we are going to rob the bank?"

Jimmie Joe doubled over with laughter at his own question.

"No, no, no. Not the bank—next door—the little building. Get in the truck, I'll show you."

Turning to look over his shoulder as he put the truck in reverse, Ángel noticed the left taillight glowing brightly as it reflected in a store window.

"Shine the headlights on that store with the writing on the window. Go ahead, put the bright lights on."

Ángel looked up and down the street. It would be stupid to be noticed flashing high beams into a storefront. A cop might take notice of what they were doing. He said nothing, knowing that Jimmie would only beat him down for questioning anything the he said.

"See," laughed Jimmie Joe. "Read that window."

The whitewashed sign in the window came into view. Ángel stared at the words and the reflected white spots from his headlights.

MORENCI RODEO AND PIONEER MINING DAYS
OCTOBER 25TH AND 26TH

CHAPTER TWENTY-ONE

As Kate headed toward the door on her way to the Garcías' place, Helen handed her a pair of day old phone messages. She apologetically explained to Deputy Steele that the messages had been accidentally stuck to the bottom of a file.

"Sheriff Hanks is on his way out to Felipe Madrigal's property. He said you would know what it was all about."

Both of the pink message slips had brief notes. The first read, 'Please call Eskadi Black Robes'. The second note was just as direct. 'Please call Josh Diamond'. Deputy Steele surmised Josh had decided after all to take the county up on paying his hospital bills and was calling her about the paperwork. Eskadi's was likely personal. She decided to handle them after she took a little trip out to the Garcías' to see if she could glean any more information.

As Sheriff Hanks approached the home of Felipe Madrigal, bright morning sunshine streamed over the top of the Peloncillo Mountain range sending short shadows over the peaceful landscape surrounding the run down adobe house that the jailed man called home.

A low groan escaped from the old windmill. Unlike earlier, Zeb was not there to bring in a suspected killer, yet his body tensed. For a brief second his mind shot back to a day at the Mexican border. He, Josh Diamond, and the now dead Darren Wendt were on routine patrol on that fateful day of Darren's death. For another, longer moment, he thought of Doreen and the loss of her husband and son. His mind began to spin with all the things in life that could go wrong and too often did. Then quickly, he remembered that he was on home turf, his turf, Graham County, and for all intents and purposes this was his own back yard. He breathed a few easy breaths when suddenly an ominous foreboding came over him. Could this be the day he breathed his last breath? He had received a bulletin from his old border patrol commanding officer on this new thing called PTSD, post-traumatic stress disorder. He had read it briefly and tossed it in the waste basket. Now he was having second thoughts about what he had read. "Don't be an asshole," he told himself. "Just be smart. Nothing to worry about. Stay calm."

In the low arroyo behind the house, an otherworldly presence seemed to beg for communication. Ears piqued, he stilled himself and listened. After a moment he shook his head knowing the present moment called for logical, rational thought, not superstition and fear. Sheriff Hanks breathed more easily as the old man's fire pit and a garbage dump caught his eye. They seemed too close to the house until he remembered Felipe Madrigal's limp and the difficulty with which he walked. Closer inspection revealed neat stacks of tin cans, glass bottles and miscellaneous unburnable items. The yard itself was full of junk and these neat stacks seemed out of place. They were probably for recycling. Maybe the old man made a few bucks this way?

Plentiful coyote, raccoon and skunk tracks lead to and away from the trash pit. He imagined the kind old man to have befriended the local critters. He assumed Felipe Madrigal suffered the fated malady of many old people, too much time, too little to do.

In the yard a skeleton of a rusted backhoe, some old machinery tires, flattened junk metal and a broken down chair were strewn about. It was a mess which likely made perfect sense to the owner. Zeb drew back from the thoughts in his head. He was beginning to feel a little too much compassion for someone who might have killed his deputy. He reminded himself yet again to stay focused and do his job.

Parked by the rustling mesquite tree was Felipe Madrigal's truck. The tire iron still propped up the hood. Approaching the truck cautiously he peeked at the engine, half expecting to find a bird's nest or perhaps a sleeping rattlesnake. At first glance the metal parts told him nothing. When he looked closer, he saw a detached wire. It led to where a distributor cap should be. He was no expert on car engines, but he knew vaguely what he was looking at. The sheriff stepped back and noticed both back tires were flat. He thought back to how the old man had described his disabled vehicle. He did not say his tires were flat. He had said his car was broken. He had said nothing about flat tires. Sheriff Hanks bent down near the rear wheels. The shade from the mesquite tree made it difficult to get a clear view. Casually running his finger along the tire's edge he felt an indentation surrounded by an unnatural rough edge. Closer examination revealed the tire had been slashed. A quick walk to the other side of the truck easily revealed that tire had also been slashed. A mostly bald spare tire sitting in the bed of the truck was also flat. It was obvious someone, perhaps Felipe himself, had wanted to make sure the truck wasn't going anywhere.

Sheriff Hanks walked to the house. He slowly poked his head inside and entered. The interior of the house was unkempt like that of an old man without a wife. In the small kitchen on the counter next to the sink sat a propane stove with an ancient coffee percolator on one burner and a much used, burn-encrusted fry pan on the other. At the back of the sink sat a water glass, a bottle of aspirin and a half-empty prescription bottle of nitroglycerin tablets with the instructions - TAKE AS NEEDED FOR ANGINA. He slipped the medication in his pocket. His prisoner might need it. Next to the coffeepot was a caned chair. Its sagging and partially torn seat spoke of many lonesome hours its owner spent staring out a partially open window. The image of an old man sitting, sipping coffee, fumbling with the bottle cap on the aspirin, placing a pill in his palm, quivering as he reached for the water glass carried the feeling of isolation, loneliness.

Through the window he had a clear line of vision to the north toward the road. The old man had taken the time to remove anything that might interfere with a straight on view of the county road. Delbert had mentioned there was hardly any traffic on this road. The old man probably did not want to miss the rare car or truck that happened by.

The second room of the house was dark. Both front windows were boarded up from the inside. A small commode and sink stood in one corner. A curtain hanging from the ceiling partially hid them. Felipe Madrigal was either very modest or thoughtful of the rare guest. Who might his visitors be? A closer look revealed cobwebs and layered dirt where the curtain abutted the wall. Felipe used little of his small space.

A dilapidated easy chair with an ancient brass floor lamp sat in the corner. The sheriff pulled the cord. The flickering light from a loose bulb revealed a stack of magazines, some of them twenty years old. As he leaned forward to tighten the bulb his foot brushed against a rusting coffee can filled with cigarette butts and ashes.

On an end table next to the lamp sat a dial phone, some yellowing, framed photographs and a clock radio. One looked to be a young Felipe Madrigal in a suit standing next to a delicate looking dark skinned Mexican or Indian woman in an ornate wedding dress. It was similar to the one Felipe carried in his billfold. Another picture was a baby in a bonnet being held by the woman in the wedding dress. Still another was a child in what looked to be a first communion dress. The fourth picture in the progression showed the same girl in a cap and gown--a high school graduation photo. Unframed and sitting on the desk was the picture of a fair skinned, long-haired boy, who looked either, or perhaps both, Mexican and Apache. The sheriff also noted the boy was rather feminine in his characteristics. He also wore a cap and gown, but looked to be only thirteen or fourteen years old. Beneath the young man's photo were some faded newspaper clippings, yellowed with age. They had been precisely cut from the Eastern Arizona Courier. One was a picture of an unnamed old man and a boy fishing. The other two were unreadable, coffee-stained police reports.

Sheriff Hanks turned on the radio and sat in the old man's chair. His big frame sank deeply into its broken seat as the radio played music from a Tucson Spanish speaking station. For the first time all day he felt at ease, incredibly calm. It was obvious that Felipe Madrigal was dirt poor but within that poverty he had every material thing he needed…or so it seemed. Sheriff Hanks' mind began to drift.

CHAPTER TWENTY-TWO

"Sheriff Hanks. Are you there?"

Deputy Steele's voice coming through his two-way radio took the sheriff away from his pondering of Felipe Madrigal. He snapped to attention quickly, knowing that perhaps Kate had found out something new from the Garcías.

"I'm here."

"Find anything interesting?" asked Kate.

"I think I have a better feel for Mr. Madrigal. But as far as evidence goes I have found nothing that I can piece together at the moment. But I do have a question for you."

"Yes?"

"Remember when Mr. Madrigal called to have us come and pick him up?"

"Yes," said Kate. "He said his truck was broken."

"That's how I remember it too. Would you consider two flat tires a broken truck?"

"No. I would call them flat tires. A broken truck would indicate something mechanical to me."

"Well he's got two flat tires and a flat spare on his truck. It looks like they have been flattened on purpose. But I believe Felipe Madrigal was telling the truth. This truck is broken. Somebody yanked the wires to the distributor cap and removed the cap itself," said Zeb. "This thing couldn't run if it wanted to. Somebody saw to it that Felipe's truck was staying put."

Zeb thought of the meek, gamy-legged Mr. Madrigal sitting in the jail cell looking forlorn and lost. He was either far more cunning than he let on or he was hiding some deep, dark secret in his soul.

"Did Mr. García remember anything new when you talked with him?" Zeb asked.

"Yes sir, he did. He said it was Mrs. García's tea leaf reading that helped him remember something. But I think it was the dead body they found in his truck that jogged his memory," said Deputy Steele.

"What did he recall?"

"Mr. García remembered a young Mexican male stopping by the house a couple of days before his truck was stolen. The young man was having car trouble a few miles up the road. His radiator hose was leaking. Mr. García gave him a bucket of water and a lift back to his car. He even helped him put some duct tape on the leaky hose."

"What made Mr. García suspicious?" asked Sheriff Hanks.

"Two things. First, he said the young man went on and on about his Chevy LUV. He asked him all sorts of questions about it. Mr. García didn't think much about it at first because everyone who sees it asks about it. You could really tell how much he loved his truck," said Deputy Steele.

"He certainly did."

"When they got the overheated car running, Mr. García headed back home. He looked in the rear view mirror and waved, you know, friendly like. The young man waved back. Then, when Mr. García went to adjust his rear view mirror, he saw something odd."

"Yes, go on," said Sheriff Hanks.

"He saw something run out of the bushes toward the car. At first Mr. García thought it might have been an animal, a coyote he supposed. He slowed down and took a look over his shoulder. He couldn't see clearly because of all the dust that had been roiled up by the other car taking off down the road. But Mr. García swore he saw two people in the little car. He pulled over to see what the deal was, but when he did, the driver of the other car made a fast U turn and headed off the other way. I guess he just sort of forgot about it until today when I was talking with him."

"Did he say what kind of car the young man was driving?" asked Sheriff Hanks.

"Yes, he most certainly did. I don't think I need to tell you he is quite an expert when it comes to cars."

Sheriff Hanks knew it for certain having talked to Lorenzo García many times since his Chevy LUV had been stolen.

"The car was a Chevrolet Vega. Mr. García said he even mentioned to the young man that he should get a different car because the aluminum engine in the Vega is nothing but trouble. He said the young man laughed and told him he was thinking about getting a new pickup, maybe one just like Mr. García's."

"Did Mr. García say what color the Vega was?" asked Sheriff Hanks.

"He said the name of the color of the car in Spanish. Amarillo."

The sheriff knew that meant yellow.

"Did he say what kind of shape the Vega was in?"

"He called it a real rust bucket. Mr. García said he couldn't believe anyone would let a car get in as bad of shape as that. He figured it was probably all the young man could afford."

The wheels spinning in Zeb's head gripped like the traction on a firm road. The description of the vehicle, yellow and rusted, was a perfect match to the recently stolen Vega. What were the odds Mr. García's truck was stolen by the young Mexican man in the Vega? Could there be a link between the young Mexican and the dead girl in Mr. García's burnt out truck.

"Deputy Steele, are you still in the vicinity of the García place?"

"Six or seven miles back toward town," replied the deputy.

"I want you to go back and get a detailed description of the driver of the Vega from Mr. García."

"I have a decent one, but I can get a better one. I will do that right now."

Kate was starting to put the same pieces together as the sheriff. Stolen yellow Vega, young man, stolen Chevy LUV pickup that the young man in the possibly stolen Vega had seen as an easy opportunity. And, a dead young Mexican woman in Mr. García's stolen pickup. It was a long shot, but it had to be considered. It was the hottest lead they had.

"Did you find out anything else?" asked Sheriff Hanks.

"Nothing specific. I did talk with four or five people out that way who complained about fast traffic. It seems an oversized pickup, a high rider with an elevated cab, has been seen speeding down those roads at what some of the people said was over a hundred miles an hour. They asked me to set up a speed trap out there. I told them that would be impossible but that we would be on the lookout for speeders, especially in big pickup trucks. I believe some of the older folks are quite scared about it, especially after Mr. García's truck was stolen."

A crosswind carried a trail of dust into the wooded dale behind the Madrigal place where it settled restlessly. Overhead, the squeaking from the windmill ceased, replaced by a constant droning hum as the wind became steady. The faint odor of dried sage surrounded Zeb as he stared at the disabled truck pondering the old man's motive. What did Felipe Madrigal have to gain by calling in a bomb threat? Why risk what little he had?

"I will see you back in town," said Sheriff Hanks, clicking off the two-way radio.

He returned to the house and grabbed the pictures from the table. Maybe being surrounded by pictures of his family would loosen the old man's tongue. It was a long shot but he needed something. Maybe Kate would find something as well.

Back in town Zeb made an official stop at Josh Diamond's gun shop. The clanging cowbell signaled his entrance as Josh's bloodhounds eyed him curiously. The proprietor was nowhere to be seen.

"I'll be right there," shouted the store owner. "I've just hard wired the place with a new security system. So don't try and walk off with anything."

Josh peeked over the swinging doors. He greeted his old border patrol buddy with a broad smile.

"Zeb, welcome back to my home away from home. I'm cleaning up an old Winchester repeater." Josh reached out to shake Zeb's hand but withdrew, noticing just how filthy his hands were. "This rifle is a real beauty. Come on back here and have a look."

Zeb slipped around the edge of the counter. The broken glass had been replaced and a new set of guns had been placed in the Elk antlers.

"Look at this. It's a Winchester 94. It's one hundred percent original, right down to the gold inlay. There aren't many of these old gals around anymore. It even has John Ulrich's name engraved. Want to see?"

Josh's infectious enthusiasm was catching and calming. Zeb found himself feeling light and happy as he watched his old pal softly run his hand along the stock and barrel of the rifle. This time his memories of the border patrol days were better ones. He remembered how Josh liked to take his weapon apart, clean it and put it back together, blindfolded, just like in the movies. It had been a difficult morning trying to dig into Felipe Madrigal's psyche. Zeb was glad for the distraction.

"Nice thirty-caliber," said Zeb eyeing the weapon.

"I'm impressed," exclaimed Josh. "I didn't know you knew these old-fashioned guns."

"What sort of a western lawman would I be if I didn't know about the most famous deer rifle in history?"

"Tell me more," said Josh, egging on Zeb. "I didn't have you pegged for the collector type."

Zeb held the gun and eyed down the sight line.

"Lever action, one of the first made, known as the true personification of the romance of the old west. Twenty-six inch barrel, forty-five inches in total length."

"Forty-four and a half."

"I was rounding up," said Zeb. "If you know so much, maybe you can tell me where the gold was mined for the inlay."

"Just north of San Francisco."

"Touché."

As he passed the gun back to Josh, Zeb eyed Josh's injuries.

"Isn't it a little tough working with a wrist cast and broken ribs?" asked Zeb.

"When a man loves what he is doing, there is no such thing as pain."

"Amen," said Zeb.

The men stood quietly for a moment as Josh wiped the rest of the grease off his hands.

"Zeb, from the look in your eyes this isn't a social call."

"Actually, it is business," replied Zeb. "I was hoping you found something which might lead me to the thieves."

"Well Zeb, actually I did find something. Here, let me show you what I found."

Josh led him to the back door. The big two inch by four inch beam still kept the door secure. But Josh had replaced the old latch with a new, complex key lock. As they passed through the door into the alley Zeb observed Josh's careful, almost measured movements. He had not changed one bit when it came to his unique eye for detail.

"Your deputy, Kate Steele, came by a few hours after you were here. She dusted for prints and made some castings of the boot prints left behind by the alleged perp. She is very competent."

"You would have to search pretty far and wide to find someone who didn't think the world of her," replied Zeb. "And I just bet you find her appealing in many ways."

"She is all right by me," said Josh. "As to how all right she is, time will tell."

Zeb nodded. He wasn't about to press the private side of Josh Diamond.

"We talked a little. While she was casting the footprints I stood around to watch. Standing there, looking at the boarded up building next to mine, I noticed something I hadn't previously seen."

Josh pointed to a piece of plywood covering a busted out basement window in the adjacent abandoned building.

"This is what I called Deputy Steele about."

Zeb looked down at the sun beaten lumber. The curled piece of wood was cracked, faded from exposure and covered with pigeon droppings. Near the center of the warped board he noticed was a brown discoloration. Beneath the stain a dried drip line ran for a few inches. It looked like a dirty board covering an old window frame. No different in appearance than when he'd originally noticed it.

Josh crouched near the window.

"Right here. This is what struck me as odd."

Zeb squatted. He ran a finger over the wood near the brown stain.

"Now take a whiff. You'll see what I'm talking about."

Zeb's furrowed eyebrows caused Josh to snicker. Zeb was well aware Josh knew things about tracking that he could only imagine, but sticking his nose next to a brown stain amid a pile of pigeon droppings seemed a little silly. Zeb did it anyway.

"What do you smell?" asked Josh.

"Pigeon shit," replied Zeb pulling his head away from the wood.

"Did you get a good smell of the brown stain?" asked Josh.

"Tobacco? It has the foul odor of chewing tobacco. Spittle, my dad used to call it."

"Very good," replied Josh. "You pass the test."

"I think I see what you're getting at, but isn't it sort of a stretch connecting it to whoever burgled your store?" asked Zeb.

"Oh, I forgot to tell you," said Josh. "I found some tobacco spittle, as you so aptly put it, in my back office, next to the ammunition. Let's go back inside. I'll show you."

Zeb examined the tobacco stain. Using a pocketknife he scraped it into a borrowed baggie.

"You haven't taken up the chew, have you?" asked Zeb.

"No. I find it a vile habit."

"Did anyone who chews tobacco come back into this area?" asked Zeb.

"The only three people that have been back here in the last week are you, your deputy and me."

"I guess there is a pretty good chance we have ourselves a tobacco chewing thief. If you find anything else, would you please let me know?"

"You can count on it, Sheriff."

Zeb smiled. Somehow it felt right to have Josh call him that.

CHAPTER TWENTY-THREE

"Sheriff Hanks just checked in. He said he wanted you to call him right away if you have anything new. Here are your phone messages."

Kate took the pink slips from Helen and headed for the communications room. The first message was from her grandmother wondering what time she was planning to stop by the Desert Rose Nursing Home. The second was from the editor of the Eastern Arizona Courier requesting an update on the school bombing investigation for the current edition of the weekly paper. The third call was from Eskadi Black Robes. He wanted her to call as soon as possible. Kate activated the radio set and signaled the sheriff's car.

"Sheriff, this is Deputy Steele. Helen said you wanted me to check in."

"I'm down in a hollow, but I can hear you pretty well. What have you got?"

"I've got some new information."

"Go ahead. Let's have it."

"You know that beat up Chevy Vega with the leaky radiator that Lorenzo García said he helped fix?"

"Yes," replied Sheriff Hanks.

"It turns out the same guy had the same water leak problem about fifteen miles further down the road. I found another man who told me a young Mexican male stopped at his house and asked for some water for his radiator."

"Did both people who saw the driver describe him the same way?"

"Yes, the given descriptions match in height, weight, hair color and length, age, right down to the silver necklace with a silver cross around his neck."

"By any chance did the second witness see anyone in the car with him?"

"Negative," replied Deputy Steele.

"Thanks, Deputy. I'm on my way back to the office now. Out."

Kate returned to her office, scribbled a few notes from her conversation with the sheriff and picked up the phone to call Eskadi. He sounded perturbed.

"Why is it when a First American calls a deputy sheriff, it takes forever to get a return call? I bet if I was some White person with a problem you would have called last night."

"Don't you even bother to say hello?" asked Kate.

On the other end of the line Eskadi Black Robes emitted a grudging grunt as a substitution for a greeting.

"To answer your question, I was working. I thought your call was personal so I was waiting until I had more time. I didn't want to have to rush when I called. What's the problem?"

"I'm sorry. It's just that I can't get any cooperation from the police anywhere. It is truly a matter of the police not giving a damn about Native Americans--even if the police have native blood flowing through their veins."

"Eskadi, getting short with me isn't going to solve anything. Please, why don't you explain to me what you're talking about?"

Kate was beginning to feel the downside of dating a tribal chairman who believed that the White man conspired against the Indian at every turn. An education at the University of California Berkeley had turned him on to the radical branch of the American Indian Movement. His politics of intolerance of Whites and other authority figures frequently rose to an unreasonable level. His position at the San Carlos Reservation had done little to quell his rage.

"The damn police in Tucson don't give a good goddamn about a missing person from the reservation. Even if they might have her body," said Eskadi.

"What are you talking about? A missing person situation?" asked Kate. "You know the reservation isn't their jurisdiction. You would raise holy heck if they came on the reservation without your permission."

"Hell, yes I would. But this is different. It's a missing kid."

"Did you report it to the reservation police?"

"They don't seem to give a shit either. No one cares if a dark-skinned, Native American child is missing. It would be an entirely different situation if it were a blond haired, blue eyed kid.

Kate knew that there was a small seed of truth in Eskadi's observation. Obviously there had been a misunderstanding somewhere along the chain of command. An angry Apache and a stubborn city cop in Tucson mixed like oil and water.

"Maybe I can help," said Kate. "Tell me what you told the police."

"I was listening to the news when they had that story on about the young girl's body," said Eskadi.

"Are you talking about the young woman who was found in a burned up truck in Tucson?"

"Yes, I am. The reporter said the truck was stolen from outside of Safford."

"That's right. The truck belonged to Lorenzo García. He lives outside of town just south of reservation land."

"The news report said the body was a young female, slight build, about five feet tall. Possibly Mexican…maybe Native American…maybe mixed blood."

"The possibly Native American part is news to me," said Kate. "Where did you hear that?"

"I didn't need to hear it. Those White cops and White coroners wouldn't know one dark skinned person from another. To them we are all the same."

"I think you're making quite a leap."

"Try seeing it through my eyes," said Eskadi.

"Tell me what you have," pressed Kate.

"Kaytee Brince's daughter, Layna, is missing. She fits the description I heard on the radio to a tee."

"What makes you think Layna is the dead girl?"

"I'll tell it to you just like I told it to everybody else. Layna and her boyfriend have been picked up twice for joy riding. They have a history of borrowing trucks that don't belong to them."

"Borrowing?"

"Kaytee Brince called me because Layna's been missing for a week. She thought she was staying over at her boyfriend's house, but he's gone too. He has been missing for a week or more as well."

"Did anyone file a missing person's report?" asked Kate.

"They're doing it today."

"Not a lot can be done until a missing person's report gets filed. Nobody would know where to begin. Did you tell Mrs. Brince to make sure to mention that her daughter has a history of vehicle theft and joy riding? Believe it or not it might actually speed up the process a bit."

"There's no history of that stuff," said Eskadi.

"But you just said--,"

"I said they got picked up for joy riding. Each time the truck was returned without any damage. Nobody pressed charges. Not everybody follows the ways of the Whites. Some people make allowances for kids who do stupid things."

"Give me a description of the two missing kids. You're in luck because the detective in charge of the case is an old friend of Sheriff Hanks. I have to talk with him anyway."

"Why don't you come up here and talk with Kaytee?" asked Eskadi. "She is pretty shook up because no one is willing to look for her daughter. It would be very helpful to me if you would drive up here, and perhaps allay her fears a little bit."

Kate was up to her ears in work. The San Carlos Reservation was technically out of her jurisdiction. Anyway, Eskadi was probably the one who got Mrs. Brince worried to begin with. If Layna and her boyfriend had a history of joyriding, they would probably show up soon. Eskadi, as usual when it came to police matters, was leapfrogging ahead of himself and the legal process. Kate glanced at her watch.

"Where does she live?"

"Just east of High Rolls off of Indian Route 9 near the Black River. When you get to the first road past the railroad crossing just north of the intersection of Indian Route 9 and Indian Route 4, hang a right. You'll see my truck," explained Eskadi.

"Is she there now?"

"No. She's sitting in my office about five feet away from me."

"Give me an hour and a half. I have to finish a couple of things here at the office."

"Thanks, Kate. I'm sorry about being short with you. It's just that in my job I am supposed to be able to get things done for my people. Sometimes dealing with the White man's bureaucracy puts me at my wit's ends."

"Forget it. If Layna Brince was the girl in the pickup, we had better know about it. If it isn't her, we need to know that too."

"There is one other thing too. I almost forgot. Somebody else reported a pair of missing license plates. This time there was an eyewitness. The thief was a White man with a big gun. I thought you would want to know."

"Do me a favor would you?" asked Kate.

"What do you need?"

"Get me a description of the White man. A description of the gun would be helpful as well."

"Might be hard to do."

"Why?"

"All those White men look the same to us reservation folk," exclaimed Eskadi.

"You're too funny for words. Just get me the descriptions and maybe I can help you."

"I'll see you in a little while at Kaytee Brince's house. Goodbye."

CHAPTER TWENTY-FOUR

The walk from his desk to the jail cell where Felipe Madrigal was being held took Sheriff Hanks less than a minute. The cold cement floor, iron bars and antiseptic feel of the holding area made his bones ache. His jail felt of pain and loneliness to him until he mentally reminded himself of its purpose.

Through a small meshed window in the heavy metal door which separated the holding cells from the rest of the jail, he eyed the old man. Sitting on the center of his cot, Felipe Madrigal slowly ate from a tray of food balanced precariously on his lap. The meal, judging from his hot plate and the number of empty cans in his garbage pit, was probably the first home cooked meal he had eaten in quite a while. He ate deliberately while staring down at his plate and chewing each bite of food thoroughly. Sheriff Hanks noticed that Felipe swallowed with some difficulty. His salt and pepper facial hair had become matted and disheveled from sleeping on the cot. His drooping mustache gave him the sad look of hopelessness. Zeb turned the key in the large metal lock and pushed open the creaking door. Felipe didn't raise his eyes to greet the sheriff until he stood over him. His aged face expressed the fear of a lost child.

"Señor Madrigal, do you feel like talking today?"

Felipe, unresponsive to the sheriff's request, shifted positions jiggling the food tray on his lap.

"I've brought you something."

The old man remained impassive, mutely staring at the floor.

"They are from your house. I thought you might like them."

Zeb held the pictures out to the prisoner, who lifted his head slightly. An unsteady hand grasped them. Clutching the photos in his gnarly fingers, Felipe pressed them to his chest. His whispered response was barely audible.

"Gracias, Señor Policía. Muchas gracias."

"The woman is beautiful. Is she your wife?" inquired Sheriff Hanks.

The old man's bespectacled gaze fixed itself firmly on the ancient, sepia photograph. Holding the wedding picture in trembling hands, his head rhythmically quivered to the restlessness of a heavy heart. The old man peered sadly into the faded photograph of his lifelong love.

"You must miss her terribly."

Tears rolled down the now softened face of the old Mexican as he tipped his head forward slightly in assent.

"I brought these also."

Sheriff Hanks handed Felipe the baby picture and the First Communion photo.

"Your daughter?"

"Sí."

"Would you like me to contact her? She must be worried about you," said Sheriff Hanks.

The old man placed the pictures on the cot next to him and leaned forward placing his head in his hands and began to weep softly. Pulling a well-traveled handkerchief from his pocket he wiped his eyes, blew his nose and returned it to his pocket before speaking.

"God has called her home. She is dead one year today," he replied.

"I'm sorry."

"Gracias. Tiene Ud. niños? Bebés?"

Sheriff Hanks shook his head, not understanding what his prisoner was asking.

"Do you have children? Babies?"

"No."

The old man put his head down and sat silently, staring at the floor. Felipe Madrigal began to tell a story that almost broke Zeb's heart. The prisoner told the sheriff of the pain his wife and daughter went through in dying from cancer. He spoke of how he tried to remain strong and faithful to God, of how he lost his faith. Felipe's eyes never met Zeb's as he talked of the pain in his heart and mind. His grandson, his only hope for the future of his family, had ended up in prison and was little more than a drunkard and a thief. Yet, Zeb felt this old man for some reason had not given up completely on his grandson. Zeb looked at Felipe and saw a man who had almost nothing to live for. This kind of man could go either way, he could try and resurrect his life or he could throw it all away. It was clear that Felipe Madrigal had said all he was going to say for the moment. Further questioning would have to wait. Zeb had breached the gate of the old man's inner being. He handed Felipe Madrigal his heart medication, asking him again if he would like to talk to a lawyer.

"I am guilty. I no need lawyer. I tell the judge that I make those phone calls."

Sheriff Hanks made a vain attempt to explain even if he did make the calls it would be better for him to have a court appointed lawyer to explain his rights.

"No lawyer. Please, I want to see priest."

Sheriff Hanks closed the cell door and watched as Felipe softly pressed his fingers on the photograph of his dead wife, tenderly caressing her image. He knew the old man needed time to think. Where that thinking would take him, Zeb could not imagine.

CHAPTER TWENTY-FIVE

Eskadi's directions were less than precise. The trip to the reservation took Kate longer than she had anticipated. By the time she arrived at the Brince house it was late afternoon.

Kate spotted Eskadi sitting at a little picnic table under a small grove of cottonwood trees on the south side of the house. Sitting next to him were a short, heavy-set Apache woman and two teenagers, a boy and a girl. The petite young girl and the tall skinny boy appeared to be in their late teens. Kate waited to get out of the car until they waved to her. Eskadi rose to greet her.

"Good news," said Eskadi. "Kayla's daughter, Layna, and her boyfriend showed up about fifteen minutes ago. They were visiting some friends over in Las Cruces. They didn't call because their friend didn't have a phone. Come on over and sit down and join the celebration. Mrs. Brince just made some fresh lemonade."

A brief chat over a cool drink with Layna and her boyfriend convinced Deputy Steele that they had not been involved with either the car or the license plate thefts. They assured her, at the ripe old age of eighteen, their wild days were behind them. As of right now, joy riding was a thing of the past. Mrs. Brince, elated at the safe return of her daughter, continually ran her fingers through her daughter's hair, periodically stopping to hug her.

With the sun resting atop the mountains to the west and an hour drive ahead of her, Kate excused herself. Eskadi walked her to the car as Mrs. Brince continued showering the returned children with affection.

"I would have tried to get a hold of you to save you the drive but the timing didn't work out," said Eskadi. "But I'm glad you drove up anyway. You have been a stranger to these parts."

"With the death of Deputy Funke we're short staffed. I have been working lots of overtime and will be for a while."

Eskadi rested his hand on her shoulder. He looked toward the shadowed western slope of the mountain as he called her by the Apache name he had given her.

"Son--ee--ah--Ray?"

The questioning and uncertainty in his voice sounded strange. His face carried a confused, pained expression.

"Have you given your heart to another man?"

Was Eskadi, the strong and brave tribal chairman of the San Carlos, jealous? The woman in her was more than a little curious as to why he was acting so strangely.

"What makes you ask?"

"You have been distant lately in a way you never have been before. It made me feel like something is wrong between us."

"I'm afraid it's just your imagination. I'm not seeing anyone but you," said Kate running a hand across his face.

While her words were essentially true, she had been having random thoughts of Josh Diamond. Those thoughts were fleeting, however, and certainly not etched into any sort of purpose or intent.

A beaming smile returned to Eskadi's face.

"Sorry, I'm running late. I have a lot of work to do yet today. Let's talk about it when we have more time."

"Then should I call you later about the White man who pulled the gun on one of my people when he was stealing those license plates?" asked Eskadi.

Kate did not appreciate Eskadi's little cat and mouse game. This was exactly the sort of thing that could make her think of the easy going, yet professional ways of Josh Diamond.

"Do you have something already?"

"I made a quick call before I came over here. I thought you would appreciate it if I did you a favor."

"Did you find anything out?"

"The White guy was not only big, he was ugly too," laughed Eskadi.

"Let's leave personal opinions out of this," replied Kate.

"No, I mean he really was big and ugly. He was wearing a cap but the witness thought it looked like he had pretty short hair, like military guys wear. His head might even have been shaved. She couldn't tell for certain."

"That narrows the list down to about fifty million people," said Kate.

"No need to get sarcastic," said Eskadi derisively. "He was also missing some fingers on his left hand."

"Missing fingers? How many?"

"Two, maybe three. She couldn't be sure because she was scared and ran away when he flashed his gun."

"Did she recognize what kind of gun it was?"

"A hand gun with a short barrel. That's all she saw."

"Do you think she would talk to me?" asked Kate.

"Not a chance. She is too scared to talk to the White police."

"Where did this happen?" asked Kate.

"Up here between the Ruidoso Ruins and Diamond Butte. She was up there gathering herbs when it happened. She said it was either last Wednesday or Thursday, just about the time when the sun was going down. He was in a great big truck, the kind of truck that sits way up high off the ground. She said after he saw her he got in the truck. Another man was driving. She thought the driver was a younger Mexican or Native, maybe even mixed blood. In either case he took off driving down the road like a crazy man."

Kate jotted down a few notes and looked over toward the mother and daughter before saying goodbye to Eskadi.

On the return trip to Safford she could only think of Felipe Madrigal. No matter how she put the pieces together, it added up to exactly nothing. The stolen cars, stolen plates and the dead body of the young girl in Lorenzo García's truck didn't seem to have a direct link. But her intuition told her otherwise. She felt trapped between the facts and what she wanted to believe.

Dusk and the hissing of the streetlights turning on overhead greeted her at the city limits of Safford.

"Deputy Steele. Step into my office would you?"

"Yes, Sheriff Hanks."

"Did you get any more information from anyone who might have seen the car thieves?"

"No..." replied Deputy Steele.

"You're hesitating," said Sheriff Hanks. "Why?"

"Nobody else had anything specific to say. I mean no one else had seen the Vega or the little guy...."

But?" said Sheriff Hanks.

She knew Zeb carried a certain amount of ill will toward Eskadi, and, as shorthanded as they were, he might not care for the fact that she had run out to the reservation to follow a lead that turned out to be nothing. On the other hand, she had garnered some information that might be of value.

"I had a lead on a missing girl who I thought might have been the dead girl in Lorenzo García's pickup. It turned out she wasn't really missing. But I did find out some other things that might be important. One in particular seems to be."

"Go on."

"Eskadi..."

Zeb rolled his eyes.

"...gave me some information. I don't know if it means anything but it might."

"I know you and Eskadi are close, but he and I have history between us."

"I know that and I get it."

"So don't be taken aback if I take anything he says with a grain of salt," said the sheriff.

"I understand completely."

"Okay, what do you have?"

"An old Indian woman was gathering herbs between the Ruidoso Ruins and Diamond Butte."

"I know that place," said Zeb.

"She saw an oversized pickup with a big White man and a younger Mexican or Native American, or maybe even mixed blood. They were stealing license plates. She got close enough to see that the big White man was missing some fingers. He pulled a gun on her when he spotted her."

"Did you talk to her?"

"Eskadi told me she is scared. She won't talk to anyone but him. He doubts she will tell him anything more than she already has. She thinks the big White man with the missing fingers is the devil himself."

"That could be very important. See if you can follow up on it. You have a better chance of getting Eskadi to do something than I do."

"Got it," said Kate. "I take it you have talked with our prisoner some more?"

"Yes, I did have a nice conversation with Madrigal. I believe he is a good man in his heart. But something is dreadfully wrong. I don't know exactly what, but I do think he will tell us eventually."

"What did you find out?"

"You might say he's more than a little down on his luck on account of his wife and daughter. They both died of cancer. First, his wife died. That was about two years ago. His poor wife died very slowly and suffered a lot. Her suffering almost killed him from the sounds of it."

"How did he express that to you?"

"It isn't as much how he said it, as what he said. Sadness, I guess. Her death broke his heart. Then just when he was starting to get over his wife's death his daughter was diagnosed with cancer too. Ovarian cancer took both of them from him. He is obviously depressed. I guess he's been that way for quite a while. He started crying when he was talking about it. To be honest, I had to do my best to keep from crying myself."

The sheriff's openness was a bit surprising. He had not really opened up in that fashion to her, ever. This new, compassionate side of her boss was as welcome as it was unnerving.

"Mr. Madrigal prayed the rosary every day for two years. He kept asking God for a miracle. He lit candles to the Blessed Virgin Mary. He even made a holy shrine. I guess he is what you would call a devout Catholic. On the other hand his faith was tested by the death of his wife and he became angry with God. When his daughter got snatched away so soon after the death of his wife, Mr. Madrigal told me that he shook his fist toward heaven and cursed God until he was so hoarse he couldn't even talk. He thinks that his actions are the root of his problems and for that he takes complete responsibility," explained Zeb.

"What exactly does that mean?" asked Kate.

"He believes his actions toward the Almighty came back on him as a personal curse."

"You mean him making the phone calls about the bombs and his being in jail?"

"No," replied the sheriff. "Not like that. It seemed like something else."

"What? What do you think he meant?"

"He feels horrible about Delbert. I am certain he is willing to go to jail for that, even if somehow he wasn't directly involved."

"If nothing else, we are absolutely certain he made the phone call."

Kate's reminder was indeed a solid fact. Felipe Madrigal had been involved with Delbert's death. Yet something felt wrong. That little man inside the sheriff, his conscience, his intuition, his gut feeling, told him something else was definitely at play. Zeb was working on a theory that someone had forced Felipe Madrigal into making those phone calls. But who? And why?

"I am becoming quite sure he didn't place the bomb in the school."

Deputy Steele reiterated that there was no doubt Felipe Madrigal had made the phone calls. "No matter how you look at it, he was complicit."

"Sometimes you learn about a man in other ways," said Zeb. "Mr. Madrigal had such a hang dog look on his face that I could almost feel sorry for him, for his situation."

Kate's return gaze spoke to the issue of becoming too compassionate with those you have under arrest. Zeb caught the look as well as its meaning.

"I wanted to get to know him better. I thought I could figure out what makes him tick. He started talking about his work. He was very proud of that. He was a truck driver for a lot of years for the company that owned the mines. Felipe had been a short haul driver for the copper mines in Morenci. He had hauled mostly for

the big mine in Morenci, but he also spent five years working at the Indian Flats mine on the southern end of the San Carlos Reservation. The limp came from a leg injury when a piece of equipment fell off a truck. After the accident he couldn't handle a clutch anymore. The union got him a job as a security guard at the credit union in Morenci. It was a desk job. He carried a gun and wore a badge, but mostly he signed people in and out of the safe deposit boxes at the credit union."

"Did he say why he called in the bomb threat?"

"We never went near that subject," replied the sheriff. "I don't think he wanted to talk about that."

"What else did he talk about?"

"Everyday things. We compared notes about different county roads we both knew. He's the only guy I ever met who has been out on those roads more than I have or more than Delbert did. He knows every landmark in the county. But most of all, I would say when he wasn't talking about truck driving he was pretty down in the dumps."

"You seem to have gotten to know him."

"Yes, I feel like I do, at least a little bit."

"Why do you think he called in the bomb threats?"

Zeb looked out the window. Deputy Steele could practically see the wheels spinning inside the sheriff's head.

"I don't want to call Felipe Madrigal a liar. But if he hadn't confessed to calling those threats in, I would swear he didn't do it. It's almost like he's making it up or covering for somebody. I listened to those tapes again. That is him on those tapes. There is no doubt about it."

"Maybe deep inside he wants to tell someone why he did what he did. Maybe that person is you, Sheriff."

"I hope so. I am going to bring him a radio so he can listen to the game tonight. He's a big baseball fan. He knows his stuff. His favorite players, back in the day, were Orlando Cepeda and the Alou brothers. What are their names again? I remember one is Felipe."

Without skipping a beat Kate replied. "Matty and Jesús are the other brothers. They're all from Domingo in the Dominican Republic. They had a fourth brother that never played ball, Boog."

"Boog Alou? Never heard..." Suddenly the sheriff caught the inside baseball joke. "Good one, you got me."

"Just keeping you on your toes, Sheriff. Actually I stole the joke from my grandma, who stole it from Gramps."

"Keeping on the subject of baseball, Felipe listens to the games on that Spanish speaking station. I also told him I would bring him some car and truck magazines. He likes them. He uses them to help practice reading English. Speaking of baseball, are you going to visit your grandmother over at the nursing home and watch the World Series game?"

"That's where I'm headed right now," said Kate. "Who do you like?"

"Yankees, of course," replied Zeb. "I like Jeter and Jorge Posada. You a Yankee fan."

"Actually, I do like the Yanks," said Deputy Steele a bit sheepishly. "I'm a big Derek Jeter fan too."

"How about your grandmother?"

"Grams, she loves the Yanks. She says Soriano reminds her of the way Grandpa used to play second base."

In the years since her move to Safford, Kate had made it an annual event to watch as many playoff and World Series games as possible with her grandmother. Tonight the rest of the world would be put on hold for a few hours while she carried on the tradition.

"Kate, enjoy yourself. Say hi to Grams.

CHAPTER TWENTY-SIX

"I'm glad you're in a little early today, Kate. Did you catch the game?"

"Man, oh man, Jeter was out of his mind. I thought the Yanks had it when Giambi smacked that homer. The nursing home gals went crazy. They even brought out a bottle of fake champagne to share--but in the end it went to Florida. It's do or die for the Yanks at this point."

"Sounds like you and Grams and the gals had fun," said Zeb. "Even if the Yankees took it on the chin."

"We had a great time. Did you and Doreen watch the game?"

"You bet we did. But after I fell asleep, Detective Muñoz called me at home. I was so tired I didn't even hear the phone ring. He and Doreen talked for half an hour. He wanted me to call him about the autopsy findings on the dead woman in Lorenzo García's truck. I'm going to call him right now. I'll put him on the speakerphone. I want you to listen in."

The switchboard at the Tucson Police Department was expecting the call.

"Detective Muñoz. How may I help you?"

"You can start by covering my behind next time a brick comes flying my way. That is what you can do."

"What the? Zeb? Zeb Hanks? Is that you?"

"It sure as hell is, pardner."

"You should be glad it wasn't a bullet you were trying to duck. That little buttercup of a gal of yours said last night you could have been hurt bad. Sorry to hear about your deputy. That has to be tough."

"It was. It is. But life goes on."

"Amen," replied Detective Muñoz.

Kate listened as the two men tossed feigned barbs and old stories back and forth before getting down to business.

"Max, I've got one of my deputies sitting here with me. Her name is Kate Steele. She lived for a while in the neighborhood where the truck and the body were found. I'm putting you on the speaker phone."

The lawmen exchanged greetings. Kate explained to Detective Muñoz that the body had been found three blocks from the house she once lived in.

"Give us what you've found out, Max," said Zeb.

"Let me begin with something Doreen brought up last night. That gal of yours is quite a talker."

"You can say that again."

"We've had some luck in identifying the dead girl. Her name is Juanita Melindez. She's a twenty year-old Mexican-American. She had no permanent address. We know about a month ago she was staying with a girlfriend in Tucson. The roommate moved back to Mexico. We have tried contacting her. No luck yet. According to the roommate's landlord, Juanita was a quiet girl. She had no social life that he knew of. He heard her mention a boyfriend but never saw one, though she did receive regular letters postmarked from the prison in Florence Junction. That could be a pen pal relationship, a brother or relative, or even a boyfriend, we don't know. Ms. Melindez worked as a waitress at a Chinese restaurant in the Village. The owners were pretty mum about her. At first I thought it was a bit of a language barrier, but it didn't take long to figure out they were paying her off the books."

"I bet I know how you got them to talk." said Zeb.

The two men began to laugh like boys in a private world.

"Do you two care to share your little secret with a fellow officer?" asked Deputy Steele.

"You tell her, Zeb," said Detective Muñoz.

"The one thing a restaurant owner hates is surprise inspections. The easiest way to get information is to send one city health inspector to the restaurant during breakfast, another one during lunch and another during supper. You get the idea. Normally we can get all the information we need, and then some, in less than twenty-four hours. In the big city it's called inter-agency cooperation," explained Zeb. "Here in Safford elections are won and lost over little things like that."

"I'll remember that," replied Kate.

"Go ahead, Max."

"It turns out the guy was paying her cash under the table," said Detective Muñoz. "I could care less. That's business for the revenue boys, not the police department. When he decided we weren't the enemy, he gave us some interesting facts."

"Such as?" asked Zeb.

"Such as the last anyone saw of Juanita Melindez was the night she disappeared. She was seen getting into a blue Chevy LUV pickup with a white male described by the Chinese man as big as an ox, uglier than a pig and wearing a military buzz cut. The truck matches the description of the one we found her in. It matches the truck belonging to Lorenzo García. When I talked with Doreen last night, she seemed to know all about Lorenzo García. When I mentioned the truck had a stolen plate on it from the San Carlos Reservation, the name of Eskadi Black Robes came up. Doreen suggested I talk with Deputy Kate Steele about that one."

Sheriff Hanks turned to Deputy Steele and pointed to the receiver.

"I know Eskadi Black Robes quite well. What do you need to know?" asked Deputy Steele.

"We got the information in a roundabout way from the State Highway Patrol. Eskadi Black Robes had called to get a vehicle ID. He wanted to get new plates for a previously non-registered vehicle. The VIN drew a match to the plates on Lorenzo García's truck. When the highway boys put that together, they called us. The discrepancy is that Lorenzo's truck is a Chevy LUV and the plates were from a Ford F-150. In my mind there is a pretty high certainty the plates on the burned up truck were indeed stolen from somewhere on the reservation."

"I think I can clear this up, Detective," said Deputy Steele.

She explained how Eugene Topy's plates had been stolen and because he had not changed registrations when he bought the vehicle he now knew he needed to get some license plates. He was worried about getting fined because he did not have current plates. She further explained how Eskadi was going to help him work his way through the system. Deputy Steele didn't mention anything about Eskadi's political beliefs. She didn't have to.

"Mr. Eskadi Black Robes doesn't seem to have much respect for authority," said Detective Muñoz. "Trying to get anything from him was like trying to pull hen's teeth."

"He can be difficult when it comes to dealing with what he refers to as the White man," said Deputy Steele.

"Did he tell you anything about the stolen plates?"

"Did he mention that someone saw a White man stealing plates up on the reservation?" asked Deputy Steele.

"He didn't mention it. But like I said, he wasn't real free with the information," replied Detective Muñoz.

"The second set of stolen plates was taken from a car up near Diamond Butte. That happened four or five days after Eugene Topy noticed his plates were missing. A woman gathering herbs saw a White man steal her plates. She got a pretty good look at him but she is awfully scared. The man she saw pointed a large hand gun in her direction and frightened her."

"Did this get reported to the police?" asked Detective Muñoz.

"I assume the reservation police took care of it. But I don't know for certain," replied Kate. "There is a bit of a jurisdictional issue."

"Of course. You said she got a decent look at him. What sort of description do you have?"

"I got the description second hand from Eskadi," said Deputy Steele. "He got it from a very frightened woman."

"I'll keep that in mind," replied the detective.

"She described a big man who was scary and ugly. She said he had a cap on but it looked like he had short hair, maybe a shaved head. He did have one distinctive trait. His left hand was missing some fingers."

"Did she notice how many?"

"Two," replied Kate. "Maybe three."

"Can you give me her name?"

"I don't have it, but I will try and get it for you. Do you want to talk with her?"

"Yes. I want to find out how sure she is about the missing fingers," said Detective Muñoz.

"She was very certain about the fact that he was missing some fingers on his left hand. She just wasn't certain of the number."

"The Chinese restaurant owner's wife told me she thought the man who picked up Juanita Melindez in the blue Chevy LUV truck had a deformed left hand."

"So you believe our murderer is a tall, not good looking, White male with a deformed hand and a buzz cut who stole a truck and switched the license plates?" asked Sheriff Hanks.

"That's what we have been able to put together. Because the truck and the plates are from your area and the girl is from mine, it sort of looks like we are working together again, doesn't it?"

"I guess it does," replied the Sheriff.

"Do you have anything else on the dead girl?" asked Deputy Steele.

"Not much. I hope to have more once we locate her family or her roommate. The autopsy had one other sort of weird thing. The young woman's neck was broken and her windpipe crushed. She was strangled before she was torched in the truck. She wore a necklace with a fairly large silver cross."

"There's nothing strange about that," said Zeb. "About half the people around here wear a cross around their necks."

"Just hold on a second. The doctor who did the autopsy is an ambitious young buck, just out of school. He is slow to get us our reports and a real pain in the ass, but he is as thorough as they come. In this case his pedantic behavior may have big dividends."

"How so?" asked Zeb.

"The broken neck was compressed down hard against her breast bone."

Zeb unconsciously pressed his chin against the top of his chest.

"The chin bone ended up resting right on top of the silver cross. The immense heat from the fire seared an impression of the cross into the breast bone and protected the metal. Although the autopsy also noted that silver melts at 1764 degrees Fahrenheit and a car fire generally can only burn at a maximum of 1300 degrees. Because the chin was resting on top of the silver cross, instead of melting, it was sort of protected in a way. It was fairly intact upon autopsy. The doctor was able to use a small scalpel to remove it in one piece. Using a high powered microscope he was able to see the cross in detail."

"What was he looking for?"

"I don't know. The guy is so obsessive about his work he does some pretty odd things. My guess is he was just curious. But who the hell knows? When he was looking at the cross, he noticed some words. Evidently the back of the cross had been inscribed and the inscription was legible."

"What did it say?"

"Three words…'Ángel loves Juanita'," said the detective. "We know who Juanita is. Now I'm looking for an Ángel."

Detective Muñoz was hedging his bets in hoping the proximity of the stolen car to the stolen plates would eventually tie into someone else who had seen the white male with missing fingers. Max made it clear his belief was that the killer was tied both to the Tucson area and to the specific area between the north central part of Graham County and the south central tip of the San Carlos Reservation. Zeb and Max ended their conversation with an agreement to keep each other closely informed.

"What do you think of the detective's theory?" asked Zeb. "Do you believe we're dealing with a creature of habit who is tied to both Tucson, Graham County and the San Carlos Reservation?"

"I certainly would like to know who the big brute with the bum hand is. But the odds of the car thief and the murderer being the same guy, based on what we know now, are nothing short of fantastic. With the evidence we currently have, Detective Muñoz's theory is little more than wishful thinking. Our job is based on facts not wishes."

"But theoretically speaking, a White male with a deformed hand last seen with a murder victim in a stolen truck with stolen plates, and also a White male with a mutilated hand seen stealing plates on the reservation does have the potential for being a good starting point in an investigation," countered Zeb.

"Your theory might have a few holes in it," Kate cautioned.

"I didn't say it was anything more than a theory. And, hell yes, it's full of holes. There is certainly more than one guy with a mangled left hand walking around, but we've got the same description from two different people and a stolen vehicle with stolen plates," explained the sheriff.

"Putting together times and places of the truck and license thefts and the murder is going to be difficult. To begin with, the plates on the Chevy LUV were from Eugene Topy's truck," said Kate. "He lives a good fifty miles from the Garcías. Why would someone steal a truck out in the middle of nowhere, drive it fifty miles onto an Indian reservation, steal some plates, and then drive it over a couple of hundred more miles to pick up a young girl, break her neck, leave her in the stolen truck and burn it? It could only make sense if we had any kind of a motive, which we don't."

"Well, Deputy Steele. Why don't you get to work and see if you can figure out exactly what the motive is? It's called doing your job."

The uncharacteristic cynicism in the sheriff's tone did not go unnoticed by his subordinate.

"The truth is, Sheriff, I am having a little trouble with motives in general these days. Sitting in our own jail we have a man who confessed to making the bomb threats. His motivation is completely lost on me," stated Deputy Steele.

Sheriff Hanks made no attempt to hide his irritation. Deputy Steele eyed the normally easy going sheriff. Maybe his gut pain was affecting his personality. Perhaps he was trying a little too hard to help an old friend solve a murder case when there was really nothing he could do.

"Deputy Steele, why don't you go back out toward the García place and see if you can find someone else who saw anyone sneaking around there."

"But you've been out there. I've been out there. We have talked to everyone more than once."

"No buts about it. It's an order," said Sheriff Hanks. "And while you're out making the rounds drop by the Madrigal place and pick up his Bible and rosary. Would that be okay with you, Deputy?"

"It's out of the way, but consider it done," said Deputy Steele sensing Sheriff Hanks' obvious frustration.

"And as long as you're out there, ask around again to see if anyone saw a big White male, sort of a nasty looking guy with a deformed left hand, missing fingers, you know the description. Try to shake loose someone's, anyone's memory. We have him linked…" Sheriff Hanks shot a glance in Deputy Steele's direction. "…make that *possibly linked* to García's truck and some stolen license plates up in that general vicinity."

"Yes, sir. Anything else?" asked Deputy Steele.

"Just do your job. People's lives may depend on it," said Sheriff Hanks.

CHAPTER TWENTY-SEVEN

"Sheriff?"

"Yes, Helen?"

"You were a little short with Deputy Steele. Are you feeling okay?"

"Other than a bombing, stolen vehicles connected to the body of a murdered young woman and Delbert's death, yeah, I guess all is well."

"Don't get short with me, Zebulon Hanks, I changed your diapers," said Helen. "Deputy Steele is doing her best. Just because you are frustrated doesn't mean you can take it out on her. You need to concentrate on your work."

Helen was right. It suddenly seemed clear to him that the actions of his brother Noah, in reverting to his pre-prison behavior of car theft, had been the turning point. Just about everything else had been going downhill since then. Maybe he was angry at the bombing and the loss of Delbert. Perhaps his frustration was in the fact that he couldn't find the stolen vehicles that might be linked to the death of a young woman. Maybe the stress of his upcoming marriage to Doreen who, thanks to her recent revelation, he wasn't even sure he knew was weighing on him. It didn't matter. Zeb wasn't being professional and he knew it. It was time to change. It was time to be a man, a good sheriff for the people of Graham County.

"Helen, you are right. I am sorry."

"Don't be sorry," said Helen. "Get to work."

Helen could not have put it more concisely. Sheriff Hanks decided it was time to pay another visit to Felipe Madrigal. Felipe Madrigal was a lonely man. He had hardly anyone to talk to since his wife and daughter had died. The sheriff knew in his heart that Felipe wasn't a bad guy, certainly wasn't the bad guy behind this. Perhaps he was just a guy who had got caught up in something over which he had no control.

The sheriff made the quick walk to Felipe's cell in the Graham County jail. The two briefly talked baseball. Quickly the subject turned to trucks and cars. Felipe loosened up a bit when the sheriff slipped him a cigarette. The former truck driver began talking about how he could rebuild an engine from the ground up in three days. Talking about pride in his mechanical abilities seemed to make Felipe a changed man. The more Felipe spoke the more Zeb realized that he was talking to a mechanical expert, at least when it came to engines. Then, like a lightning bolt it struck the sheriff. Felipe Madrigal was a liar.

"Felipe, have you been telling me the truth?"

Sheriff Hanks tried playing the old good cop routine.

"Sí, Señor Sheriff. I never tell lie."

"Are you a good mechanic?" asked the sheriff.

"Sí, sí, the best. I can fix anything on engine."

Sheriff Hanks left the cell, returned to his office and came back with the tape recording of Felipe Madrigal calling in and asking to be arrested. Sheriff Hanks played it for his prisoner. Felipe said nothing. The sheriff waited. His prisoner said nothing.

"Felipe, you said your truck was broken."

"Sí, sí, it was broken."

"Why didn't you fix it?"

"I don't have no spare tire," said Felipe sheepishly.

"That's it?" asked Sheriff Hanks. "No spare tire?"

"Sí."

Felipe suddenly looked like a treed polecat. He began to look around the cell as if seeking a place to hide from the sheriff's questions.

"The flat tires were the only reason your truck didn't work?"

Felipe Madrigal held steadfastly to his lie.

"I'm no mechanic, but I noticed the distributor cap was missing and the lead wires had been yanked off. Don't tell me you didn't see that?" asked Sheriff Hanks.

Felipe was a cornered mouse. He had lied. Sheriff Hanks could read the falsity of it in the man's words, the sound of his voice and the expression on his face.

"I don't have no spare parts in my truck or in the house."

"Don't lie to me, Felipe."

Felipe was visibly shaken and sweat beaded on his upper lip.

"I tell you the truth. Only the truth. That is what I tell you, the truth."

Sheriff Hanks stood next to his seated prisoner. He inhaled, expanding all six and half feet of his height and two hundred forty pounds of his weight. Felipe cowered. The look on the sheriff's face made Felipe wonder if the sheriff was going to strike him. Felipe slid to the back of his bed protectively. Sheriff Hanks paced back and forth menacingly. He knew Felipe Madrigal was lying to him. How could he get him to tell the truth?

"Why didn't you have spare parts? You know your way around an engine. Why wouldn't you have a spare tire or two, everyone does."

Felipe shrugged nervously. "I don't know. I don't have no extra distributor cap. I had spare tires. I thought I did but when I look they were gone, stolen."

Felipe's lies were getting larger. Not having a distributor cap was one thing, but not noticing the theft of spare tires was quite another, especially to a man who had so much time on his hands. Sheriff Hanks tried to bluff Felipe.

"I'll tell you what," said the sheriff. "I'll call my deputy on the two-way radio and have her take another look around. Maybe she can find the distributor cap?"

The prisoner nodded sheepishly, like a child caught in a lie. Sheriff Hanks made the call to his deputy.

"Deputy Steele," said Sheriff Hanks. "What have you got for me? Did you find Mr. Madrigal's religious items?"

"Yes, I did. They were right where he said they were, but I found something else too."

"What have you got?" asked the sheriff.

"I sat down in his chair to tie my shoe. When I sat down, some loose change fell out of my pocket. I reached in behind the cushions to grab it."

Sheriff Hanks, thinking of his own easy chair, imagined what sort of junk might have fallen down there over the years since Felipe's wife had died.

"There was quite a collection of miscellaneous debris stuffed under there, matches, half-smoked cigarettes and some hard candy with lint stuck all over it."

"Is that it?"

"There was something else--something that is very important."

"What is it, Deputy?"

"A handwritten note."

"Read it to me."

It took exactly five words for the sheriff to know exactly what it was. He had listened to those exact words a hundred times before. Felipe Madrigal had written out the bomb threat. He had been reading it when he called it in. That was why the tone of his voice on the tape had sounded so unnatural. Why hadn't he figured that out before? Now as Deputy Steele read the threat, it was all very obvious.

"It's the bomb threat, verbatim" said Deputy Steele.

"Get that note to me ASAP," said the sheriff.

"Yes, sir, and Sheriff? Now that I take a look at Felipe's handwriting closely...for an old man, who probably wasn't schooled in English, he has excellent handwriting. It is as neat as a pin. It's better than either yours or mine. I'll be there in about twenty minutes. Goodbye."

Sheriff Hanks opened the Madrigal file and turned to the old man's handwritten admission of guilt.

Felipe Madrigal's handwriting was barely legible.

CHAPTER TWENTY-EIGHT

Ángel opened his eyes; instantly he squeezed them shut again. Certain he had awakened in the middle of a perfect dream, Ángel made a vain attempt to fool the sandman and slip back into the sweet fantasy. It was for naught. He was awake.

Slowly Ángel reopened his eyes, fearful of returning to the reality he knew awaited him. Ángel touched his face and rubbed his eyes, looking around the spacious bedroom. To his right, a large picture window overlooked the river. The huge bed he lay on was soft, crisp and clean. He sat up and swung his feet onto the plush carpet nearly kicking over a half full bottle of tequila. Disoriented, his eyes darted around the room a second time. He pinched himself to make certain he wasn't dreaming. Maybe he had died. Maybe this was heaven. His pounding headache told him otherwise. Where was he? How did he get here? A rustling noise in the next room drew his attention. Quietly he opened the door and peeked through. At the kitchen table he saw the shadow of a large man cleaning a gun.

"You trying to sneak up on me, amigo?"

The gruff voice was Jimmie Joe's. In fits and starts memories came slowly drifting in. He and Jimmie Joe had broken into a rich man's house. They had spent the night drinking, laughing and playing music.

Jimmie Joe turned to Ángel.

"Did you get your beauty rest, muchacha? I don't think it worked. You are just as ugly as you were yesterday."

Ángel pressed his thumbs against his eyeballs. The previous night came back to him, the drinking, the partying, even stumbling into the fancy bed pretending he was kissing his darling Juanita.

"Coffee with a double shot of tequila, amigo? It'll kick those nasty demons out of your head."

"Sure, Jimmie Joe."

The big man pointed with his chin to a coffeepot on the counter. Ángel grabbed a cup and pulled a chair to the kitchen table. A recent copy of the Eastern Arizona Courier was spread out on the table. On the paper were the five handguns Jimmie Joe had heisted on his recent venture into Safford. Next to the guns were cleaning push rods, brass bore brushes, solvents, lubricants and patches. Some of the weapons were broken down into parts for cleaning. Others had already been meticulously taken care of. The big man worked slowly, using the contents of the Otis Elite gun cleaning kit to make certain each of the weapons was perfectly clean and in superior working order.

Ángel sipped his liquored up coffee. Even with missing fingers, the big man deftly manipulated the guns. Ángel's eyes fell on the scar tissue around the missing finger stubs. The grotesquely misshapen hand was a perfect match for the ugly face. Ángel thought back to the story he had heard in prison of how Jimmie Joe lost his fingers and gained his nickname, Diablo Blanco. Only at this moment, for some strange reason, Ángel wondered whether it was true. Had Jimmie Joe Walker chopped three of his own fingers off with a single swing of an ax? Had he taken the three fingers and cooked and eaten them as some people said? Had he done such a thing to destroy his fingerprints? Only a crazy man or the devil himself would do such a thing. When other men would ask him why he would do such a thing, he would only let out a diabolical laugh and brag that the devil had taken possession of his soul.

"The big day is about to arrive. Are you ready to become a rich man, Ángel?"

Ángel looked at his surroundings. He liked what he saw. He was ready to have the big money that would change his life. He lusted after the cash that would allow him and Juanita to raise a family on the beach in Mexico. He thought about the rush of the surf lapping against the beach. The time had come. Now Jimmie Joe would tell him what the plan was and when it would happen. Ángel looked at his partner who was staring down the open chambers of a .38 caliber pistol.

"One million dollars each. That's what you promised. Right?" asked Ángel.

"Maybe even more," replied Jimmie Joe. "A million dollars is big money, the kind of cash that could take care of a man for the rest of his life."

Holding the gun in his right hand the big man spread out newspaper with the clawlike stub on his left hand and pointed at two stories he had circled repeatedly with a red pen.

"Read this story."

Ángel picked up a .38 that was covering the article and set it off to the side.

MORENCI COPPER MINING DAYS BEGIN ON SATURDAY

The 53RD annual Copper Days Festival is set to begin on Saturday, October 25. This year the event marks the longest continuously running local event in southern Arizona. The Festival kicks off with the Annual Copper Days Parade featuring ten area marching bands, over eighty floats, and a half dozen beauty queens including the World's Best Rodeo Gal, Bobbie Jo Crenshaw, from right here in Safford. Starting Saturday afternoon and continuing on into Sunday, the Rodeo and Roping Events expect to draw over five thousand people. Cash prizes in excess of $150,000 will be awarded.

Jimmie Joe had underlined the $150,000 twice.

"One hundred fifty thousand dollars in prize money and five thousand people paying five bucks a head to get in the door and that's just for starters. Ángel, my partner, read this one."

Ángel's eyes darted to the second circled article.

PROFIT SHARING ANNOUNCED

The Morenci Copper Mine today announced annual bonuses for all hourly employees will set a record this year. Over $2,500 will be given to each employee in conjunction with Copper Mining Days. The Credit Union will be open both Saturday and Sunday so union members can cash their checks.

Ángel set his coffee cup down. His hand began to tremble. Now it all made sense. Hiding out in the middle of nowhere for the last few weeks, driving the back roads, Jimmie Joe's gun theft, scouting out the town of Morenci. If Ángel had known they were going to rob a credit union with guns, he would have run off with Juanita. If he had seen his grandfather, he would have been too ashamed to do such a thing. He now understood why Jimmie Joe had insisted he stay away from Juanita and his grandfather.

"There are over one thousand five hundred employees at that mine up there. Figure it out," said Jimmie Joe.

Ángel couldn't do the math in his head.

"I don't know. How much is that?"

"Almost four million in bonus money alone. Even if half of those men pick up their checks on Saturday, there will be close to two million bucks, plus the prize money of a hundred fifty thousand, the gate admission of twenty five grand and there's always the popcorn and peanut money. The way I got it figured the absolute worst we could do is a cool million each. What do you think about that?"

Ángel's trembling fingers began to shake. He held one hand down with the other. They could never pull off such a big job. It was crazy to even think about the two of them doing it. The local police and the sheriff's department would be keeping an eye on things along with the armed security that would surely be guarding the money. The town would be packed with visitors.

"It's an awful lot of money. I don't see how we can do it. I've been in that building. It's like a fort," said Ángel. "We could get shot by the guards before we ever see the money. It's a crazy idea."

"Here, have a cigarette and quit worrying. I've got the whole job all planned out, from soup to nuts."

Ángel took a cigarette from the open pack. He inhaled deeply. The tobacco had a soothing effect. He began to think more clearly.

The big man silently cleaned the gun barrel of the .38, sliding with cautious precision the clean white patch through the shaft of the weapon with a push rod. Ángel nervously smoked one cigarette after another. He put the idea of getting shot as far out of his mind as possible. With over four million dollars in cash at the credit union, the guards would certainly be heavily armed. He did not want to die before he held Juanita in his arms. But he did want to be rich.

"When?" asked Ángel.

"Tomorrow," said Jimmie Joe. "Saturday night...round midnight."

Ángel had celebrated Copper Days in the past by drinking late into the night. If this year was like every other, the partying would rise to fever pitch by eleven p.m. The bars stayed open until two or three and the street dance kept going until the police shut it down.

"But Jimmie Joe, the streets are going to be packed with people. Someone will see us. Shouldn't we pick a better time?"

Jimmie Joe grabbed the smallest of the guns, the .22. He had already cleaned it. He knew it was the perfect gun to be used up close and personal. It was the perfect gun for an assassination. Jimmie Joe was thinking one of the guards might wander upon them and a quick shot to the head would kill him. It was unlikely Ángel would actually shoot to kill, but if his life was in danger, it was best to be prepared. Handing it to Ángel he simply said, "Here, just in case you need to shoot someone."

Ángel held the .22 in his hands. "I'm not going to shoot anyone."

"Not even to protect your partner?" asked Jimmie Joe with a malicious grin.

Ángel stared blankly at Jimmie Joe. "Well, I won't kill anybody."

The big man pointed the empty .38 at Ángel and slowly squeezed the trigger over and over again.

"Bang...bang...bang...bang...bang and fucking bang! You will if I tell you to, muchacha. Amigo, you are nothing short of a fucking idiot. A crowd is perfect, you dumb asshole. We can use them to our advantage," said Jimmie Joe. "The more people out on the streets the merrier."

"What are you talking about?" asked Ángel.

A ray of sunlight sneaked through the open window. It glinted off the freshly polished gun barrel. A zinging ray of sparkling light darted past the corner of Ángel's eye and landed on a statue of Jesus. Ángel was certain it was a sign from God.

"Do you think for one freaking minute some security guard is going to fire willy-nilly into a crowd? They would have to be nuts. Besides, the way I have it figured we will be in and out in less than twenty minutes. No one will be the wiser until they re-open the credit union the next morning."

It was early in the day to drink heavily, even for Ángel, but his boozing reflex sent his hand reaching for the bottle. Tomorrow might be the last day of his life. His head throbbed. His heart ached for Juanita. He thought of his grandfather. A rush of fear sent the little hairs on his arms straight up. His father had died in a car accident outside of Morenci. His grandfather had mangled his foot while working at the Copper Mine in Morenci. The town had cursed the men of his family. Would the bad luck streak run like a dagger through his heart as well? He grabbed the half-empty bottle of tequila.

"A shot of courage for my little brother?" asked Jimmie Joe.

Ángel started to pour more liquor into his coffee but stopped short and downed a slug straight from the bottle. The first swallow of the day burned like fire. A second swig cut the scum from his teeth. Once again confidence and ease began to ripple through his veins.

CHAPTER TWENTY-NINE

"What's the plan, Jimmie Joe? How are we going to get in? How are we going to get out?"

Jimmie Joe wiped his hands on a clean kitchen towel and tossed it carelessly into a corner.

"I thought you'd never ask. Take a seat in the living room. I'll show you."

The Diablo Blanco disappeared into a bedroom. He returned with a notebook, the kind Ángel had used in school. He laid it out on the coffee table and opened it. The first page was a detailed sketch of the top of the credit union building. The next page was a map of the ventilation shaft leading to the vault that held the safe, a safe that for the last five years had a broken lock. Above the vault was a small grate with a notation indicating it was twenty inches by sixteen inches. Page three had the floor plan of the inside of the credit union. Large black X's marked the spots where armed guards would be posted.

"Where did you get all of this information?" asked Ángel. "No one except people who work inside that building knows about this stuff."

"Let's just say I had some inside dope," replied Jimmie Joe. "I got a little birdie to sing for me."

The Diablo Blanco's sinister howl made Ángel cringe. People who knew the inside secrets of a bank didn't give out that sort of information unless someone had a gun pointed at them. And some people, like his grandfather, the proud Felipe Madrigal, would take a bullet in the head before giving up such information. Ángel's heart stopped.

The Diablo Blanco had gone to his grandfather's house to let him know his Ángel was okay. Ángel's heart sank even further as he remembered one lonesome night in the jail cell when he was thinking about his family. He had talked to Jimmie Joe about his grandfather. He had confided everything about his grandfather's truck driving days for the mines, his foot injury and how the mining company gave him a job as a security guard at the credit union in Morenci.

"My grandfather would never betray the mining company. He would never do that. He loved his job at the mines. He would never give you all this information."

"Take it easy. He didn't do it for me, my little muchacha. He did it for you," said Jimmie Joe. "He just wanted to make sure your life was going--somewhere. Let me put it another way. He was looking out for your future...as well as his own."

The Diablo Blanco's remark confused Ángel. The scheming laughter didn't. Unless Jimmie Joe had threatened his grandfather he would never have given him any information. Ángel was afraid to ask the details. He shuddered at the thought of what Jimmie Joe might have done to Felipe. Another shot of tequila flowed down his gullet.

"Don't worry about your grandfather. He's a righteous dude. He did his job. It's time you started thinking like a rich man."

Jimmie Joe opened a street map of Morenci and laid it next to the floor plan of the credit union.

"It's a simple plan, one even you can follow, my little muchacha," chided Jimmie Joe.

Ángel's heart beat faster with every word. He would drive the big truck into town and park in the alley behind the credit union building. Jimmie Joe would hop out and scout the alley while Ángel waited in the truck with the guns. When he was certain it was clear, Jimmie Joe would return to the truck, put on the flak jacket and slip the four handguns into the pair of double holsters he would be wearing.

"You can carry your .22 in your pants along with your knives. You though I didn't know about that shiv you carry in your boot? And that little pouch in the back of your pants? You think you could hide that from Jimmie Joe's eyes?"

Ángel knew now that nothing could be hidden from the White Devil. He had eyes in the back of his head.

"At the other end of the alley is a fire escape," continued Jimmie Joe. "It goes up to the top of the building. The roof slants toward the alley, away from the street. We can move along the top of the buildings without being seen. Once we're up there we have to go across six buildings before we get to the credit union."

Jimmie Joe flipped a page in his notebook to a detailed drawing of the roof of the credit union. Dead center was a large air conditioning unit. Next to it was an air exchange vent. It led directly to the vault.

"We could go in through the air vent…if we have to. But there is a better way," said Jimmie Joe. The big man tapped the drawing with his deformed hand. "Next to the air vent is a trap door. "It leads to the top floor of the building. It's old and weak. I plan on yanking it open with my hands."

Jimmie Joe smiled and winked as he flexed his big, tattooed muscles for Ángel.

"Why do you think I spent so much time lifting weights in the slammer?"

Ángel nodded remembering him lifting big weights in the prison yard.

"But just in case it's padlocked from the inside, we'll take a crow bar with us. You can carry that. When we get inside--"Jimmie Joe's voice became calmer the more excited he got. "--when we get inside, we go right down the stairs and, BINGO, we are directly over the top of the vault."

"How do we get in?"

Jimmie Joe turned another page.

"Here." His mutilated hand once again tapped the page. "In the crawl space between the vault and the ceiling is the air duct that leads into the vault. It's sixteen by twenty inches, just like the one inside the vault. We can cut it open with metal shears. My little friend, you are going to crawl through the duct, kick off the grate and get the money."

Ángel would put the money into two laundry bags and push them back up through the vent to Jimmie Joe. The escape route would be the reverse of the way in.

"Do you think I can get into a space that small?" asked Ángel.

"If you can't, we're doing this for nothing. I'll bring a can of grease along, just in case."

"If we aren't going into the bank where the guards are, how come we need so much fire power?"

"Better safe than sorry, amigo. I'd just as soon creep in like a gato and sneak out like a thief in the night. But you never know who or what might screw up. That includes you."

What was the Diablo Blanco thinking? That Ángel was going to double cross him? Why would he? They were partners in this deal. They would both be rich when it was over. There was more than enough money for both of them to live the rich man's life until the day they died--a day he hoped wouldn't come soon.

CHAPTER THIRTY

With Deputy Steele at his side Sheriff Hanks replayed the tape recording for the umpteenth time. This time, however, it was different. This time Zeb held in his hand the note Kate had found in Felipe Madrigal's chair. When he was certain of his next step, they made the short walk to his prisoner's cell. Felipe Madrigal, head in hands apparently lost in thought, did not hear them approach.

"Mr. Madrigal, I need to ask you a few questions," said Sheriff Hanks.

Felipe kept his eyes averted, his lips remained sealed. Zeb handed Kate the note she had found in Felipe's chair. She handed it to Felipe. The prisoner took the piece of paper in his hand without looking up.

"Have you ever seen this note before?" Sheriff Hanks' voice was firm, direct.

The old man could not escape the question. His weary eyes, bloodshot from the fatigue that accompanies uneasy sleep in strange surroundings, slid the paper into focus. His aged hands clung tenuously to the note as though it might explode. He shook slightly. His voice was a stutter.

"I d-don't know. Maybe."

Sheriff Hanks gritted his teeth. It was as close as Felipe Madrigal had come to admitting anything other than making the phone calls. The sheriff knew this note was the key to getting him to talk. He chose his words cautiously.

"Deputy Steele found it at your house when she went to get your rosary and your Bible. Maybe it's a sign from the Holy Mother. Maybe the Blessed Virgin wants you to talk to us?"

Deputy Steele nodded in agreement. Felipe returned the piece of paper.

"I would like to make confession," mumbled Felipe.

"Of course," said the sheriff.

"That would be good for you," added Kate.

"I see a priest?"

Both Kate and Zeb were taken aback by the request for a priest.

"Are you sure there isn't something you would like to tell me first?" asked Zeb.

The old man closed his eyes and shook his head. He would only talk to the priest.

A call to Father Ortiz brought no immediate solution. The priest apologized for his busy schedule. He had a wedding service, a church service at the Desert Rose Nursing Home, and he had to hear confessions. Saturday, he said, was even busier than Sunday for a priest. He could be there by twelve-thirty on Sunday, earlier only if someone was dying and needed Extreme Unction. The law would have to wait for the Lord.

Zeb reminded himself to be patient. Seeking to change the ways of the Lord would only create anxiety. Justice moved at its own speed. Yet, his entire investigation of the bombing would move forward so much more easily if Felipe would just talk.

"Deputy Steele, I need to clear my head a little. I believe a cup of tea over at the Town Talk might just do the trick."

"Sounds good. Bring me back a cup of Doreen's best coffee, would you?"

"You got it."

Zeb headed out the door to the Town Talk.

Kate remained at the office. She wracked her brain, thinking of how to break through Felipe Madrigal's stubbornness. Her musing was interrupted by the ringing of her direct phone line. It was Eskadi reminding her of their date.

"Have you ever been to the cowboy rodeo?" he asked.

"I've never been to a rodeo, not even once," replied Kate. "But if it's as good as you claim, I can hardly wait."

"It really is a lot of fun. Let's get there early. Some of the reservation boys are riding the big broncos. I don't want to miss that. There's a street dance afterward. Geronimo's Cadillac, the only all Apache rock and roll band on the planet, is going to be playing some good ol' rock and roll."

For the first time in weeks Eskadi carried genuine excitement in his voice. His tone was beautiful compared to the anger and jealousy he had been exuding lately.

Eskadi gave her a rundown of the events. His animation rose as he described bareback riding, bucking broncos and calf roping. It came to a fever pitch when he went off on a tirade about the history of rodeo clowns, their importance to the rodeo and how they had originally been a part of the sacred Indian culture. He even jokingly hypothesized the whole idea of rodeo clowns was yet another idea co-opted by the cowboy White man from the Native Americans. When he laughed at the silliness of his own statement, Kate felt maybe Eskadi was once again becoming the man she had fallen in love with.

"Oh, there's one more thing," said Eskadi. "You know that tape you had me listen to? The one with the bomb threats?"

"Yes. We've got the man who made the calls in jail."

"Everyone knows that," said Eskadi. "That old Mexican, Felipe Madrigal. The old men up here on the reservation who worked with him down at the Morenci Copper Mine say he was the best guy they ever worked with. He would hang out with the Natives because the Whites didn't like him anymore than they liked the Mestizos or Mexicans. They would eat lunch together every day. Felipe's wife, who was both Mescalero Apache and Mexican, was a great cook, and she made food for some of the guys who weren't married. Old man Madrigal even learned some Apache language. He would tell a story in Spanish, and they would tell him the same story in Apache. Telling all those stories in two languages and listening to his wife's accent is how he got the Apache accent in his voice. He even claims he has a little Mescalero Apache blood in his veins. I believe him, even if it is only because he married into it."

"Did they say anything else about him?"

"Not much else except he was a better mechanic than any of the White guys. Oh, there was on other thing. He used to bring his grandson, a little pipsqueak of a kid, with him in the truck. When that kid wasn't even ten years old, the old man used to let him drive that big truck all by himself. I guess that little squirt was a hell of a good driver."

Eskadi promised to pick her up by five o'clock. Kate hung up the phone.

By the time Kate got done with her paperwork it was three o'clock and Zeb was back in the office. He handed her the cup of coffee she had requested.

"Before everyone heads off to the rodeo, did you learn anything new on your rounds today?" he asked.

"I got four more complaints about fast drivers. Some fella in a big truck has been going like a bat out of hell...pardon my language...out that way. But I didn't see any speeders all afternoon. I sometimes think those ranchers out there complain just to have something to talk about or somebody to talk to."

"I imagine some of those folks go for weeks without talking to anyone new," he added.

"You know them better than I do," said Kate. "And then there was one old couple who said a young Mexican kid came to their door asking for water for his car's radiator. The car was parked down the road a piece so they couldn't say for sure if it was a Vega, but it was yellow. The wife thought she might have seen a second person sitting in the car, but she couldn't be sure because the kid came to the door by himself."

"I'd sure like to find the kid driving that yellow Vega and figure out what that is all about."

"We will," said Kate. "What was the word over at the diner?"

"I didn't think I was ever going to get out of the Town Talk. Every time I stopped to talk to somebody all they wanted to talk about was the rodeo. By the time I get cleaned up and Doreen and I get up there, it will be five or six. The rodeo starts at two. I would hate to miss three or four hours of it. It's Doreen's first time at the rodeo with me."

Kate was glad to see a little less stress on the sheriff's face.

"It goes on until nine or ten," said Kate. "In fact Eskadi told me most of the best events are after five o'clock."

"I guess you're right. I sure don't want Doreen to miss it when they let the bulls out to chase the clowns. I know she will just love that."

"I would say it sounds more like you who doesn't want to miss it, Zeb." said Deputy Steele.

The sheriff chuckled. She was right. Ever since he was a little kid the bulls chasing the rodeo clowns around the arena had been his favorite part of the rodeo.

"Eskadi told me the clown show was at seven-thirty," Kate continued. "He says that's the best part."

"It is a heckuva lot of fun," replied Zeb. "Enjoy yourself."

"You too, Sheriff. Relax. Have a little fun. Not much bad can happen at a rodeo."

CHAPTER THIRTY-ONE

"Pull in that alley over there," ordered Jimmie Joe.

Ángel took a right, then a left and pulled the pickup truck into the alleyway that ran behind the Morenci Credit Union. Both men, on high alert, kept an eye out for anything unusual. For the most part the small road was full of cars and trucks. Anyone looking for a parking spot at this hour would be looking elsewhere. These prime spots would have been taken hours ago. Ángel glanced at his watch. It was twenty two minutes past midnight. So far everything was right on schedule.

"Luck is with us, amigo," said Jimmie Joe. "Look."

Using his ugly, deformed hand Jimmie Joe pointed out a small drive to a loading dock. It was posted with a no parking sign. It couldn't have been more perfect for their needs. It was an easy in and out. There was no way someone could accidentally block them in. Even more than that they could back in and use the back of the pickup to grab onto the fire escape ladder. From there they could easily reach the rooftop of the buildings. Ángel maneuvered the truck into the small driveway, put it into park and shut it off. He double checked to see if the second set of keys he had made were under the mat. It was a precaution his grandfather had taught him in case he lost his keys. Without a word Jimmie Joe hopped out of the truck and did a quick reconnaissance of the alley. He briefly checked each car and truck to make sure someone wasn't passed out drunk in it or sitting and waiting for someone. It took less than five minutes to check everything out. In the meantime Ángel double checked the gear. Jimmie Joe's flak jacket, double holsters and handguns were where he had stashed them. The crow bar was under the seat, easy to grab. Ángel checked the access. Under his feet were two canvas bags to carry the loot. Last, he reached into the pouch in his pants where his trusty .22 was ready for action. Oddly, the little peashooter as Jimmie Joe called it, gave him the most comfort.

"We're all set to go. You ready?"

All Ángel could think about was the money, Juanita and the beach in Mexico. Jimmie Joe shook him by the shoulder.

"Pay attention, amigo. This is a once in a lifetime opportunity. Don't you dare fucking blow this for me."

Ángel snapped to attention. He grabbed the canvas bags and the crow bar. "Don't worry about me, Jimmie Joe. I am ready to be a rich man."

The ugly hand pointed to the fire escape ladder. "Señorita first." Ángel shot Jimmie Joe an angry look. "It's only a joke," said Jimmie Joe. "Don't get your panties in a bunch now. We've got serious business to attend to."

Ángel scooted up the fire escape ladder with Jimmie Joe close on his heels. Little did Ángel know that Jimmie Joe wanted him to go first in case there was a guard on the roof. If that were the cas,e Ángel would take the bullet. The music from the street dance was suddenly louder on the angled roof top. Ángel glanced across the tops of the buildings to make sure no one had decided to watch the street party or listen to the music from up there. It was clear.

"Move it. Rápido."

Ángel scooted low on the roof top. Jimmie Joe also kept low. Ángel knew precisely when they were on top of the credit union. It looked exactly as Jimmie Joe had drawn it out in his notebook. At the center of the building was the air conditioning unit. Next to it was the grate-covered air exchange vent that led directly to the vault. Next to that was the trap door, their first choice of entry. Jimmie Joe jammed the crow bar hard into the edge of the trap door. It banged hard against cement. Someone had sealed it off from the inside. A couple of hard whacks and a few curse words later it became obvious that entering by the trap door was not going to happen. Ángel remembered all the times Jimmie Joe spent lifting weights in the prison yard. He would need dynamite instead of brute strength to get through the trap door.

"Plan B. You go in through the vent," said Jimmie Joe reaching inside his vest and grabbing a can of WD-40. "Strip to your undies and close your eyes."

"No," said Ángel. "I can make it through there without that stuff on me."

Jimmie Joe hesitated, stunned momentarily by Ángel's defiance. He looked at the opening, at Ángel. He smiled.

"You are a fucking crazy fuck. I like that. Okay, go on, but you had better squeeze your skinny ass through there without any trouble."

In the street below, Geronimo's Cadillac was playing a tribute to Paul Revere and the Raiders. The song *Kicks* came through the air. The words kicks just keep getting harder to find caused Jimmie Joe to chuckle and comment, "Ain't that the truth?" Ángel didn't know what the crazy devil was even talking about.

This time Jimmie Joe yanked so hard against the grate that he stumbled backward as it came off easily. He slid it aside and ordered Ángel into the opening. Ángel slipped through the opening and quickly found himself in the crawl space. He lifted a single vent and stepped down onto the top of the old safe. It creaked under his weight. Jumping to the floor he eyed the vault. Would it open as easily as Jimmie Joe had promised? Ángel tugged hard. Nothing. He tugged again. The door seemed to come a bit loose. One last time he pulled at the handle with all he had. This time it was his turn to be surprised as the door flew open and Ángel stumbled backward. He regained his footing and stared into the open safe. It held his dreams of freedom and the rich man's life.

"What's going on down there?" Jimmie Joe's voice echoing through the ventilation system seemed to be coming from a million miles away.

Ángel walked over to the vent and in a whispering shout said, "I'm in."

"Hurry the fuck up."

Ángel jammed the stacks of money into the two bags. Each bag was about the same size when the stacks of bills were in them. Ángel was surprised that they were as small as they were. Maybe there was less money than Jimmie Joe had promised. He jumped back onto the top of the safe after yanking the bags tightly shut. He tossed them into the ventilator shaft and crawled up after them. He made his way to the shaft.

"Jimmie Joe."

"Toss up the money bags."

For a brief second Ángel considered that Jimmie Joe might take the money and run. He tossed up one bag and quickly hooked the drawstring on the second bag tightly around his ankle.

"Where is the other bag?"

"I had to tie it to my ankle. Now hand me the crow bar."

Jimmie Joe stuck it down the shaft and pulled Ángel to safety.

"Let's get the hell out of here," said Ángel.

Keeping low, the pair scooted across the building tops and down the fire escape to their truck. Three minutes later they were past the outskirts of Morenci and on the road to freedom.

CHAPTER THIRTY-TWO

The rodeo had turned out far better than Kate expected. The rodeo clowns were even funnier than Eskadi had described. There was hardly a single event that didn't have the crowd on its feet cheering, whistling, making noise and just generally having a great time. At the end of the night things took an exhilarating turn as Eskadi whispered in her ear.

"Why don't you spend the night with me?"

Kate's words came without hesitation. "I was waiting for your invitation."

Eskadi's gentle touch had returned. His edgy jealousy seemed a distant memory.

Kate was deep asleep in Eskadi's arms when her slumber was broken by the ringing of her cell phone. It was Sheriff Hanks.

"Did I wake you?" he asked gruffly.

Kate reached over and ran her hand over Eskadi's broad back and shoulders.

"Yes."

Kate looked at the clock. It was nearly nine. She had not slept this late in years.

"What's going on?"

"Did you go to the rodeo up in Morenci last night?"

"Yes."

"Did you see anything funny? Was anyone acting suspiciously?"

"The clowns were funny. I didn't see anything suspicious. What's this about?"

"I just got a call from the Morenci PD. There was one hell of a robbery up there last night. Maybe a million or more bucks was taken," said the sheriff.

"A million dollars? What's that kind of cash doing in Morenci? A rodeo doesn't bring in that kind of money."

Sheriff Hanks explained the profit sharing money and rodeo prize money totaled over four million dollars. The local police had asked for their assistance. He wanted her to meet him in Morenci right away. She said she would be there ASAP.

"Somebody stole a million dollars from the credit union in Morenci?" asked Eskadi wiping the sleep from his eyes. "That greedy corporation has too much money. Maybe they should learn to share their wealth."

"They were. It was profit sharing money for the workers. I've got to run. I don't know when I'll be back. I'm meeting Sheriff Hanks in Morenci."

Kate got dressed, pulled her long hair into a ponytail, kissed Eskadi goodbye and headed out the door. Zeb was standing inside the credit union's walk-in vault when she arrived. He introduced her to Morenci's finest.

"They're a hundred percent certain it was an inside job," said Sheriff Hanks. "The robbers came in through the roof, then through a grate-covered air vent that runs through a crawl space just above the safe. The safe itself is over a hundred years old. It has a heavy door but the lock mechanism is faulty. One good hard tug opened it."

"Why did they have a safe with a faulty locking mechanism?" asked Deputy Steele.

"No one wants to answer that question. Everyone possibly in charge of fixing keeps pointing the finger at the next guy."

One of the Morenci policemen took Sheriff Hanks and Deputy Steele to the roof and ran them through the presumed order of events. As far as the local police knew no one had seen or heard anything. They believed the robbers came after midnight but before five in the morning. The street music was so loud that the two guards posted inside the building didn't hear anything. The music continued on until almost three a.m. The money was mostly in unmarked twenties, fifties and hundreds. The vault also contained safe deposit boxes, none of which were touched. Most of the stolen cash was the bonus money promised to the copper miners. The rodeo prize money had also been stolen. By the time the FBI agents arrived from Tucson it appeared like the perfect crime had been committed.

Hours later Sheriff Hanks and Deputy Steele returned to their Safford office in time to see Father Ortiz exiting their jail.

"Father Ortiz," said the sheriff. "Bringing the word of the Lord to our prisoner?"

"Yes, Sheriff Hanks. I was offering him a temporary cleansing of his troubled soul," replied the priest.

"I know you can't discuss anything he told you in confidence," said Sheriff Hanks. "But is there anything we should talk to him about? Anything we can do to make the load he is carrying a little lighter?"

"He seems to trust you. He has wanted for some time now to tell you what he knows. He hasn't because he has been afraid. I think his mind is clearer now." Sheriff Hanks thanked the priest. "My vows of silence won't allow me to tell you anything he told me, but I would highly suggest you get in there and talk to him on the double."

The men shook hands. Zeb once again thanked the priest who parted with an ominous warning.

"Please hurry. But not only for the sake of the old man."

Zeb hustled past Helen who seemed to know already what was going on. "I think Mr. Madrigal confessed to Father Ortiz. If I know how Catholics think, now that Mr. Madrigal has made his peace, he is ready to talk to you."

Zeb's mind was spinning. He glanced through the glass partition in the door leading to the cells. Where should he begin? He knew the old man loved the rodeo. Talking about all the action at the rodeo might ease Felipe's mind and get him talking. The look on the old man's face, as he knelt beside his bed praying the rosary, told the sheriff something very heavy was weighing on his mind. Felipe Madrigal carried a look of life and death in his eyes. Sheriff Hanks wondered whose life it was that Felipe was worried about.

Zeb removed his weapon from his holster, took off his hat, tugged at his pants and took a deep breath as he walked into the jail cell. Sheriff Hanks momentarily kept a respectful distance as Felipe continued to pray. When he finished, he made the sign of the cross, turned and began to speak.

"Señor Sheriff, I have done some bad things. Because of these bad things my grandson may die. I was only trying to protect him. But I have done something very terrible."

"Felipe, please slow down. Tell me how you got into this mess to begin with?" asked Sheriff Hanks.

"This diablo gringo, he comes to my house. I don't know him. I never even see him before. But he says he is a friend of my grandson, Ángel. So I invite him into my house. I give him a cup of coffee, and he tells me he knows my grandson from in the Florence Junction prison."

"Why was your grandson in prison?"

"My grandson, Ángel, he ges the diablo inside when he drinks," said Felipe. "He ges drunk and steals cars. I'm ashamed because I teach him to drive...and I give him his first drink. I thought one little beer wouldn't hurt him. But he no can handle liquor. He's no bad boy. See, this is his picture."

Felipe handed the picture of the girlish looking young man to Sheriff Hanks.

"So I look at this diablo blanco grande who knows my grandson in the Florence Junction prison, and I know there is trouble. I don't know what happens in prison. But I hear bad stories. I think Ángel is in big trouble because this man look very mean. He look crazy in the eyes."

"Why did he come to your house? Did he have a message from your grandson?"

"Sí, sí! That is what he said. The big man said..."

"Did this friend of your grandson have a name, Felipe?" asked Sheriff Hanks.

"His name was James. Señor James Walker."

"What message did he bring?"

"He told me Ángel wants to come and visit me. But first Ángel has job to do. Señor Walker says when you get out of prison they make you have a job to go to. He said when Ángel ges a day off from his job he will come and visit me right away. But when I ask where he is working, the big man does not know. So I ask him if he knows my Ángel like such good friends, how come he don't know where he works."

"Did he give you an answer?

"No, no, he just ges very mad at me. He don't explain nothing. He ges real mad and says I don't do what he wants I would never see Ángel again. He said he would kill him, shoot him in the head with big gun. Then he pulled out big gun and point it at me. Then he ask me for piece of paper. I give it to him. He write down that note about bombing. He make me read it to him to make sure I get it right."

"Señor James Walker wrote the note?" asked Delbert.

"Sí, it is true. He tells me to call sheriff's office at 8:30 exactly and tell them I plant a bomb at high school and it will explode at 9:00 a.m.. Then at 12:30, I call sheriff again and tell him bomb will explode at grade school. He said do it or Ángel is dead meat."

"Why didn't you call the police and tell them the truth?" asked Sheriff Hanks. "We believe people like you."

"The bad man said if I breathe one word to anyone he kill Ángel and rip his heart out of his chest. Then he would come back here to cut my throat and burn my house down. I believe him," said the old man.

"Was Señor James Walker missing fingers on his left hand?"

"Sí, sí, sí. That is right. Do you know him?"

Sheriff Hanks took a second look at the picture of Felipe's grandson. He could be the young Mexican kid in the yellow Vega that people had been describing.

"Then bad man said he wanted one more thing from me and he would leave me alone."

"What was that?" asked Sheriff Hanks.

The old man began to tremble. He kissed the rosary he held tightly in his hand and made the sign of the cross.

"I think I do something very terrible. I have made much trouble for many people, even my Ángel. I pray with good priest to Blessed Virgin for answer. Mother María tells me good sheriff can fix it."

"I'm not Catholic," replied Sheriff Hanks.

"The Blessed Virgin, she no care about that," said Felipe.

"Did she tell you what I should do?"

"I don't know. I just pray. The answer come to me…tell Señor Sheriff," said Felipe.

Everything Felipe Madrigal had told him was important.

"Tell me what? When you prayed, what did the Blessed Virgin Mary tell you to tell me."

"She tell me to tell you bad man hold a gun to my head and make me draw up everything I know about credit union building in Morenci where I worked as security guard. I tell him way to get in through roof. I tell him safe door is broken."

Felipe held his weary head in his hands.

"I tell everything I know about the credit union. I want only to save my grandson. I am so scared. I don't know what to do when devil is at my house.

Sheriff Hanks was stunned at the seeming connection between everything that had been going on. "You did what?"

"I was afraid. I knew he would kill Ángel. Then I have no family. I was so afraid. I don't know what to do."

Zeb's gut rumbled. His heart raced with anticipation. Ángel's life was certainly in danger now that Jimmie Joe Walker had the money.

"Can you save Ángel? Is he still alive?"

"I hope so, Felipe. Say a little prayer."

Zeb bolted from the jail holding block, through the heavy door and into his office.

"Deputy Steele. The robbery in Morenci. It was Felipe."

"What are you talking about, Sheriff? Felipe was here in jail last night. He didn't have anything to do with it." said Deputy Steele.

"No, no! Listen to me..."

Deputy Steele listened as Sheriff Hanks relayed the story he has just heard from the old man--the bomb threats--the big man who held the gun and threatened to kill Ángel--the drawings of the floor plans at the credit union in Morenci--and finally the knowledge that Felipe's grandson, Ángel, was a partner in the crime.

"...and I think I know where they might be," said Sheriff Hanks.

"Where?"

"Felipe showed me a picture of his grandson, Ángel. If my hunch is right, I believe I know where Ángel is. Yesterday a man told me that halfway between Morenci and County Road 6 he thought he saw a yellow car at an abandoned trailer house. He told me right where it was."

"Deputy Steele, grab a rifle." said Sheriff Hanks. "It's forty minutes, forty-five tops, to get to that trailer. You follow me. I'll lead the way. We'll stop a quarter mile or so short of the trailer. If they are still there, don't let them get the drop on you. I am one hundred percent certain they are heavily armed and very dangerous."

Deputy Steele grabbed a rifle from the gun cabinet. The race was on and her heart was pounding.

CHAPTER THIRTY-THREE

"Come on, Ángel. It's time to get the hell out of here."

Ángel opened his eyes with a great deal of difficulty. His head felt like it was going to explode. He couldn't think straight. His mouth tasted like moldy socks. He put his fingers on his tongue to see if something had found its way in there while he slept.

"I think you celebrated a little too much last night," Jimmie Joe chuckled.

Two empty tequila bottles lay at Ángel's feet. Then he remembered the robbery. Sneaking up to the roof, breaking into the credit union, sliding through the small vent into the vault and all that money. Two big sacks full of cash. He opened his eyes a little further and saw Jimmie Joe towering over him. One big sack of money tucked under each of his arms.

"Let's go. Drain your lizard and let's blow this pop stand."

"Where are we going, Jimmie Joe?" said Ángel rising to his feet. "I thought we were going to split the money up and each go our own way?"

"Come on, move it. That's exactly what we are going to do. But first we got to move away from this place in case somebody saw us come back."

Ángel gathered his things and scampered outside.

"Put your things in the Vega. I'll take the truck. Follow me," commanded Jimmie Joe.

"Where are we going?" asked Ángel.

"I told you from the very beginning…don't ask questions. But if you really need to know, we're going to a safe place to split up the money, a real safe place. I've got a beautiful candy-apple-red Corvette stashed away for you over in Tucson as a little going away bonus."

"How did you get that?"

"Remember our friend Noah Hanks? The car thief from prison? He got you the car."

Ángel thought he remembered something else he had heard about Noah as hopped behind the wheel of the Vega, that his brother was a sheriff somewhere in southern Arizona. In the back seat were five gallon jugs of water in case the radiator hose started leaking again. Jimmie Joe peeled out of the driveway and headed east at full speed; Ángel tailed close behind. Near the Gila River just past the Riparian Preserve and into a valley, a sickening feeling overcame Ángel as Jimmie Joe turned the truck north on County Road 6. Jimmie Joe was headed directly to Grandfather Felipe's house.

As Ángel pulled into his grandfather's driveway Jimmie Joe was already standing outside his truck smoking a cigarette. A cool northern wind sneaking under the prevailing westerly wind created a downdraft. The old windmill squawked loudly as it fought against the opposing winds. Trembling, Ángel thought of something his grandfather told him as a child…northern winds carry bad luck. He looked over at his grandfather's truck. The propped open hood could mean only one thing…his grandfather must be in the house. What would he think when he saw Ángel with Jimmie Joe? What could Ángel say to his grandfather?

"Let's go somewhere else and split things up," said Ángel. "I don't think we're safe here."

"Why?" asked Jimmie Joe. "All you ever talked about in prison was seeing your precious Juanita and your loving grandfather."

"Jimmie--"

"He's not here anyway, so don't sweat it," said Jimmie Joe. "You are still his precious little Ángel."

"His truck is here. He never goes anywhere without his truck. How do you know he's not here?"

Ángel dashed past the Diablo Blanco and ran into the small house.

"Abuelo! Abuelo Felipe? Grandfather??"

Ángel turned around to see his partner in crime standing in the doorway.

"I told you, he's not here. You should listen to me. You don't trust me do you?"

"Where is he? Where is my Abuelo? Where is my grandfather? Tell me where is Felipe Madrigal?" Ángel roared in a voice that even he had never heard come out of his own mouth.

"You're a regular little firecracker when you get your undies in a bunch, aren't you?"

"Where is my grandfather?" demanded Ángel threateningly. "Tell me now or else!"

"Or else what? Don't tell me you're going to pull out that little peashooter of yours and put a bullet in me?" chided Jimmie Joe. "I don't think your man enough to try that. Go ahead if you think you are."

Ángel knew he would end up on the short end of the stick if he tried anything, but in a moment of madness he put his head down and charged ahead, full speed, at Jimmie Joe's big belly.

In his agitated state Ángel did not see the much bigger man pull the .38 from his holster. He only felt the steel handle as it cracked against his skull sending him into a cartoonish swirl of dancing stars. Crashing to the ground, Ángel became strangely lucid. Would he ever see Juanita again? Was his grandfather alive? Would Jimmie Joe's next move be to place the gun behind his ear, slowly pull back on the trigger and put a bullet into his brain? This final thought, as consciousness drifted away, brought a smile to his face. The pain of getting hit over the head would certainly give him a headache. If he wasn't dead, when he woke up he could deal with the pain.

Jimmie held a loose finger on the trigger of the .38 as he caressed Ángel's ear with the barrel of the gun. A demonic smile covered his face as he bent down and spoke to the unconscious Ángel. "I ought to blow your fucking stupid ass brains to Kingdom come, my little muchacha. But I know you will suffer so much more knowing that you killed your lovely gata, Juanita, and put your grandfather in jail. And I don't think the sheriff is going to be happy when he knows that little red Corvette that got his brother killed has your things in the trunk. It would just be too nice of a final gesture to kill your sorry ass. Goodbye, little one. See you in hell."

Ángel did not hear Jimmie Joe's pickup back out of the driveway. But when he came, to the truck's tire tracks gave the Diablo Blanco away. The big man was heading north, up County Road 6, toward the San Carlos Reservation. Ángel knew the road. He knew Jimmie Joe had only two escape routes from there, Indian Route 11 to the northwest or the old mining road that led to the long abandoned Indian Flats Mine. Ángel stumbled over to his grandfather's truck. If he could get it running, it would be a much better option than the Vega. One quick look at the engine and his decision was made. Without a distributor cap it wasn't going anywhere.

Ángel tasted the blood pouring from his head as he stumbled along the outside of the house and made his way to the door. Inside, respectful of his grandfather's house, he wrapped his head in a towel before falling into his grandfather's chair as visions of his dead mother and dead grandmother surrounded him.

"Maybe I am to die for my bad deeds," he muttered aloud.

Ángel fell off a deep abyss into unconsciousness. He had visited many a nightmarish place in his alcohol induced stupors, but nothing scared him like the dreadful feeling of falling into a bottomless hole as he passed out in his grandfather's chair.

Demons nipping at his heels howled with the same terrible cackling he had heard come from Jimmie Joe. In his hallucinogenic dream state Ángel found himself covered in blood. Off in the hazy distance his mother and grandmother cried out to God to forgive Ángel and save the soul of their poor boy. He called out to them. His words fell on deaf ears as the images of his loved ones drifted further and further away. In despair he fell to his knees, ready to die, when he felt the presence of his grandfather.

"Grandfather…save me. Please help me. I will never drink again. Please. Please."

A powerful gust of wind blew open the door to the small house, then slammed it shut again. Ángel stirred. A second gust of wind buffeted the door and his eyes fluttered. A third and he awoke.

"Grandfather? Is that you?"

Ángel tried to stand, but his legs failed him. He slumped deeper down in his grandfather's chair. Blood, some dried and caked, some flowing, covered his aching head. He swooned with each attempted motion. He knew he was alive because only living men know they are bleeding. Stumbling to the sink he washed his face and wiped away the blood with his grandfather's towel. Lifting his head to the mirror he saw only shame in what he had become.

"What have I done to my family?"

The wind slapping against the screened door startled Ángel. He instinctively reached for his knife. What had he become? Now, understanding the hopelessness of his situation, Ángel began to sob. He begged for an answer. Struggling to his car Ángel stuck his hand under the seat and grabbed a paper bag, money he had taken when Jimmie Joe wasn't looking. It was maybe ten thousand dollars. He stuffed it behind the seat of his grandfather's truck.

Returning to the rusted out Vega he turned on the radio to the Spanish speaking station. A newswoman reporting on the Morenci robbery said the bandits had gotten away with almost two million dollars. The police had no suspects and were asking people to call in for a big reward if they knew anything. Ángel glanced up and down County Road 6. Better to escape and be with his beloved than to have dirty money.

The newscaster flashed a sudden update on the story. Police were looking for a large White male, thirty-five to forty years old, for a murder in Tucson. Ángel felt a chill enshroud him. The White male suspect had a deformed left hand and was missing two or three fingers. He reached for the silver cross necklace around his neck. The victim was a twenty-year-old Mexican woman. She was found with a broken neck, in a burned out blue Chevrolet LUV pickup truck. She had no known connection to her believed assailant, the large White male with short hair and a deformed hand. If anyone knew anything about the incident, they were to call Detective Max Muñoz at the police department in Tucson.

"The woman worked as a waitress at the El Charo restaurant in Tucson..."

Ángel felt his heart being squeezed, then crushed by an unseen force.

"...she has been identified as Juanita Melindez."

Ángel screamed and bolted from the car. He ran until his knees buckled beneath him. Choking on bloody vomit and stricken with grief Ángel was unable to lift his heavy head. He felt nothing but hatred in his broken heart; he cursed eternal revenge upon the Diablo Blanco.

CHAPTER THIRTY-FOUR

Sheriff Hanks and Deputy Steele stood less than fifty feet away from the abandoned trailer, weapons drawn.

"I don't see anyone," whispered Sheriff Hanks. "I'll sneak around back. Cover me. Keep an eye on the front door."

Crouching low and trotting quietly alongside the trailer, Zeb stopped suddenly, shot upward like an alert chipmunk and poked his head up to the lower edge of a window. Looking back at Deputy Steele he shook his head and moved to the next window. Each of the four windows of the trailer brought the same response. Zeb signaled Kate to remain at the west side of the trailer and edge near the door. His hand signaled her that he was going in and to draw close, just in case. With that he smashed through the back door using his shoulder. The trailer was abandoned.

"The coast is clear," he shouted. "They've high-tailed it out of here."

Kate joined him inside the trailer. Empty tequila and whiskey bottles, crushed beer cans, dirty dishes, fast food wrappers and cigarette butts were everywhere. Two sleeping bags were in the living room, each haphazardly heaped into a pile.

"Somebody's been here recently. I'm sure we'll find enough prints to ID them. Deputy Steele, get on the radio. Call the state prison up in Florence Junction. Talk to the warden. Find out who Ángel Gómez was friends with in the joint. See if you can connect him to a big white guy with missing fingers. I'll use the two-way and have Helen call

Police Chief Haugerud in Morenci to let him know what we've got going on here. Bring the county map from the glove compartment when you come back."

Kate raced to the cruiser. Zeb continued his search of the trailer. As Zeb stepped on one of the sleeping bags, he felt something with his foot. Reaching in, he pulled out a notebook. Inside were pages of definite proof that they were at the right place.

Kate was back in minutes.

"What did you find out from the warden?" asked the sheriff.

"I was lucky. I got right through to him. He had heard about the robbery on the news. He knew exactly who I was asking about. Ángel Gómez ended up under the wing of Jimmie Joe Walker, a career criminal with everything but murder convictions on his rap sheet. He fits the description--six four, two hundred forty pounds, missing three fingers on his left hand. He's got an IQ of 160, but he's a sociopath and psychological deviant. Coincidentally, they were both on the same cell block as your brother."

This information was news to Sheriff Hanks. He shuddered at the possibility of his miscreant brother being involved with all of this.

"According to the warden Walker abused Ángel and just about everyone else around him. He ran the cell block like a dictator when he wasn't pumping iron and reading up on explosives and bomb making in the prison library."

"What did the warden say Jimmie Joe had on Ángel?" asked Sheriff Hanks.

"Ángel's a hard core alcoholic. Walker controlled the contraband, including booze."

"Did Helen get anything from Chief Haugerud in Morenci?"

"Yes," said Deputy Steele. "Helen told him what we've got and he told me what they've got."

"What is it?"

"Someone saw two men prowling around the alley behind the credit union a little after midnight."

"They get a look at them?" asked the sheriff.

"White male, tall, Native American or Mexican male, short. They saw them getting out of an oversized pickup truck, the kind set way up off the ground. The description of the truck matches exactly the one stolen two weeks ago in Tucson."

"The same day the Chevy Vega was stolen," interrupted the sheriff. "Probably the same Vega that's been seen multiple times around these parts being driven by a young male that appeared to be either Mexican or Native."

"Deputy Steele, where would you go?"

The sheriff scoured the notebook.

"What?"

"If you had a million bucks?" asked the sheriff. "Where would you go?"

"I suppose I would leave the country as quickly as possible," replied Deputy Steele.

"How about if you stole a million bucks and this was your starting point? Right here at this trailer. You have a million dollars in cold, hard cash. Where would you go so no one would find you?"

Deputy Steele took no time in answering.

"Instinct would tell me to head straight for the Mexican border. But that is what the authorities would figure as well. Any criminal would have to assume the state police and federal authorities would be thinking the same thing and have that escape route covered with an APB."

"Even young Ángel probably has that figured out," said Sheriff Hanks.

"The second place I might think of going is north onto the reservation, at least until things cooled off a little bit. There aren't many people up there. There is plenty of open space and more hiding places than anyone could ever get at. Everyone knows the tribal police aren't much for cooperating with outside agencies."

"Do you think Eskadi would work with us, help us get tribal police cooperation on this one?"

"I doubt it. I am sure he views this as the evil White man's corporation getting what's coming to him."

"Even if one of the thieves was White?"

Deputy Steele could only shrug her shoulders. Sheriff Hanks understood her meaning.

"Deputy Steele, call the Border Patrol. Have them be on the alert for a twenty-one-year old Mexican, about five foot four, a hundred fifteen pounds, feminine looking, long hair, drinking problem and a white male, thirty-five to forty years of age, six foot four, two hundred forty pounds, with missing fingers on his left hand. Let them know they should be considered armed and dangerous."

"Yes, sir."

Deputy Steele once again raced to her vehicle and relayed the information. Sheriff Hanks walked slowly down the driveway of the trailer. He pointed to the ground as Deputy Steele joined him.

"We know they've got at least two vehicles," said Sheriff Hanks. "Look at the two sets of tracks. One is oversized and the other undersized and bald on the outer edges."

"One for each of them. They probably split up the money and headed in opposite directions," added Deputy Steele.

"Maybe, but think about it for a second," said Sheriff Hanks. "According to the warden, Jimmie Joe Walker is a sociopath with a genius IQ. For the last two years he has been psychologically and likely physically abusing Ángel routinely. I think I know where we might be able to find them both."

"You're a step ahead of me, Sheriff. Where?"

"Jimmie Joe could complete the circle of his crime by returning to Felipe Madrigal's house. Ángel grew up there. It's where Jimmie Joe coerced the old man to give up the floor plan of the credit union, and it's where he got Felipe to call in the bomb threats. It would be the perfect way to further psychologically abuse Ángel," said Sheriff Hanks. "Jimmie Joe is clever and cunning. He is also a fucked up head case.

He might be taking Ángel back there to kill him. That way he would get his kicks from abusing Ángel one last time while ridding himself of the one person who could truly rat him out."

"It would also be a way to torture the old man forever," added Deputy Steele. "What's the quickest route to Madrigal's house?"

"We can head cross country on a couple of back roads and catch County 6," said Zeb. "Ángel and Jimmie Joe might be there now."

"How long will it take us to get there?" asked Kate.

"Twenty minutes, maybe twenty-five."

"Lead the way. I'll be right behind you."

Zeb called Josh Diamond on his cell phone. The service was spotty but he got through.

"Meet Deputy Steele and me at the Madrigal place." He filled his old border patrol pal and expert tracker in on what was going down. "Bring your dogs. We'll need them."

A steady southerly crosswind blew Zeb's dust and dirt trail away from Kate's trailing car as they headed west. At County Road 6 both vehicles turned north.

Sheriff Hanks assumed that either one or both of the suspects were going to be in the oversized vehicle heading up the old Indian Flats Mine road, with a disappearing act in mind. He had Josh Diamond bring his dogs as he was expecting they would ultimately end up tracking the criminals on foot. Sheriff Hanks' car-to-car radio buzzed.

"Eskadi told me the tribe has done a quite a bit of work to make sure no one drives on that road," said Deputy Steele. "The Apache don't want anyone in there, especially us."

"By making the road impassable, Eskadi may have inadvertently done us a favor," said the sheriff.

At the Madrigal house Sheriff Hanks pulled over and took a rifle from the trunk. Deputy Steele pulled in behind him.

"I don't see any signs of life," said the sheriff.

They both knew the layout of the Madrigal place. The wind died down. A strange atmosphere permeated the homestead. Inside the house the trail became red hot.

"The blood in the sink and on the towel is fresh," said Deputy Steele

"And so was the vomit in the ditch."

The lawmen turned to see Josh Diamond standing in the doorway.

"Based on two fresh sets of tire tracks," said Josh. "I'd say you got a big truck and a small car that have been here recently. Whoever was driving the small car is wearing tennis shoes. And, from the upchucked bile and blood, I'd say there is a pretty good chance he's got an ulcer. Care to bring me up to date?"

Zeb pulled the map from his back pocket and laid it out on the kitchen table.

"The tracks head north at the end of the driveway," said Josh. "The most likely route is County Road 6 to Indian Route 11. If they make it onto the reservation, they have a thousand places to disappear."

"I don't like the sounds of that," said Zeb. "We've got to see to it that they don't make it. We don't want to lose them up there."

"What about this old mining road that goes up to Indian Flats?" asked Josh.

"None of our vehicles are going to get far on that road," said Zeb. "After three or four miles it's in real tough shape. We likely will end up on foot."

"My guess is that's where they are going. If they took off down that road, it won't be hard to tell. Let's go have a look. Deputy Steele, you go with Josh. Josh, follow me."

A broad grin swept across Josh Diamond's face.

"Just like old times, eh, Zeb."

The sheriff tipped his cap and hopped into his vehicle. The look on his face was dead serious.

CHAPTER THIRTY-FIVE

The twenty mile trip to the old Indian Flats Mine road gave Deputy Steele time to let Josh in on her theory concerning the guns stolen from his store. In addition, she gave him the details she had on Jimmie Joe Walker and his pathological mindset. When she explained they would likely be hunting the men on foot, Josh's demeanor became intensely focused.

"Understanding human nature is an art as well as a science," said Josh. "Human behavior is as varied as the individual. From what you've told me, tracking down Jimmie Joe Walker will be like hunting a rabid coyote. Ángel will be like stalking an injured rabbit in his own territory."

His directness about human hunting led Kate to ask the question, "How does it feel to track someone knowing you might have to shoot them?"

"My shooting days are over. After six months in Kuwait I vowed never to point a weapon at another human being," he answered. "Working for the border patrol confirmed that decision."

Josh's response took Kate a bit by surprise. Her intuitive response was to check her weapon.

"I apologize for being so abrupt," said Kate. "That was way too personal."

"No need to apologize, Kate. It probably isn't one of those questions that has an easy answer. I hunted people--under direct orders. In war it's kill or be killed. You are hunting or tracking down someone who wants to kill you. Our unit had a single mission. Our job was to track down and eliminate, when possible, the commanders of the Iraqi forces who were ordering the deaths of Kuwaiti civilians."

"I saw the picture in your office. You were playing with a yoyo, and a bunch of kids were watching you and laughing."

Josh cleared his throat. He hesitated a moment before speaking.

"There's a story behind that picture. It's not one I've told many people."

"You don't have to tell me if you don't want to," said Kate.

"Normally I wouldn't, but somehow it seems like I should. It's not really a pretty story. Are you sure you want to hear it?"

Kate did, and did not, want the facts. She sensed it was important but did not want to intrude too deeply into Josh's personal life. Somewhat hesitatingly she answered yes.

"That picture was taken on what can only be described as both the best and the worst day of my life. We were operating on the Kuwait-Iraq border after hostilities had ceased. We were providing food and medical care. The Iraqi Red Guard had poisoned the only water supply the village had so we were working on drilling a new well. In return we wanted information about any locals who had been working with the Iraqis. It was a simple trade off, water for information. Most of the villagers were poor farmers. They weren't political. They didn't want anything to do with the war. The village leader agreed to help us if we would drill the well and build a soccer field for the kids. We did. The night before the first game operatives sneaked in and planted some land mines in the middle of the field. Four of those kids in that picture were killed when one detonated."

"I am so sorry," replied Kate.

Josh cleared his throat again. As he began to speak his words were raspy.

"I was in charge of security. It was my fault. I became insanely angry. I vowed to track down the men responsible and kill them. But my squad leader, God bless him, yanked me out of there. He talked with the commanding officer, and I was put on the next plane back to the states. Someone else literally saved my life. The nightmare of those children dying still haunts me. It took me years to realize that if I had killed the men who killed those kids nothing would have changed, except I would have ended up fighting even more demons."

Josh stopped talking and looked out the window across the desert toward the western mountains. His incredible tale left Kate with a hollow feeling in the pit of her stomach. She knew that if she pulled the trigger on Jimmie Joe or Ángel it would be out of duty, not hatred. Still, it might boil down to just that, her pulling the trigger and ending a human life. In the heat of the moment, what would she do? Time would tell.

At the turnoff to the old mine road, Zeb pulled over. He got out of the car and crouched in the middle of the road. Two sets of tire tracks headed up the old mine road. One set was extra wide with a deep tread. The other set of tracks indicated small tires with little tread. Josh had guessed right.

Zeb picked up some dirt in his hand. It was sifting through his fingers when the ringer on his cell phone buzzed loudly.

"Sheriff Hanks."

"Zeb, Max Muñoz. Do you have a minute?"

"Not really."

"Zeb, it's about your brother, Noah."

Zeb immediately felt his blood pressure rising. His fucked up brother was always inserting himself into his life at the worst possible moment.

"Did your men find him and that goddamn stolen Corvette?"

"He's dead, Zeb, assassinated with a single shot to the head. He's been dead for almost a week. We've got an eyewitness."

Zeb's heart squeezed tightly in his chest. The pit of his stomach sank like a stone. Noah had led a bad life, but he did not deserve to die like this.

"Who, what, how?"

"The eyewitness is one of your brother's pals. They were going to get together after Noah delivered the Corvette to an ex-con named Jimmie Joe Walker. Walker was supposedly paying him five hundred bucks to deliver the vehicle. The witness was going to meet Noah, but he was running late. When he came on the scene, there was a big argument between Noah and Walker. He stayed hidden and watched as the two exchanged words. Without warning vehicle. The witness was going to meet Noah, but he was running late. When he came on the scene, there was a big argument between Noah and Walker. He stayed hidden and watched as the two exchanged words. Without warning Walker pulled his weapon, plugged him point blank and took off in the Vette. We've got an APB on the car. I am so sorry."

"We are hot on Jimmie Joe Walker's trail as we speak. I'll get that son of a bitch."

"Stay cool. If you act in anger, you're likely to make a mistake."

"I'll try and keep that in mind. But give it one second's thought as though it were your brother who was murdered in cold blood. Goodbye."

Zeb was ready, maybe even eager in the heat of the moment, to kill the man who killed his brother. His red hot anger was juxtaposed by the strange blend of anxiety and cool calmness that comes with having been tested under stress.

Josh pulled his vehicle up behind Zeb's. Josh got his dogs from the truck's kennel. Kate stepped out of the vehicle. The look on Sheriff Hanks' face told her something was wrong.

"What is it, Sheriff?" asked Deputy Steele.

"The Corvette. Noah stole it."

"Did they find it?"

"No."

"What then?"

"The theft was a consignment job for Jimmie Joe Walker. When Noah delivered it..."

Sheriff Hanks found himself choking back tears as the words he spoke made it suddenly all too real. Just as quickly he stuffed his emotions, another little trick he had learned in his hard life.

"Jimmie Joe Walker murdered him. Shot him in the head."

Kate and Josh were stunned silent.

"You good enough to carry on, Zeb?" asked Josh. "We will understand if you can't."

Zeb stared ahead blankly. A hawk swooped down, grabbed a baby rabbit and broke his line of sight. When he spoke again, his voice was calm, assured.

"We've got a killer to find," said Sheriff Zeb Hanks. "I've been on the first part of this road before. It gets pretty rough about three miles in. Are your dogs going to be okay in the back of your rig?"

"They're pretty tough old boys," replied Josh.

"Are they going to give us away in close quarters?" asked the sheriff.

The dogs were pawing around, snorting, whimpering and tugging against their leashes.

Josh unleashed the dogs, gave another hand signal that apparently meant "kennel up", and like soldiers instantly obeying a command, they were back in the vehicle, fully poised, at attention and ready to go.

"Follow me," said Sheriff Hanks.

CHAPTER THIRTY-SIX

The first couple miles of the ill-maintained mining road were covered with wild sagebrush and a variety of scrub trees. It was passable...with careful maneuvering. Large boulders placed every quarter mile were evidence of the tribal desire to close the road to outsiders. Roughly three miles off the main road the landscape changed dramatically. What had been a flat, straightaway became a series of switchbacks, blind curves and washouts as the road began to climb through a series of ever increasing elevations.

"What's that? Over there." Deputy Steele pointed into a distant crevasse where reflected light flickered against the brown landscape.

"It could be windshield glass," said Josh.

She removed a small pair of binoculars from a case on her belt. "Bingo. We've got ourselves a yellow Vega."

"Scan the surrounding area," said Josh. "Do you see anyone moving around?"

She saw nothing. Five minutes later at the top of a stone plateau the team stood around the abandoned, rusted out, yellow Vega. Sheriff Hanks popped open the hood.

"It still has a leaky radiator," he said. "This baby isn't going another foot."

Ahead, where the road once again turned to hardened dirt and crushed gravel, Zeb examined a single set of oversized tire tracks. In the Vega, Kate found blood on the steering wheel. Josh leashed his dogs and made half circles fifty feet away from the car searching for human tracks. He then placed some equipment into a small backpack and joined Kate.

"Zeb, I've got some tracks here. They are identical to the ones at the trailer and at the Madrigal place, said Josh. "A small man's tennis shoe."

Sheriff Hanks did a slow three-hundred-sixty degree scan of the area.

"What do you think, Josh?" he asked.

"I think we're hunting a hunter. I'm fairly certain Ángel is going cross country to try and catch up with Jimmie Walker. My guess is Jimmie Joe double crossed him and Ángel is eager for a little vengeance."

"That young kid would be taking a helluva chance in this country going against a highly armed sociopath," said Deputy Steele.

"But he's got one distinct advantage," said Sheriff Hanks. "He knows this road like the back of his hand. His grandfather taught him to drive on this road when he was a trucker for the mines," said Zeb.

"Ángel started driving this road when he was ten years old," added Kate. "Eskadi got that information for me from some Apaches who worked with Felipe Madrigal."

"Unless that young kid is completely out of his mind we can assume he's got at least some kind of weapon," said the sheriff. "That makes him dangerous to us."

"Here."

Josh handed his truck keys to Sheriff Hanks.

"I'll follow him. He should be easy to track. I don't think he's going to do much to cover his trail."

"Josh, take this rifle," said Sheriff Hanks.

"Keep it for yourself," replied Josh.

"I guess with your arm in that cast you're not going to be much of a shot," said Sheriff Hanks.

"I've got the dogs. Besides which, I don't plan on shooting anyone…unless my life or one of yours is in imminent danger," replied Josh. "I gave that shit up."

Kate knew exactly what was behind Josh's statement. Zeb had a pretty good idea.

"We had better get moving," said Zeb.

"Right now we've only got a couple hours of good daylight ahead of us. I expect Ángel is going to try and surprise Jimmie Joe up ahead," said Josh. "But if what Eskadi says about the road is right, Walker may well have to abandon his truck sooner than he planned."

"Jimmie Joe may or may not know Ángel is after him," said the sheriff. "He may think that we have him. We had better assume Jimmie Joe figures we're not too far behind him. Remember Jimmie Joe will be listening for us or anything out of the ordinary. We don't want him to end up hearing us. Do your best to keep any noise to a minimum. If we have an element of surprise on our side, we don't want to lose it," said Josh.

"I've got a set of walkie-talkies in the trunk," said the sheriff. "I want you to take one so we can keep in contact. In these hills and canyons I don't know how much good they'll do, but they're better than nothing."

Zeb, Kate and Josh all switched their walkie-talkies to silent signal mode, opting for a continual dual flash of the red light and a buzz as a signal for requested communication. In the event of an emergency it was agreed that flipping the override switch would be the best form of instant verbal communication. Josh's vehicle had four-wheel drive and would make the trip better than the police vehicle.

Zeb shifted Josh's truck into low gear. Haltingly he made his way along the treacherous winding road. Josh and Kate headed out on foot, following the tracks of Ángel Gómez. As they moved stealthily through a run off wash, Josh crouched to the ground every hundred yards or so, his animal like senses honed in on the world around him. An hour passed before he spoke.

"Ángel's lost blood," said Josh. "He is tiring and beginning to stumble."

Kate had seen two smeared bloodstains on rocks earlier, but other than the occasional impression of a sneaker in the sand she had spotted little else.

"He's bleeding from the head," said Josh.

"How do you know that?" she asked.

"The blood pattern on the rock back there. The one you noticed. That blood was from his hand."

Josh rubbed his hand against an imaginary cut on his face, squatted near a rock and used a flat hand to push himself up. His muted explanation was perfect. Blood on the fingers would leave exactly the smear mark she had seen.

"I noticed three other splatter patterns on the rocks. It was very faint or I'm sure you would have seen it. Blood falling from up here--"

Josh gently rubbed his hand against her forehead.

"--would create a central point with a small splatter pattern when it hit the ground or something on the ground."

"Shouldn't the blood from his wound be clotting after this amount of time?"

"Maybe it's a big cut. Or maybe he keeps touching it and irritating it. It could be a gunshot wound."

"How do you know he's stumbling?"

"He is walking on the outside front part of his foot, rolling it over and pushing off his big toe," explained Josh. "He's faltering forward as he walks. It could be from fatigue or pain or both. He had a big night last night. In all the excitement he probably didn't get much sleep. There's a pretty good chance he's dehydrated too. He's probably running on sheer force of will at this point. To say nothing of the fact that it must be quite an adrenaline rush to steal a million dollars."

"I'm sure it is," replied the deputy. "Most people would do just about anything for a million dollars."

"Some people don't know there's more to life than money," said Josh.

"Like the thrill of the chase, maybe?"

"You tell me," replied Josh.

Josh Diamond's double entendre was all too obvious. Kate took a deep breath.

"Did you see evidence at the Madrigal place which makes you think he's been shot?" asked Deputy Steele.

"There was a bloody towel in the driveway culvert. I gave it to the sheriff. My suspicion was that, with this kind of money involved, Jimmie Joe shot Ángel and left him for dead."

With the gradual change in daylight from the sun beginning to disappear behind the higher hills, the desert temperature cooled down quickly. Josh's dogs became only slightly excited as they began to sense the onset of early evening animal activity. These were the most well trained dogs Kate had ever observed.

"The setting sun is working against us," remarked Kate. "Ángel or Jimmie Joe could be hiding in the shadows just about anywhere out there."

"Good call. You're right. We should move very carefully until we can use nature to our advantage. We need the advantage of dusk. Let's rest very briefly, then get moving."

Josh took a position on a rock just into the shadows. Even from fifteen feet away Kate would have missed him if she hadn't known he was sitting there.

"Drink some water," he advised. "I've done a lot of remote desert reconnaissance work. It's very easy to get dehydrated and not even know it, especially under stress."

She sat, removed a canteen from her hip and took a long drink. In the distance something scurried in the underbrush.

"Small animal, not our man," said Josh without moving a muscle. "But we are getting close. Look."

Josh shined a small flashlight on a spot half way between them. It was fresh blood.

"The dogs found it," he said. "Mutt is trained to point his tail downward when he smells human blood."

CHAPTER THIRTY-SEVEN

A nearly translucent moon was rising in the eastern sky. Sunlight was lessening more quickly than was ideal for tracking purposes. Josh surveyed the area with his binoculars.

"We've got forty-five minutes, maybe an hour, until darkness plays a huge factor. We need to keep moving, but we have to be careful. Let's roll."

Moving through the desert undergrowth in sparse light proved much easier than Kate had imagined. Following Josh's lead they moved as if a single person. At three minute intervals he directed her with hand signals to stop and listen. Josh shined the directed light of a laser flashlight ahead and motioned for Kate to have a look. A mother skunk, teaching her children how to survive and hunt in the night, stared disdainfully at them. Another quarter mile on, Kate and Josh halted simultaneously. Ahead, around a corner in a small box canyon, a muted noise came drifting through the darkness. As they moved closer the shrill sound of satanic laughter became hauntingly clear.

"We'll move up along the base of the canyon wall," whispered Josh. "Stay low. When we get to the outcropping, stay put. I'll move ahead, see what's going on."

Deputy Steele knew Josh could see the slight nod of her head as dusk crept over them.

"Make sure you are feeling everything with your feet. I do not want anything to give us away now."

It was a point well taken. Josh suddenly signaled her to stay put. He sneaked away from the protection of the canyon wall, sliding into the underbrush on his stomach using his elbows to propel himself forward. She watched as he noiselessly disappeared into the desert underbrush. She was amazed that even one arm in a cast didn't deter him from his mission.

The quiet desert air carried every sound from the canyon to Kate's sharpened ears. Words suddenly became clear. One man with a deep voice was speaking. The gringo accent made her certain it was Jimmie Joe. His voice became clearer as the anger in his voice increased.

"Fool. You should never have followed me."

"You killed Juanita." Ángel's voice was full of defiance, hatred and anger.

"Yes," taunted Jimmie Joe. "Yes I killed your lovely Juanita. Her throat crushed as easily as a hummingbird's."

Ángel vomited.

"Do you want to know what her last words were? She begged me not to kill you. She pleaded for your life to be spared as I was taking hers. Oh, she was loyal to you, muchacha. Very soon that loyalty will be rewarded when you join her in hell."

Deputy Steele gasped quietly as Josh slithered out from beneath the undergrowth not three feet from her.

"We got ourselves a bad situation," he whispered. "We are going to have to move fast. Jimmie Joe has the kid tied to small tree. He is ranting and raving and telling Ángel how he killed his girlfriend. It sounds like he broke her neck and torched her."

"What exactly do you think Jimmie Joe has in mind?" asked Deputy Steele. "Torture?"

"Whatever it is, it isn't good. Looks like he's pistol-whipped Ángel. He has taken the blood from Ángel's wound and used it to paint a bulls-eye on his face, another on his chest and one near each arm. I don't know how quickly this guy likes to kill or how much of the Marquis de Sade he's got in him, but I would say Ángel's life could be measured in heartbeats not minutes, unless we move fast."

"We'd better get going."

"We've got a second problem. Zeb is directly opposite us. We don't want anyone to get caught in crossfire."

Kate checked her weapon.

"How far do I have to move out from here before I can get a clear look at things?" she asked.

"Fifty feet out and you will be dead center of the small canyon. The small tree he's got the kid tied to is about fifteen feet away from the canyon wall. It will be on your left. Your shooting distance will be seventy-five, give or take a few feet. Zeb is less than one hundred feet directly opposite us and behind the tree where Ángel is tied. I don't think he knows we're here. Follow me." Josh hand signaled his dogs to crouch and remain silent.

Deputy Steele snaked along the ground close enough to the heels of Josh's boots to smell sandy dirt ground into the rubber soles. Reaching the spot with a clear view he stopped. Drawing half way on his knees, using the cast on his left arm as support, Josh viewed the men through his binoculars.

"If we try and surprise them by getting any closer, we stand a good chance of getting hurt," whispered Josh loosening his holster strap. "And, we lose the element of surprise."

In the distance Jimmie Joe's voice became crystal clear as he lectured his young, helpless captive.

"You stupid, fucking, little bastard. What the hell is wrong with you? I literally saved your ass in prison. I get you in on the biggest heist of your wretched life and how do you pay me back? By sneaking up on me like I'm some sort of stupid rookie con? I made a mistake by letting you live earlier. I should have killed you at your grandfather's house."

Deputy Steele watched the pair through the rifle's scope. Josh eyed them through his binoculars.

Jimmie Joe suddenly grabbed Ángel by the hair. He forced the gun into his cheek, howling with delight as he distorted his prey's face. Drawing back he pointed the gun barrel at Ángel's head. His expression turned vile as he repeatedly brought the handle of the gun down hard on Ángel's face and neck. Standing back, the big man grunted discordantly before kicking Ángel in the ribs and spitting on him.

"I don't know what the hell I'm waiting for. I ought to shoot you right now and get it over with. What good is your fucking, rotten life anyway? Your girlfriend's dead--your grandfather's in jail, your mother and your grandmother are dead. I'd be doing you a hell of a favor by having you join them."

"Ángel's not moving," whispered Deputy Steele.

"If he has an ounce of smarts, he's playing possum," answered Josh.

Jimmie Joe also noticed his prey wasn't stirring. He grabbed a tree branch for balance and brought the heel of his boot against the bridge of Ángel's nose. Angrily he bore down with the full weight of his massive body. Blood hurled through the air.

"Wake up, you little, brown traitor. It's no time for a siesta."

The insane laughter of the big man echoed in the canyon rousting a pair of night birds whose fluttering wings whooshed in the distance.

"I never killed a man I couldn't look in the eye and I'm not starting now. So wake the fuck up." shouted Jimmie Joe. "I said, wake the fuck up."

Half lying on his side, head tilted back, Ángel didn't stir.

"Maybe he's dead already," whispered Deputy Steele.

"He's not. Zero in on his hands. He's a tough little soldier."

Deputy Steele sighted the scope toward Ángel's hands. Tied behind his back, around the thin base of the mesquite tree, Ángel's fingers were clawing at the ground, gathering sand and dirt, possible weapons for one last stand. She returned the aim of her rifle back toward Jimmie Joe who had now tucked his gun under his arm. He opened a water bottle, twisted Ángel's neck toward the ground so his nose was pointing upward and began pouring water into his nostrils. Ángel sputtered reflexively.

"So the little muchacha is awake now, is he?"

"Go to hell, Jimmie Joe. You son of a bitch. Go straight to hell!"

The stillness of the night provided no resistance for the raw tension of barbed hatred zinging through the air. Deputy Steele raised the 30.06 to her eye. She drew a bead just above Jimmie Joe's ear. The big man began to pace slowly back and forth, repeatedly checking his weapon. Directly behind him, in her scope, she saw Sheriff Hanks moving through the underbrush toward Jimmie Joe. If she missed or the bullet passed through Jimmie Joe, it would head directly toward the sheriff. Josh held a rock in his good hand. He set his .45 at his side so he could quickly pick it up once he tossed the rock. Setting his gun down was a gamble. It was a risk he had to take if his plan was going to be executed. Moreover, he was hoping he wouldn't have to use his .45.

"Time is running out," he whispered. "If we are going to act, it has to be now."

The utter calmness in his voice sent a chill down Kate's spine. Her heart raced as she looked through the scope. Deputy Kate Steele could practically hear the wings of the Angel of Death approaching.

"I'm going to throw this rock directly between us and him. I'm hoping Jimmie Joe will turn directly toward you when he hears the noise. He may crouch down so be ready for that. You will have three, maybe four seconds to get your best shot. If we don't do this now, Ángel is a dead man. It's up to you to save that young man and rid the world of a wicked one."

Through the scope she eyed Jimmie Joe Walker. For the first time in her life she recognized what pure evil looked like. If she pulled the trigger, this devil would be dead. But the line of her aim was such that she would almost certainly hit Zeb as well. If she did nothing, Ángel Gómez would most certainly die.

"It is time to save the life of an Ángel," she whispered. "Don't throw that rock yet. Give me thirty seconds to sneak around behind Jimmie Joe, then throw the rock. I need a clear, safe shot."

"I don't like it," said Josh. "That is dangerous for you and we increase the risk of Jimmie Joe killing Ángel."

Before Josh could complete his sentence Kate was moving stealthily through the underbrush behind Jimmie Joe. Through his binoculars he watched as she slipped behind a split cactus tree, not more than a dozen feet behind Jimmie Joe. She found Jimmie Joe in the scope, looked toward Josh, nodded and looked back through her scope. She took one step forward to steady her position. At that instant her foot caught between two rocks and she stumbled forward falling on top of her weapon. Simultaneously Josh tossed the rock. One second later the .45 was in his hand, pointed at Jimmie Joe. Life then became a series of slow motion events.

Kate's sense of hearing became so exacting that the rock arcing through the thin night air brought a clear whistling sound to her ear. Overhead, a pair of mated killdeer gracefully shifted their unified flight pattern as the stone descended onto a small bush breaking a branch, rustling dead leaves. Behind Jimmie Joe, Zeb, on bended knee with his finger resting on the trigger, aimed his rifle toward the big man who suddenly disappeared into the undergrowth.

Jimmie Joe smiled as he pointed his weapon directly into the face of Deputy Steele. Slowly he pulled the rifle from beneath her.

"Bad day to be you," he whispered. "One sound out of your mouth and you are a dead woman. Got that?"

She nodded. Jimmie Joe pulled a filthy bandana from his pocket, ripped in in half and quickly tied Kate's hands behind her back and gagged her. She knew Sheriff Hanks and Josh were out there and could possibly save her life. What she had not figured on was how quickly Jimmie Joe assessed the situation.

"Sheriff, are you listening?"

No response was forthcoming.

"I know you see my little friend tied to the mesquite tree."

Jimmie Joe quickly pulled the weapon Kate had been carrying to his shoulder.

"Thanks for the scope, Deputy," he said as he pointed the gun at the helpless Ángel. "Adiós Ángel."

The gunshot took less than a fraction of a second to tear Ángel's chest apart. He gasped once, lightly. His head fell forward. His life was over.

"Your deputy is next, Sheriff. You've got thirty seconds to come out with your weapon over your head or she dies. You know I will do it."

The seconds began ticking off the clock inside Zeb's head. He knew Josh was near but didn't know where. Ten seconds passed. The guilt of Deputy Funke dying under his command raced through his head. He couldn't let Deputy Steele die. He had to risk his own life for the slim possibility of saving hers.

"Twenty seconds, Sheriff. Your deputy is breathing her final breaths unless you do something now."

Silence.

"Fifteen seconds. My finger is getting itchy."

Zeb lifted his weapon over his head and walked into the open space next to the murdered Ángel Gómez.

"Good move, Sheriff. Now put the weapon down in front of you."

Zeb did as ordered. Jimmie Joe once again put the weapon to his shoulder. Josh Diamond was watching all of this through his binoculars. With a silent move of two fingers he ordered his dogs to attack. As they flew through the brush Jimmie Joe turned and Deputy Steele swung her legs around knocking him off balance. Falling, his shot went wide. Zeb hit the dirt.

Jimmie Joe righted himself, turned and found himself staring down a gun barrel. He reached for his holstered .38. Josh's weapon was aimed directly between Jimmy Joe's eyes. His finger felt weightless as it rested lightly against the trigger. Exhaling slowly he felt the warm flesh of his finger squeezing against the cold metal of the trigger. He had vowed never to fire on another human being. Suddenly his dogs were within feet of Jimmie Joe Walker. Walker instinctively pointed his weapon at the dogs. It was his last mistake. Josh exhaled, and pulled the trigger. The shot was true. It split the skull of Jimmie Joe Walker. As his body buckled, his crumbling legs gave way to the onrushing forces of certain death. Landing on his knees in a praying position, his body paused momentarily. A cry of devilish despair erupted from his bloodstained lips. Abruptly his head snapped back and then jerked forward again. Jimmie Joe Walker breathed his last tormented breath, crashing face first into the jagged underbrush.

The killdeer overhead curved further away. The dogs raced circles around the dead man. Kate freed her hands from the bandana, removed the gag from her mouth and spit. Her mind was numbed. Never had she seen so much death so close up. Zeb picked up his weapon and stood over the body of Jimmie Joe Walker. Josh appeared out of the darkness.

The sight of a massacred Ángel shook Kate to her core. Josh looked at her, his dogs, the gun in his hand and the dead body of Jimmie Joe. He had broken his vow to never shoot another human being. He felt an overwhelming rush of emptiness and sadness. The sorrow of death hung heavily over Josh and Kate. They looked at each other, each seeing the anguish in the other, each feeling the sanctity of life. An unspoken bond of trust, of love, of loss, of giving passed between them. Josh reached out to Kate. They held each other compassionately.

Zeb stood amidst the death and carnage. An overwhelming number of thoughts rushed through his mind. What he saw in front of him was nearly incomprehensible yet intensely real. His eyes landed on Josh, who had literally saved the day, and on his deputy, Kate Steele, who had come within seconds of death. At his feet was the dead Ángel, a foolish young man caught in a deceitful trap of lies, which were not of his own making. Ángel's horrible choices had ruined the life of his grandfather, Felipe Madrigal, caused the death of his beloved, Juanita, and had led to the death of Zeb's friend, Deputy Delbert Funke. Delbert, poor dead Delbert. Corita Funke his lonely, heartbroken mother would spend the rest of her days thinking of what her son might have become.

The destroyed life of Felipe Madrigal, the death of his dissolute brother Noah bore down on his being. The deepening confusion regarding Doreen circled in his mind. Zeb stared at the dead body of Jimmie Joe Walker. All he saw was evil, the evil of one man, the evil the heart and mind can carry and the evil that dwells so constantly in this world. Despair over the loss of innocent lives sunk his heart, while rage and anger rose in his mind as he thought of the evil he had to deal with to do his job the way it had to be done.

His life had once again changed. But it would always be changing. He was beginning to see that is how it would always be. There would always be innocent victims. The said truth was evil would always co-exist with good.

CHAPTER THIRTY EIGHT

It was late. Just over twenty-four hours earlier Zeb had witnessed the murder of Ángel Gómez and the killing of Jimmie Joe Walker. Zeb reflected on the craziness that had been his life over the past weeks. The spectre of death haunted him. He could live with the death of Ángel and Jimmie Joe. That was his job. But he was having a very hard time dealing with the death of his longtime deputy and friend, Delbert Funke. Yesterday, Deputy Kate Steele had come within seconds of losing her life too.

He wrapped his knuckles on the desk monotonously for several minutes. The sound of bone and flesh on wood helped his thoughts to slow down. Zeb knew he should just get away from the office, but he clung to the familiar setting like a life line. When his mind calmed, his thoughts turned to Doreen. He glanced at the clock. As late as it was he was in no hurry to go home to Doreen. The revelation of her past had thrown him for a loop. Zeb couldn't understand why she had kept her past a secret, especially from him. Why hadn't she trusted him, and how could he now trust her? He knew he was going to have to deal with it rather than let it fester under his skin.

Zeb stared at his reflection in the window and thought hard. He was definitely in a place he had never been before. Was it exhaustion? Yesterday's brutal events? His brother's death? Doreen's inability to put her trust in him? Zeb couldn't quite put his finger on what was sticking in his craw. The only thing he was certain of was everything was changing--he was changing. After all Doreen had been through in her life, it simply wouldn't be fair to marry her now when his very foundation was on shifting sand.

In the late night quiet his senses became acute. The sound of Kate's pen scratching across a piece of paper echoed down the hallway. Zeb sensed that Kate, too, was using the office and paperwork as a hideaway. She had been through hell. Zeb listened to Kate's chair scoot across the worn wooden floor of her office. He listened to her footsteps coming down the hall. He looked up to see her standing in the doorway of his office.

"Zeb, do you have a minute?"

Zeb motioned to the chair sitting directly in front of his desk.

"What's up?" he asked.

Kate got right to the point. "I've been doing a lot of thinking," she replied. "About my job, my future, my relationships--you name it, I've been thinking about it."

"Join the club," replied Zeb.

"I think I should talk to someone."

"About yesterday?" asked Zeb.

"About a lot of things. Yesterday--well--I know I could have died, but I don't think that's it. I understand the potential for death and injury come with this job. I accept that. Actually, I find it exciting. I guess it's what I don't feel that has me confused."

"Meaning what?" asked Zeb.

"Meaning this job affects everyone around me. I don't know how close I want to get to Eskadi right now. I don't think it's fair to him if I can't give one hundred percent to the relationship.

Zeb nodded. His lips pursed in a half smile. He understood completely. Years ago Jimmy Song Bird and former sheriff Jake Dablo had told him when you face difficult problems in your life you never really know where answers will come from. Both of these men firmly believed that the universe would always provide answers at precisely the moment you needed them. Both men were flawed in their own way, yet both understood the ways of the world.

"Might I suggest you have a heart to heart chat with Jimmy Song Bird and Jake Dablo?

Kate thought for a few short moments before responding, "Good idea. Thank you."

"No, Kate, thank you."

Kate eyed Zeb inquisitively. Zeb's face gave away nothing.

"Let's call it a night. The paperwork can wait for one more day," said Zeb.

They both stood to leave. Zeb reached out. Expecting a handshake, Kate was confused when Zeb gave her a big hug. Once again he thanked her. The thank you was for something she didn't fully understand.

Zeb pulled into the driveway. Doreen was waiting for him with a cup of decaffeinated tea. They hugged and walked in silence to the living room.

"How's my sugah…"

Zeb raised a solitary finger to his lips. As Doreen looked into the face of the man she loved, a single tear rolled down her cheek and died on her lips.

"You can't marry me, can you?"

"No," he replied. "I can't. Not now. With all that's been going on, I..."

Now it was Doreen's turn to put a finger to her lips.

"I understand." Doreen's response was sad but not heartbroken. "I can wait."

"Doe, I can't really explain exactly what's going through my heart. If I could tell you when or if I'll be ready to move forward, I would. You have a right to know, but I don't know myself. Right now I feel like I might only cause you more heartache. You don't deserve that."

Zeb sipped his tea. He felt completely numb.

Doreen knew uncertainty and loss all too well. Zeb's words hung over her like the clouds clinging to the face of Mount Graham.

42221274R00156

Made in the USA
Lexington, KY
17 June 2015